Long Past Dawn

The Cowboys of Bison Ridge, Book Two

Katie Mettner

ISBN: 9798431474989

Dedication

Remember me every time a bird flies over the horizon, when the apple blossoms bloom on the trees, and when the waves wash over your toes.

In loving memory of Linda Mettner

Prologue

Twenty years ago

When I met Blaze McAwley at the start of third grade, I knew we would be best friends. He was funny and loved to get into trouble with mean Mrs. Hasselback as much as I did. When I found out he lived on a ranch, I was so excited. I'd always wanted to ride a horse and rope a steer, but living in the middle of town made that impossible, even in the heart of Texas. Things were so much different now, though. I was alone, and if it weren't for Blaze, I'd probably be on the street.

I slipped into his daddy's barn through the side door the way he'd shown me when we hatched our plan. I checked around the barn to make sure all the hands had left for the night before letting my guard down even the slightest little bit. I would have from ten p.m. until five a.m. to sleep before I had to leave the barn again and hide out somewhere else on the ranch. Thankfully, they had thousands of acres, so it wasn't hard to keep myself hidden during the day. If school were in session, I'd stay there, but since it's the middle of July, that's impossible. At least when Blaze can get away from his daddy for a few hours, he always hunts me down to go for a swim.

I checked the old digital watch he'd given me when I first got here. It had an alarm on it, so I would know when to get up and leave the barn. It also told me he'd be by soon to drop off some food to eat for the night. It had been our routine for the last two weeks, and it worked okay. During the day, I could snack on apples and carrots I'd steal from the barn bins. I didn't think the horses would mind much if I ate a couple of their treats.

Blaze had made me a bed of hay in the loft and kept blankets and a pillow hidden for me to get out every night. We didn't want any ranch hands getting suspicious and reporting to Blaze's daddy that someone was in the barn.

The shower at the end of the stalls called to me. It was so hot today, so I was dusty and dirty. Since I only had two sets of clothes, the one I was wearing when I ran away, and the one Blaze was letting me borrow, I would have to wash them tonight and dry them tomorrow in the sunshine.

I checked the watch again, nervously chewing on my lip. It was half-past ten, and Blaze was usually here by now. Maybe he fell asleep and forgot about me. If he had, I'd grab another apple and go to bed, hoping tomorrow he'd show up with breakfast. My stomach grumbled at the thought of food, and I rubbed it absently. It had been so long since I'd eaten three meals a day that I couldn't remember the last time. It was probably back when school was open. That was two months ago now. Before that, it was when my momma was alive. I leaned against a bale of hay and let out a heavy breath. I didn't like thinking about Momma. I missed her so much. My foster family used to tell me I had to stop talking about her since she'd been dead for a year. I didn't think that was right. The counselor at school told me I could talk about her as much as I wanted. I didn't know who to believe anymore, so I just believed in Blaze. He'd never done me wrong and never would.

I didn't talk about Momma anymore, though. Instead, I thought about her in my mind and wrote down all the stories I could remember about her. My foster family told me I'd forget what she looked like one day, and I didn't want that to happen. I had pictures of her saved in a secret place where no one would find them, and I had my notebook full of stories. That was all I had now besides Blaze. Living out here like this was hard. I was so scared of being found out, but I was more scared of going back to foster care.

There were footfalls on the gravel outside, and my heart started pumping hard in my chest. I pushed off the bale of hay and ducked behind it until I knew for sure it was Blaze. If a ranch hand forgot something or needed to check on an animal, I didn't want him to find me.

Blaze called out softly. "The horses are quiet tonight."

That was our secret phrase, so I knew it was safe to come out.

I jumped up, anxious to see what he brought me for supper. I was starving. "I didn't think you were coming tonight," I said, stepping around the bale of hay.

What I saw froze my feet and my words in place. Blaze stood there with his daddy holding one arm and his momma holding the other. He didn't have any food, and his eyes told me he was scared. My gaze darted around, looking for a way out. The closest door was the one I came in, and I ran for it, my legs pumping as hard as I could make them on what little food I'd eaten today. My heart was pounding, and I was almost there when a hand grabbed the back of my shirt.

"Stop now, son."

It was Blaze's daddy, Ash. He was gruff and bossy with his ranch hands, but Blaze always said he was a good man.

I swallowed hard and hoped he'd see reason. "I—I was just leaving, sir," I said, my voice shaking. "I stop—stopped on by to sa-see Blaze. You know how long it stays lig—light in the summertime," I yammered, praying he'd let me go. I didn't know where I'd go, but as long as it wasn't back to that awful foster family, I didn't care.

It was Blaze's momma who spoke once I quieted. "Why don't you come inside the house, Beau? I've got leftover burgers from dinner and some apple pie."

"Thanks, Mrs. McAwley, but I-I-I will ba-be on my way," I said. My stomach chose that moment to rumble, and I willed it to be quiet.

"Son," Mr. McAwley said, "Blaze told us what's been going on out here. We'd like you to come inside now."

I hung my head and shuffled my feet toward the door where Blaze still stood with his momma. He slipped his hand in mine because he knew I was scared even though we were eleven now.

"I'm sorry," he whispered, "Momma caught me trying to get the food tonight. I didn't snitch on purpose."

I nodded but didn't answer. I couldn't. I was afraid I'd cry. I was going to have to leave my best friend now and go back to that awful place. Mrs. McAwley motioned for me to sit at the table once we were inside the large, open kitchen I'd come to love since I met Blaze. It was always bright, warm, and smelled of apple pie and fresh bread.

I hesitated, but finally, Blaze sat, so I grabbed the chair next to him. "I don't mean to be na—n—no trouble. I can disappear as f—fa—fas as I appeared," I promised, my stutter heavy from fatigue and fear.

"You're no trouble, Beau," Mrs. McAwley assured me. "Relax and eat." She set a plate of food in front of me that was too hard to pass up.

I ate half the burger before I looked up to see that Blaze's parents had sat opposite us. I wiped my lips with my hand. "You always make the best food," I said, offering a rare smile. "I—I—go once I'm done," I promised, attacking the pile of fries and washing it down with the giant glass of milk Mrs. McAwley had set in front of me. When I finished, she pushed a piece of apple pie in front of me and handed me a fork.

I ate that much slower, savoring the sweet cinnamon apples and the buttery pie crust. It might be the last piece of pie I ever got from Blaze's momma, and I wanted to hold onto the memory as hard as I held onto the memory of my momma. A tear dripped onto the plate, now almost empty, which meant it was time to leave them and find my own way. Another tear fell, and I swiped it away with my shoulder while I finished the last bite of pie and swallowed the last of the cold milk.

I pushed the plate away and stood. "Thank you. I'll sa—see you around," I said, but Mr. McAwley stood and motioned for me to sit my butt down in the chair.

I lowered myself into the seat again and hung my head, the tears falling faster now that they weren't going to let me leave. I was in trouble. Big trouble. I ran away from the foster home, and now they'd probably put me in a home for boys and make me dig holes. I heard they even carried guns and used big dogs.

"You're not going anywhere, Beau," Mr. McAwley said, his voice booming in the quiet of the room.

"But I—I don't wa—want to dig holes," I said, my voice quivering. "I don't even like d—da—dogs."

"What are you talking about, son?" Mrs. McAwley asked. "You don't have to dig holes."

Blaze sighed from where he sat next to me. "We read *Holes* in class at the end of the year. Beau's worried he's going to get sent away to a camp to dig holes. That's why I had to keep him a secret." I could hear how upset Blaze was, and I felt bad for putting him in a position where he had to lie to his parents.

"Do-don't be upset with Bla-Blaze," I stuttered, my problem evident now that I was upset. "I ma—made him pra—prom—promise not to tell."

Mrs. McAwley held up her hand. "We're not upset with either of you, Beau."

I nodded once and tried to smile, but the stupid tears made my lips shake. "Than—thank you. I don't want n-no one to get in trouble, so I'll be ga—goin'. Da-don-do not tell anyone I was ha-here."

"Social services is already aware of your whereabouts," Mr. McAwley said. "We've known you were here since you set foot on the property. We didn't tell Blaze because we wanted to keep you here. If you were here, you were safe."

I glanced between the two adults in confusion. "Why didn't they come get ma—me? I ran away from the foster ho—ho–," I cleared my throat and tried again. "Home."

"Son, they were just happy to know you were safe and that you had a place to stay," Mr. McAwley said. "We did some paperwork with social services over the last few weeks, and now you're going to be staying here."

I was confused, and my voice shook when I spoke. "I'm staying he—here? In the ba-ba-barn?"

Blaze's momma laughed and shook her head. "No, you'll be staying next door to Blaze, in his brother's room."

I swallowed again and eyed her carefully. "But—but Bix just left for call—college. He—he'll be back."

"We have plenty of room here when Bix comes home. You need a place to call your own, and Bix already said it was okay," she explained patiently.

"Fo—for sure?" I asked, still suspicious.

"We're positive, son," Mr. McAwley said, offering a rare smile. Blaze was right. He was a good man. "There will be chores to do, of course. We'll expect them done in a timely fashion each day. Blaze will teach you. He tells me you like horses?"

I nodded eagerly. "Yes, sa—sir."

"Good, then you'll have your own to take care of, along with several others. You'll have to keep the stalls clean and the water troughs full. Can you do that?"

I nodded because I couldn't speak. I was worried the tears were going to start again.

Mrs. McAwley stood and motioned for me to get up. She tucked me under her arm and walked with me toward the stairs to the second floor of the giant home. "Tomorrow, we'll drive into town and get your things from the social worker. We'll also pick up some proper boots and work clothes for the ranch. Good enough?" she asked, squeezing me gently. It had been a long time since I'd gotten a hug from someone who cared about me the way a momma would.

I turned and hugged her, burying my face in her side to hide my tears. "Than—thank you," I wept. "I won't la-la—let you down," I promised, my body crumbling to the ground from the tears, exhaustion, and relief.

It was Mr. McAwley who scooped me up and carried me to the shower, patiently helping me get clean of the day's dirt and the terror of the last few months. I would never forget that look on his face for the rest of my life. It was the same look he wore whenever he helped any of his boys. The fact he was wearin' it now told me I was home.

One

Present Day

The fire snapped and popped every time the wind blew across it, and it pulled me from my memories. Memories of a time like this one where I didn't know who I was or where I was going. The difference was, this wasn't Texas. This was northern Wisconsin, and Mother Nature hadn't had her fill of winter yet. We'd had a warm spell in February, and March rolled in like a lamb, but she was going out like a lion. The bite in the air tonight assured me of it. The animals I was tending wouldn't mind the cold since bison love snow, but my hide was a lot thinner and less hardy than theirs was.

"Beau?" a sweet voice called out, and I turned, surprised to see Dawn riding toward me on her horse, Black Beauty.

"By the fire," I called back, standing and grabbing the reins from her so she could dismount. "What's up?" I asked, hooking Black Beauty to the line where my horse, Cloudy Day, was hanging out.

"Blaze sent me up to check on you. There's bad weather coming."

"I'm aware." I pointed at the walkie by the fire. "He radioed up. He's such a worrywart these days. I'm not afraid of a little wind."

Dawn shook her head and rubbed her arms up and down in the chilly night. "Try wind and snow. The weathermen are saying half a foot by morning. You have to stop playing home on the range and go back to the ranch, Beau."

I motioned her over to the fire so she could warm up. She sat on the old wooden log I used as a backrest and held her hands out to the fire. Her hands always captivated me. They were strong, capable, and should be rough and dry with jagged nails, considering how hard she worked, but they never were. Her hands were always soft, and she wore her nails done up in a sassy purple.

Sassy was an excellent word to describe Dawn Briar Lee. She was fiercely protective of her tribe, and once you were part of that tribe, you were part of it forever. Under her warm Carhartt stocking cap was a pile of strawberry blonde hair I would love to run my fingers through every night. Her eyes were the color of a bison, except for the flecks of gold that dotted them when the firelight was just right. I shifted on the log and tore my gaze from the woman before she caught me gawking. Dawn Lee was so pretty she'd make any man plow through a stump, myself included.

"I'm not playing home on the range," I insisted, throwing some exasperation in there for good measure.

"You've been staying out here for months, Beau. What gives? I know you love camping in the summer, but this is March in Wisconsin. It's time to go inside before you catch your death of a cold."

My gaze landed on the small tent set up to the side that admittedly was becoming ridiculously cold. "I'm fine. The fire keeps me warm, and I have my bison coat and blanket. I'm probably warmer than you are."

She shook her head while rubbing her upper arms through her old barn coat. "Beau, you can't keep dancing around this issue forever. Blaze and Heaven are getting married, but that doesn't mean you can't stay in the house. There are plenty of bedrooms."

I brushed my hand at her with a shake of my head. "Please. I'd sooner sleep in the barn than in the same house with a couple of newlyweds. Ick."

Dawn giggled, and the sound shot straight through me like an arrow. I loved her giggles, and she didn't laugh nearly enough anymore. I hadn't decided why that was yet, but eventually, I'd get to the bottom of it. There were many things about Dawn Briar Lee that I wanted to get to the bottom of if I was honest. I'd had a crush on her for the entire six years I'd known her, but no way in hell was I going to ruin our friendship to scratch an itch. If Blaze weren't my best friend, Dawn would be. I guess I had two best friends at the end of the day, and not everyone could say that.

"You're so romantic, Beau," she cooed, holding her hands near her chin and batting her eyelashes at me.

I didn't respond, but I did let my gaze roam over her in the firelight. Something was wrong with Dawn Briar Lee. The light in her eyes had gone out, and she carried an air of sadness about her now. Maybe she was sad for the same reason I was. Our lives were changing, and we didn't have any control over it anymore.

"If I had to guess, I'd say you're finding it hard to accept that Blaze is getting married again," she said, her hands stretched toward the fire.

"If all your brains were dynamite, you couldn't blow your nose," I muttered, tipping up a cup of hot coffee to my lips. I didn't offer Dawn any in hopes she'd go away and stop bugging me about leaving the ridge.

"Where do you come up with all these ridiculous sayings?" she asked, shaking her head. "Is there a book of stupid Texas sayings that you memorized?"

I refused to answer her, biting my tongue to keep from chewing her out. I wanted her to leave me alone, but I didn't want to hurt her in the process.

Dawn stood and grabbed Black Beauty's reins from the line. "I don't much care what you do, Beau Hanson. Stay, leave, whatever, but I'm not going to lose any sleep over your dead, frozen body." She hauled herself into the saddle, and I noticed she grimaced and sucked in a breath before she finally righted herself. "As for me, I'm going home to a warm house where I'm going to drink hot chocolate with Heaven while we discuss wedding plans."

"Is Heaven staying at Heavenly Lane tonight?" I asked, standing up and tucking my hands in my back pockets.

"She is. We have interviews for the cook position tomorrow. Let's go, Black Beauty," she said, giving the horse a tap with her heels.

I watched her ride off into the darkness and sighed with resignation. I hated that she was right, and not just about the weather. Life was changing again, and I had no idea where my place was in it anymore.

The back door slammed shut, and I gingerly tugged my gloves off. The cold had seeped into my joints in the short thirty minutes I was out there, and I was going to pay for it tomorrow. I tucked my hat in my coat pocket and hung the coat on the hook near the back door. Now that Heaven was living at Bison Ridge, and for the most part, I had this old farmhouse to myself, loneliness was all that permeated the space. I used to come in from doing chores in the barn and share dinner with Heaven, where we'd discuss business or events of the day. Then we'd grab a beer and sit outside by a fire or make hot cocoa and watch movies on the Hallmark Channel. Sure, I still had Tex around, but he lived in the new foreman's cottage next to the old bunkhouse, and he rarely came into the house now. That meant nothing but silence filled the space, giving my mind time to play out all my problems on an endless loop. I'm sure I thought I'd come up with answers eventually, but I never did. I had no answers for the situations I was facing. Well, I had answers, but none of them were good.

I sat down on the bed with a heavy sigh after changing into my pajamas. How was I going to keep going like this? How would I find the strength to keep a smile on my face when all I felt was sadness? It had been a long, lonely winter. Maybe that was all it was. Seasonal depression that would improve when the sun stayed out longer, and the air warmed in the spring. I could hope, but the truth was, I already knew that was only *part* of the problem. I glanced down at my hands and came face-to-face with the rest of it.

A tear ran down my cheek, and I swiped it away before I stood and walked back to the kitchen. I couldn't pretend everything was going to be fine any longer. If I did, I would lose my job here at Heavenly Lane *and* everyone I loved. That wasn't acceptable. Tomorrow, I would have to make the call that I'd been putting off. I kept saying 'maybe tomorrow,' but now there was no more maybe.

I set the saucepan on the stove to start warming the milk for our sweet treat. Heaven would be here soon if she weren't already in the barn putting Grover up for the night. She always rode her horse to Blaze's ranch, so I made sure to keep his stall empty for him when she was here. That wouldn't be for much longer, though. They were getting married in a few months, and then Heaven would be gone from Heavenly Lane Dude Ranch for good.

I grunted at myself as I pulled mugs from the cupboard and got the chocolate mix ready. "Not for good, Dawn. Heavenly Lane is her property. She just won't be sleeping here anymore."

I hated that I had started talking to myself just to fill the silence. I would be grateful when we hired a cook who would live in the house with me. When Heaven decided to turn Heavenly Lane into a dude and guest ranch, I was surprised by how quickly people signed on the dotted line and paid a hefty fee to be a cowboy for a week. Heaven hired a team to put the riding ring up in a matter of weeks, and the new bunkhouse was renovated and insulated for winter. Since the first of the month, we'd had guests here, but it was too much work for me to carry all the responsibilities. Once we hired someone to do the cooking, I could concentrate on the guest services we wanted to offer and stop spending all my time in the kitchen.

I stirred the chocolate into the milk absently while staring out the farmhouse window at the dark ridge beyond. I loved cooking for my friends, but not for overgrown boys who wanted to gorge themselves on steak and eggs. Besides, the way my body had turned on me lately, I couldn't do it for much longer. I prayed every night that if I could stay out of the kitchen, my hands and feet would stop hurting so much. Sometimes the pain was so bad it stole my breath, and I had to stop walking or risk falling. I didn't know how much longer I could hide it, but it helped that Heaven didn't live here anymore. If she did, I was sure she'd already be going on about it.

The back door opened, and a gust of cold wind accompanied my best friend through the door. "Damn, it's going to be ugly by morning. Did you find Beau?" Heaven asked as she unzipped her coat and stomped her feet.

I nodded without turning, busying myself with pouring the hot chocolate into the mugs. "I found him, but I can't say he's going to listen to me. He's crankier than a bear with no honey."

Heaven chuckled and pulled out a kitchen chair to sit. "By the sounds of that, I'd say you've been hanging out with the boy too much."

"Wrong," I corrected her, carrying the hot mugs to the table carefully. "I haven't been hanging out with Beau much at all anymore."

She sipped her cocoa and raised a brow over the mug. "Because?"

"We've been busy, and he's always up on that ridge. I have other things to do, and I'm not the least bit interested in sitting out in the cold all night."

"If you ask me, you're as cranky as a bison ready to calve."

"I didn't ask you," I said, lowering the mug. "I've got enough to worry about here, is what I'm saying. I don't need to be worrying about Beau Hanson, too. If he doesn't want to talk, I sure as hell can't make him."

Heaven held up her hand and waved it. "Blaze is just worried about him, that's all."

I nodded and bit my lip for a moment before I made eye contact with her again. "I am, too. He's going to kill himself out there. I told him I wasn't going to lose any sleep over his dead, frozen body, but you know I would."

"I know you would. Beau's your best guy friend, but I'm your best friend, of course, and it better stay that way, even after

I get married." Her hand was on mine now, and the way she rubbed it belayed the undertone of her joking.

"I wouldn't have it any other way," I promised on a wink. "How are the plans coming to merge the two ranches?" I asked as we carried our cocoa into the living room to get more comfortable. It was warmer in there, too, which wasn't a bad thing on a blustery night like tonight.

We turned on our favorite movie about a haunting in a small town, but all I could see was the haunted eyes of my best guy friend. That seemed to be a theme around here. Most of us were haunted by the past in some way or another. None of us knew how to talk about it. We didn't know *if* we should talk about it. Beau was usually always the first to offer a smile and the last to leave the party. That had changed recently, but none of us knew why.

"And then I told Blaze I was going to sell Grover and buy a Clydesdale to ride," Heaven said.

"Leave Grover here. I'll take care of him," I muttered, my mind still on Beau's sad chocolate eyes.

Heaven tipped my chin toward her. "I just told you I was buying a Clydesdale, babe. What the hell is up with you?"

"I'm worried about Beau." I leaned my head back on the couch. "Like, really worried."

Heaven wiped a tear off my face and ran her fingers through my hair like she does when she wants to say something without making me mad. "I know you are. We're all worried, but I think it's more than that. You're losing weight at a record pace and grimace every time you move wrong. At first, I thought you'd hurt yourself, but I don't think that's the case anymore. I'm not so blinded by the changes in my life that I can't see the changes in yours. I'm still your best friend, Dawn Lee, and I know something is wrong."

I could tell her the truth, but to what end? It would just worry her, and I didn't want to do that when trying to get the dude ranch off the ground *and* plan a wedding. "I did hurt myself. The injury is hanging on, but it's improving, so don't worry."

"I do worry because you're working too hard. I'm glad we had so many applicants for the cook position. That's going to help take a huge load off you every day."

I nodded and offered her a smile that I didn't feel. "I agree. I'm burning the candle at both ends, and it's starting to show. Aren't we supposed to be talking about the wedding plans?" I asked, sitting up and forcing my mind away from that cold cowboy on the ridge and back to my best girl-friend.

"Yes, until I noticed the slump of your shoulders and the pain etched across your face. I decided the plans could wait, and we'd just spend the night watching movies and relaxing. We have plenty of time to talk about the wedding."

I pushed myself up off the couch and grabbed her mug and mine. "In that case, let me get some popcorn and a little Jim Beam. It's not a movie marathon without them."

Heaven laughed, and while the sound was light and airy, I could tell she was forcing it. As I walked away, it was hard to pretend that the look in her eye was anything but worry.

Two

I set a platter of biscuits down on the table and poured myself a cup of coffee. It had been almost a week since I had seen Dawn up on the ridge. Since then, she'd been incognito, which was unusual. We were nearing April, and while it was getting warmer as the sun stayed out later each day, I was still forced to sleep inside for shelter. For the most part, I stayed in the barn unless Heaven was at her ranch, then I slept in the house.

This morning, I'd showered and changed, then made a platter of biscuits to avoid going out to do chores. The end of March offered nothing but cold, blowing snow, which made trying to get work done efficiently almost impossible.

"Smells good in here," Blaze said from the doorway.

I motioned at the platter on the table. "Beau's sausage biscuits are on the menu. Help yourself. There's coffee in the pot."

Blaze strode into the room, his usual cocky swagger firmly in place, even without his boots. He poured himself a cup of coffee and sat at the table, snagging a biscuit, and biting into it. His eyes rolled around in his head, and he moaned, finishing the whole thing before he spoke.

"I swear, Beau, you could market these. They're like heaven."

"And you know heaven."

He pointed at me and gave me the same cheeky grin he'd given me way back in third grade. "I do know Heaven. She's at the ranch getting ready to help the new cook with dinner."

I sipped my coffee and stretched my leg out under the table. "I'm glad Heaven found someone. Now Dawn will have less to do. Did you notice that Dawn lost a lot of weight over the winter?"

He nodded while he chewed his biscuit. "We have. Heaven's terribly worried, but Dawn refuses to talk about it. Maybe you should be the one to ask Dawn about it."

I snorted and almost choked on the swallow of coffee in my mouth. "Dude, do I look dumb as a watermelon? You don't ask a woman something like that." I shook my head at the thickheaded fool in front of me. "That would be the perfect way to end a friendship."

"Maybe not. It might sound like you're concerned about Dawn's wellbeing." He had leaned back to sip his coffee now that he snarfed down two biscuits. I hated it when he eyed me like he knew all my secrets. He thought he did, but he didn't, not anymore.

"Not happening," I said firmly. "What do we have going today?"

His smirk told me he knew I was changing the subject. "Nothing outside if we can avoid it. It's nasty out there and not conducive to anything but frustration and illness. I was hoping you'd run into town for me and pick up a few things while I do some paperwork."

"Not a problem. Give me a list, and I'll get it done. I have some work to do in the barn and something I need to finish in the workshop when I get back."

"That's fine since there isn't much we can do in this kind of weather. The lawyer is coming out later. We'll be drawing up the paperwork to put safeguards in place regarding the ranches. That way, if something were to occur, we're all protected."

"You're getting a prenup?" I asked, surprised. "I thought you trusted each other."

"It's not a prenup like you're thinking. It's more like a trust, and Heaven agrees we need to do it."

"Well, I'm glad Heaven was there to help you make decisions about our ranch." The sarcasm dripped heavily from my words.

Blaze leaned forward and thumped the table with his finger. "You got something to say, boy, then say it."

I sat mutely, sipping my coffee and eyeing the plate of biscuits. I carried them to the counter and packaged them up, planning to drop them by Heavenly Lane for Tex on my way to town. When I turned back to the table, he was still sitting there, but now steam poured from his ears.

"If you want to get me that list, I'll head into town." I leaned on the counter and waited for him to either get the list or explode. There was never any in-between with Blaze.

He pointed at the chair I'd exited and lifted a brow. Looks like he done chose explode. I slid into the seat and rested my arm on the table, tapping my fingers on the old wooden top. I looked relaxed, but I was steeling myself for the tongue lashing to come. You don't badmouth Miss Heaven without getting a butt chewing.

"What's your problem with Heaven?"

"I ain't got a problem with Miss Heaven." I made sure my voice was steady and sickeningly sweet.

"Then what's your problem with me because you sure as hell have a problem with someone."

"I don't have a problem, Blaze. Let it go. It's been a long winter. I'm ready for some warmth and sunshine."

"And I fell off a bison and landed in a bed of roses," he drawled.

My laughter echoed around the room, and I had to wipe the tears from my eyes. "Good Lord almighty, son! You suck at Texan phrases. Holy man," I said, laughter bubbling up every time I thought of it. "You never could use them right."

Blaze waited out my giggles until I was quiet again. "I can't help but notice you haven't slept more than a night or two in the house since January."

"That's not all that unusual," I said, motioning around the kitchen. "I sleep all over the place on this ranch. Work has to get done, and someone has to do it who isn't shacking up for a long winter's nap."

"There it is." A smirk filled his face, but it wasn't his usual sarcastic one. This one looked dangerous.

"There what is? You asked, and I answered."

"I have more brains than a bumblebee, Beau. I can see what's going on. I haven't said anything in hopes you'd talk to me, but you aren't, so now I'm going to speak my piece. I'm worried about your mental state."

"My mental state is just fine. Don't go getting all touchy-feely on me."

Blaze shook his head and crossed his arms over his chest, one brow going up in the air. "I don't think it is. What I can't understand is why you're so upset about me marrying Heaven. You didn't so much as blink when Callie and I got married."

Callie was Blaze's first wife. When Blaze's daddy sent us up here to this frozen tundra to learn how to ranch bison, she refused to stay behind, even though Blaze tried to break it off with her. She stayed, worked the ranch, and died at the hands of one of the animals up on the ridge. That had been almost six years ago now. I didn't begrudge Blaze's happiness. He'd suffered enough here, and so had Miss Heaven. She was injured trying to save Callie, and now her left arm was completely paralyzed. That girl had seen enough hardship, too.

"Listen, I'm glad you've found happiness again. Can we leave it at that?" I asked, not making eye contact with the man who I had known for over twenty years. We were more than friends. We were brothers. I just wasn't sure I could find a place here now that he was marrying his meant to be. They'd be starting a family once they were married, I had no doubt, and where did that leave me? No place that I wanted to be. That's where.

"No, we can't leave it at that. I may have found happiness again, but you are the furthest thing from it. Are you unhappy here? Do you want to return to Texas? If you do, I'll understand, Beau. I won't like it, but I'll understand and honor your wishes."

"I told you before, and I'll tell you again, Wisconsin is my home now. There ain't nothing for me back in Texas other than another ranch that means nothing to me anymore. If it makes you happy, I'll make sure to be inside by eleven every night for curfew," I said sarcastically.

Blaze shook his head slowly while his fingers tapped out a rhythm on the table. "I'm more concerned about what makes you happy, Beau."

"I used to think I knew what that was, Blaze. I'm not so sure anymore," I admitted. "Listen, it's nothing against you or Miss Heaven. I'm glad you two finally got your heads out of the backside of a bull to see what the rest of us could see. I'm going to be here to take care of this place while you get hitched."

"And then you're going to stay and keep working this land with me, right?" he asked, leaning forward. "You're the reason this place stayed alive after Callie. We both know it."

"Water under the bridge, Blaze." I flicked my hand at my wrist to shoo that nonsense away. "Can I go to town now? I'm uncomfortable."

"Because I'm expressing my appreciation for your hard work or because you know I know you're in a bad place right now?"

I stared over his shoulder toward the empty doorway. "Both."

"You still haven't answered my question. Why are you so worked up about me marrying Heaven?"

"Callie was a known to me, Blaze. Miss Heaven is not."

His brows furrowed for a beat before he answered. "You've known Heaven for eight years. What makes her an unknown?"

"I don't know. That's just how it feels, oh—oh—okay? I didn't say I could explain it. You're the one in—insis—sistin' I do."

"I won't push you on it then, but I will push you on these two things. You start sleeping in the house. I don't like worrying about where you are or if you're safe. Feel free to move upstairs if you don't want to run into Heaven when she's here. If that's making you uncomfortable, I won't take offense."

"Fine, done, but only until calving season, then I'm on the ridge again."

"I don't understand why. There's nothing you can do out there to help the cows give birth."

I tipped my head at him in confusion. Had he dropped his brains out his Stetson when he decided to get hitched again? "Well, of course not, but I can make sure the wolves don't go after the little ones."

"They won't. Wolves don't mess with bison."

"I like being out there, is that oh—kay?" I asked angrily. "I just like being out there su-su-sometimes."

"It's fine, Beau. Just make sure you're safe when you're out there. Rifle at the ready at all times."

I saluted, and he rolled his eyes in feigned sarcasm. Unfortunately, I could see the look in his eyes that said he was more than a little worried and not just about my safety.

"What's the second thing?" I asked, tired of making small talk. I'd rather work until I dropped than talk to Blaze McAwley about our feelings.

"I want you to think about talking to someone about your momma. I can see the date on the calendar, Beau. You're staring down twenty years since you lost her. I know that must be hard, but I think it's more than time you lay her to rest."

I stood, grabbed the bag of biscuits and my coat, then slammed the back door behind me without another word.

Screw him.

I'd never lay my momma to rest. He could ride all the way to hell on the high and mighty horse he rode in on first.

The truck rumbled under me on this cold morning, making it clear it didn't want to be out here. Neither did I, but I had a job to do, and by God, I was going to do it. I didn't care what Blaze McAwley thought. I made my trip into Wellspring for the things we needed, and I was ready to head back when I noticed a familiar figure walking down the sidewalk to my right. When I had dropped off the biscuits at Heavenly Lane earlier, Tex told me Dawn had gone into town for the morning. Looks like I just found her.

I slowed and rolled the truck window down before I called out to her. "Dawn? Where's your truck? It's too cold out to be walking."

"Go away, Beau."

Hmm, not the greeting I wanted. Dawn's thin shoulders were hunched nearly to her ears to block the wind, but I couldn't figure out where she was going. She surely hadn't walked into town when the ranch was ten miles out in the sticks. Her coat hung on her now that she'd lost so much weight, but she was still as gorgeous as she ever was. If only she weren't the only friend I had left in this town, I would take this woman out for dinner, dancin' and a little romancin'.

"I'm not going to do that, Dawn. Get in the truck, and I'll take you to your car."

Her shoulders slumped, but she stopped walking and waited for me to bring the truck to a stop. Once I did, she pulled herself up into it and slammed the door. I rolled the window up and cranked the heater to high, warding off the chill of the morning.

"What's going on? Tex told me you went to town, but he didn't know why."

"So you came looking for me?" she snapped. "I can take care of myself, Beau. I don't need you following me around like a red dog follows his cow."

I tipped my head at her, the steady rhythm of the flashers the only sound in the truck. "I know you can, and I wasn't following you. Blaze texted me a list of things to pick up for the ranch. I was in town and noticed you walking down the street. Where's your truck? I'll drive you up there."

"I wasn't going to my truck. I had to go to the pharmacy, and it wasn't that far."

The pharmacy was at least three more blocks up the street, so I let off the brake and signaled onto the almost deserted road. The town of Wellspring, Wisconsin, wasn't a busy metropolis on a good day, but no one even poked their head out if they could avoid it on a day like today. Wellspring had a clinic, pharmacy, feed store, café, and several mom-and-pop shops that kept the townspeople from having to drive another ten miles to a bigger city. When Blaze and I blew into town, we were a bit taken aback. We lived in a small town in Texas, but even that town was three times the size of this one.

The ride to the pharmacy was silent, and even an obtuse cowboy like me could feel the anxiety and sadness rolling off her in waves. I parked in front of the pharmacy and waited for her to open the door. "I'll wait here, and then I'll drive you back to your truck."

Dawn slammed the truck door without a word and stole into the pharmacy. I watched her through the windows as she stood in front of the counter talking to the pharmacist. While I waited, I tried not to think about what Blaze had said to me earlier today, but that was impossible now that I was alone again. His words rolled through my head like the annoying lyrics of a famous pop song. The truth had little to do with Heaven being at Bison Ridge now. The truth had everything to do with being unhappy that Blaze was getting a second chance at happiness when I hadn't gotten my first.

Contrary to his opinion, it had nothing to do with my momma's death, either. It had everything to do with the beautiful, pain-filled eyes of the woman standing in the pharmacy. Something was wrong with her, but I didn't know what it was. I did know it was killing me to watch her become someone I didn't recognize—both physically and emotionally. We had been best friends for years, but this winter, that all changed. She had changed. She stopped laughing. Tex told me he'd even found her crying on more than one occasion. I wanted to help her, but I didn't know how. That was the hardest pill to swallow. She was within reach, but she was going to slip away and drown because she refused to take my hand.

When Dawn turned from the counter with a bag in her hand and her head hanging in defeat, I saw the answer to the question I didn't want to ask. Regardless, the time had come to get the root of her problem out in the open, even if that meant she never talked to me again.

Three

Why was Beau so good at showing up in the wrong place at the wrong time? He was always around when I didn't want him to be and never around when I did. I guess that's what made him one of my best friends. He sensed when I needed him, even if I never spoke the words. His big brown eyes held a level of heat to them when he gazed at me that both excited and scared me. He was tall and lanky, but every scrap of his one hundred and seventy pounds was muscle. He wore his hair in a typical Texas cowboy shag that was always in need of a cut but rarely got one. Today he wore a Stetson over the shag, one he'd made himself from bison leather. He was the quintessential Texas cowboy right down to the vocabulary he used to express himself. He'd lived in Wisconsin for years, but that didn't mean a hill of beans, as he would say. He still spoke as though he had just walked off the ranch in Texas.

Beau was a proud man. He was proud of his profession and the work he did. He also insisted he wasn't intelligent, but that wasn't even close to the truth. He was wise in all the ways it mattered, including matters of friendship and family. He was intensely loyal to his friends, which made him one of those guys you knew you could count on, no matter what.

This morning, those sienna eyes were unnerving me from across the booth at the small café in Wellspring. When I left the pharmacy, he refused to take me back to the truck and insisted I have coffee with him first. I wasn't in the mood to do that, but I couldn't convince him I needed to get back to the ranch. From what he tells me, he'd already been by there this morning, and Tex told him I was off for the day. Thanks, Tex. I blew out a breath as I stared at the black brew in my mug. It wasn't Tex's fault, I guess. I didn't tell anyone why I was going into town. Not even Heaven.

"You okay?" he asked, settling his rough and tumble hand over mine on the table.

I inhaled sharply, and he lifted it again instantly. His gaze tracked downward until it came face-to-face with my hand. He glanced up immediately. "What the hell, Dawn Lee? Your fingers are all red and swollen. Did you hurt them at the ranch? Is that why you were at the clinic?"

I lowered my hand to my lap and lifted my mug to my lips with my right hand to avoid answering him. Unfortunately, he was a patient man. He was ridiculously good at waiting people out when they didn't want to talk. Beau sipped his coffee some more and waited until finally, I couldn't take those eyes staring at me in silence any longer.

"I'm fine, Beau. Leave it alone."

He settled back into the cushioned red booth and frowned the way only Beau could. His lips went down, his cheeks fell, and his eyes followed. I never knew that eyes could frown, but Beau's deep all-knowing eyes could. "I'd like to believe that you're fine, but you're not. You've easily lost fifty pounds since last summer, and you didn't have it to lose to begin with."

"Seventy-five and I had plenty of extra padding," I said smartly, my lips going back to the cup so they wouldn't keep talking.

Beau lifted the other brow. "That didn't help your case, Dawn. I'm worried about you, so is everyone else at the two ranches. You don't have to pretend that something isn't wrong if it is."

I shook my head and didn't make eye contact with him. If I started crying, I would never stop, and I didn't have time for that. I didn't even have time to sit here and drink coffee with the guy I couldn't stop thinking about every minute of every day. I had a job to do, and I had to get back to the ranch and do it. Considering what the doctor told me today, I would need that job just to stay alive. "I'm not talking about this right now. Besides, I could say the same thing about you. You haven't been yourself lately either, Beau Hanson. If you ask anyone in a ten-mile radius, they'd say you've been meaner than a momma wasp."

He was going for nonchalant, but the shrug he gave me was jerky and filled with an emotion I couldn't put my finger on. Something told me I better figure it out sooner rather than later if I wanted to keep him in my life. "It's been a long winter, nothing more. I'm tired of being cooped up. I need sunshine and some warmer temperatures." He said it as if he recited it to the mirror every morning before he left the house. It rolled off his tongue too quickly for it to be the truth.

My hand chose that moment to throb, and my breath hitched. I had to drag in short staccato breaths for a moment while I held my hand to my chest. Beau reached out and lowered my hand to his warm ones, cradling it and letting the heat of his hands ease the aching. He didn't touch the fingers or do anything but hold it for me until I could speak. "I know what you mean," I finally agreed. I didn't want to look into his sweet eyes, so I stared out the window at the fat snowflakes as they fell. When they hit the ground, they melted into drops of wet slush. "At least we're getting closer to spring. "

"I heard Heaven was able to hire a cook for the dude ranch. Good news, right?" he asked. The question was small talk, but his attention was focused on my hand in his. He was studying it as though he was memorizing the mottled skin and had plans to report back to Heaven about it. As if she couldn't see it with her own eyes.

I pulled my hand back and tucked it under the table, even though that was just going to make it throb. I would bite my tongue off before I showed weakness in front of him again, though.

"I was thrilled to hear it," I admitted. "Considering Heaven's getting married in a few months and won't be living at the ranch at all, I will need the help. I can't do it all. I helped her with the interviews, and I think Cecelia will fit in perfectly at Heavenly Lane."

Beau's fingers tapped on the table while we both stared out the window. "I'm still trying to figure out how it's all going to work, you know?"

"Me, too," I admitted. "The ranches aren't that far apart, but she won't be at Heavenly Lane at all once she's married."

"And that changes the dynamics equally as much at Bison Ridge."

I glanced down at my cup and back to him. "I know you're not happy living there anymore, Beau. I can understand why, so I thought maybe you should move into the house on Heavenly Lane."

He lowered his cup slowly and lifted one brow. It was always sexy as hell. I pictured him doing that at night after a shower wearing nothing but a towel. The image made me squirm in my seat, and I forced myself to put those thoughts and feelings aside. I couldn't fall for Beau Hanson. He was about to be the only best friend I'd have around. I rolled my eyes at myself internally. *You can't fall for Beau Hanson.* That horse left the barn years ago.

"You want me to move into Heaven's house? With you?" he asked, as though he was clarifying the statement.

I nodded but still didn't make eye contact. "I've gotten the vibe that you don't want to live in the house at Bison Ridge."

Beau chuckled his famous *Texas get 'em* chuckle. What was a *Texas get 'em* chuckle? It was the sound he made to get a woman to do whatever he wanted. Only this time, I suspected it was more of a nervous laugh covered by his signature sound to distract me. Either way, my stomach swooped at the sound. I wanted to lay my lips on his, which meant his chuckle got me every time.

"What gave you that vibe?"

I leaned back on the booth and eyed him. "Oh, I don't know. Maybe the fact that you've been anywhere but there since Blaze and Heaven got engaged." He didn't answer, just stared out the window at the falling snow. I set my mug down and rested my hand on his wrist. "You've been part of Blaze's life for as long as you can remember, Beau. Things change the moment he marries Heaven. Even more so than they did when he married Callie. I understand that. Heaven and Blaze understand that. You don't have to pretend something different out of deference to them."

His gaze flicked to mine for a breath, and the swirling anger and discontent I saw in his now dark tumultuous globes made my breath pause in my chest. He was in worse shape than I had suspected, and I didn't know what to do about it anymore.

Beau shook my hand off his arm, stood, and walked out of the café, leaving me with tears in my eyes and regret in my heart.

Where in the hell does she get off acting like she knows what's going on in my head? That's rich coming from her. Obviously, she thought she knew something she didn't. My foot hesitated on the gas before I pulled away from the café. Was I leaving her stranded? Nah, screw it. Dawn was a big girl. She knew where her truck was and could find her way back to it. I had better things to do. I pressed down on the accelerator, ready to get back to the ranch. Anger made the blood run hot through my veins and hurt dropped a cloudy haze over my vision.

I was angry at myself. I was mad as hell at Blaze. Now I was ticked off at Dawn.

Dawn didn't do anything wrong, Beau, a quiet voice said.

I flicked it away with my hand and refused to listen to it. Everyone wanted to be in my business while trying to keep their own a secret. I wasn't playing that game anymore. Ever since Blaze got engaged to Heaven, he's been different. Not necessarily different bad, but different enough that I no longer felt welcome on the ranch.

I pounded my fist into the steering wheel and turned the truck down the gravel road toward Bison Ridge. Blaze was at the house doing paperwork, and I didn't want to talk to him, so I'd unload the supplies from town and then head to the shop to finish up a few things before it was time to do chores again. When Bison Ridge came into view, my heart stuttered in my chest.

How many more times was I going to see this beautiful land stretch out before me?

How many more times was I going to get up in the morning and keep doing my job when no one cared either way if I did or not?

The answer used to be 'until I took my last breath' for both, but I wasn't so sure anymore. If I took Dawn Lee up on her offer to move into the house on Heavenly Lane, I could still wake up and do my job every morning. Riding down the road every day to Bison Ridge wouldn't be a big deal, but sleeping in the same house with Dawn and not being able to touch her would be a deal-breaker.

At the thought of Dawn, I swallowed hard and shook my head, shame filling me. I could still feel her hot, swollen hand in mine and could hear her sharp intake of breath at the pain. My groan filled the cab of the truck, and I pounded the steering wheel again. I should never have left her there alone. I knew she had her vehicle there, but I should have given her a ride back to it. My momma would not be happy with my decisions today.

I turned the truck into the driveway and noticed Heaven struggling to get off Grover's back. I rolled my window down and yelled as I threw the truck into park. "Wait, and I'll help you, Miss Heaven!"

I jumped out of the truck and jogged toward Grover as he patiently waited for his rider to dismount. Grover was probably thinking the same thing I was. *Why was she so stubborn?* Heaven was always trying to do things that were going to get her hurt or killed.

I held tight to her waist and lifted her tiny frame down off the horse. "Where's Blaze, and why isn't he helping you?" I asked as soon as she was firmly on the ground.

"I wanted to put Grover right into the barn, but Blaze was on the phone."

I shook my head and grabbed the horse's reins. "I picked up your dismounting stairs. They're in the truck. Why don't we put

Grover in the barn, and you can tell me where you'd like the stairs set up?"

Heaven walked with me into the barn. "Bison Ridge has a better barn set up than Heavenly Lane does. If we put them right outside his stall, that would make it easiest," she answered while I pulled the saddle off Grover, and she started brushing him out.

"Sure, that makes sense. The stairs will be out of the way there, too. Let me grab them." I pulled the handcart to the truck and loaded them up. When I brought them back into the barn, Heaven was leaning on the stall waiting for me.

I unloaded them silently until they were set up and secured together again. "Will that work for you?" I motioned at them, and she nodded, but she never took her eyes off me. I was starting to feel exposed. I didn't like it one bit. Hopefully, she went into the house soon so I could do my work without her eyes boring holes in my back.

"I just talked to Dawn. She's on her way back to my ranch. She sounded upset. Can you saddle Grover again, so I can go check on her?"

I refused to stay in the barn and play, so I walked into the house and to Blaze's office, where he was drinking coffee and doing paperwork. "Miss Heaven is in the barn. She needs a ride back to the—"

I got whiplash before the words were out of my mouth. When I finished the forced spin, I came face-to-face with Heaven, who was steaming mad. I could tell by the way her eyes were half squinted closed, and her breathing was heavy. She had the strength of ten men with only one working arm. She could kick my butt if she had two.

She backed me up against the office door and stuck her finger in my chest. "Did you leave Dawn sitting in a café in town a mile away from her truck, or did you not?"

"She wasn't a mile away from her truck. It wasn't more than four blocks." I stared at the floor to hide the shame I felt being read the riot act by this tiny thing. An hour old red dog weighed more than this woman, but I was far more scared of her than I was of a red dog.

Blaze took his almost-wife's finger out of my face and held her against his chest. I was thankful. At least I could breathe again. "Did you leave Dawn in town? Were you supposed to bring her home?"

I tossed up my arms and let them fall. "No. We ran into each other and went for ca—cof—fee at the café. Dawn had her truck."

"A truck that was parked a ten-minute walk away," Heaven said again. "And it's snowing, and she hurt herself, which is the reason she was at the clinic!"

"I took her to the pharmacy, but she didn't say what she needed. I noticed her hand was swollen. She refused to tell me why, so I left."

"Maybe if you had stayed in the café with her, instead of leaving in a huff, she would have told you," Heaven said, her words dripping with sarcasm.

"For your information, I tried to fa—ind out!" Wa—wa—at do you want from me? I can't make her say something she da—don—t want to say!"

Blaze shook his head in shock and probably disappointment, but I was too hot to care. "And you still chose to leave her there? Did she tell you she didn't need a ride back to the truck?"

"No," I answered without making eye contact with either one of them. "She had her truck, so I knew she wasn't ster—an—ded. It was better that I left. What's the b—ba—big deal?"

Blaze scratched the back of his head in confusion. "I just … I don't know you anymore, Beauregard Hanson. You're not the same guy I drove up here with twelve years ago."

The heat crept up my cheeks when I tossed my hands onto my hips to keep from punching him out. "We were eighteen-year-old ka—kids the day we left Texas. Ya—yor—you're not the same person I drove up here in that truck with either, Blaze McAwley! I—I—d poured my blood, sweat, and tears into this pull—ace out of respect to your family for what they did for me when I was a kid! I stood by you when you were the biggest jerk ah—aft—fter Callie died. For years! I did that because I knew you were hurting, and I—I—I couldn't fix things for you, but I—I could make sure this place didn't go to hell in a han—ha—handbasket. You act like I'm supposed to be some ha—p—happy go lucky backwoods hick twenty-four se—se—ven. La—la—ike, I can't have a thought in my head that you didn't put there. Well, guess wa—what? I'm tired! I'm tired of running this place while you get to pa—lay. I'm tired of pretending that my life doesn't suck. I'm tired of telling ma—ma—self that you need me, and that's why I st—stay. Is that what you wanted to ha—ear? Does that fill you with the tu—tu—touchy-feels? I'm miserable, but you can bet your sweet Texas ah—as—butt that I'm going to be here working still. That's what I was tasked to do, and tha—hat is what I'll do. I don't give one ba—bison turd if you like it or not."

I turned my back to them and walked down the hallway with my head held high. You could hear a pin drop other than the slap of my boot heels on the old hardwood floor and then the slam of the front door when I walked out, maybe for the last time. I probably just lit a match to a bridge already soaked in kerosene. Truth be told, I didn't even care. It was a bridge that was falling apart around my ears anyway.

There was a thumping on the door, and I checked the clock. It was after midnight, which forced a sigh from my lips. My daddy always said nothing good happened after midnight. I sighed again and tossed my feet over the bed, then grabbed my robe. It was probably Tex. Maybe we had a problem with one of the guests, and he needed help. He would have called, though, and he wouldn't knock on the front door.

I pulled the curtain back, and there was a face that I'd been worried about for days. I wasn't the only one, either. I yanked the door open and planted a hand on my hip. Complete relief filled me that I made sure to cover with feigned anger. "What the hell, Beau Hanson?" I demanded.

He was lounging against the doorframe and offered me his famous Beauregard smile. "Hey, sweetheart, mind if I come in?" The slur of his words and the stink of booze wafting toward me as soon as he opened his mouth told me he was drunker than a skunk.

I pulled him in the door, and he nearly fell face-first onto the carpet. He righted himself in time and kicked his boots off, then threw his coat on the floor. "Did you miss me?"

I shoved him in the shoulder with real anger this time. "Everyone has been worried sick! Where the hell have you been?"

"Around. If Blaze took his head out of his backside, he'd have noticed that my chores were done," Beau said, his words slurring heavily.

I shoved him again, and this time he stumbled backward and landed on the couch. Beau's laughter filled the room. It would have been a relief to hear if it weren't for the fact it was simply alcohol-induced. "Ooh-wee, this here little gal is in a horn-tossing ma—mood!"

I shook my head at him and walked to the kitchen, hitting the brew button on the coffee pot that I'd set up last night for the morning. I grabbed my phone and punched a familiar button, then waited for it to be picked up.

"Hello?"

"Blaze? It's Dawn. Beau just showed up at my door."

He released a heavy sigh. "Thank God. Is he okay?"

"Drunker than a skunk and smells just as bad but otherwise fine. Beau said he was doing his chores, so you should have known he was fine."

"Doing his chores and being fine are two different things. That boy would do his chores if he were dead."

I bit back my laughter so Beau wouldn't hear me. "Good point. I'll sober him up and let him sleep upstairs. I'll make sure he gets home safely tomorrow morning for his chores."

"If it weren't freezing out, I'd tell you to leave him hanging the same way he left you the other day, but he'd probably pass out and die."

"Considering he's leaking whiskey from his pores, that's a good possibility."

"Want me to come around and collect him?"

"Nope," I answered immediately. "Something tells me that would be a bad idea. Just let me talk to him for a bit. I'll get some coffee in him, too. Go to sleep. I know you've been looking for him late every night."

Blaze sighed, and I could almost see him nodding. "I'm on Rapunzel now. I was just heading back in since it's so cold. I can't risk my horse because he's a stupid fool."

I chuckled and turned to grab two mugs from the cupboard. "I feel like that's a saying that should come out of Beau's mouth. You'll see him in the morning. Night, Blaze."

I hung up the phone, tucked it in my robe pocket again, then poured two cups of coffee, carrying them to the couch. I handed Beau one, and he took it, swigging back most of it before he took a breath. It had to have burned the skin right off his tongue, but he didn't look bothered.

"Had to call my daddy and report my whereabouts?"

I handed him my entire cup of coffee and carried his cup back into the kitchen. I grabbed a clean mug for myself and refilled it, then wandered back to sit in the chair opposite the couch. If he decided to puke, I wanted to be out of his projectile range.

"No, I called your best friend and told him you hadn't frozen to death in a ditch. He was out on Rapunzel looking for you, just like he has been the last three nights."

"I didn't ask him to be. He knew I was fine. I did my chores."

"Which you already pointed out," I agreed. "And as Blaze pointed out, you'd do your chores if you were dead. I don't honestly care, Beau. I have my own problems, and you're interrupting my sleep. You're welcome to crash upstairs for the night. It's time to sober up. Drunk doesn't look good on you."

"I'm not that drunk," he said, his words slurring slightly. "I've been drunker."

I leaned forward, a thought seeping into my sleep-deprived brain. "How did you get here? Did you drive? Is Cloudy Day outside in the cold?"

I forced myself not to roll my eyes at the name of his horse. He named him Cloudy Day because his markings look like clouds in the sky. He wasn't wrong, but it was still a ridiculous name for a horse.

"No, Mommy, I didn't drive, and my horse is in the stable. Ding-ding that should have been another clue that I was still alive and ka—icking."

"I know you didn't walk in from town, so where have you been?" I asked, leaning back in my chair, ready to be entertained by this story.

"I do—do not have to tell you my sa—see—crets."

"Does that secret involve Jim Beam? Because that's not much of a secret," I said, waving my hand in front of my face. "You smell like a distillery."

"Jack Daniels and only half a bottle." He tipped his mug up and finished it. When he stood, he stumbled to the side several times on his way to the kitchen. He returned with another cup of coffee that spilled over the side of the cup with every step. He finally stopped in the middle of the floor and drank the rest of it. "I'm going to the bathroom. Be ri—ri back," he slurred, then jogged down the hallway and shut the door.

My phone beeped, and I grabbed it from my pocket while I shook my head at the man in the can. What the heck was going on with him? I didn't know this Beau Hanson. The part that bothered me the most was that I didn't think Beau knew that guy either. That was scaring him. I opened my phone and read the text from Heaven. She was wondering if I was okay or if she should come home. I quickly typed back that I was okay and could more than handle Beau Hanson with one hand tied behind my back.

I used to think that was true, but this new Beau was a wild card I couldn't predict. Was I in physical danger? No. Beau would never hurt me physically. Emotionally he absolutely could, and if the other day at the café were any indication, he absolutely would without a second thought. He knew how to cut right to my core without even trying. I would have to encourage him to go to bed tonight and then talk to him in the morning when he was sober. I tapped my phone in my hand. Then again, perhaps talking to him drunk wasn't a terrible idea. With his inhibitions gone, he might tell me what the hell was eating him up inside.

The bathroom door popped open, and he strode back into the room, his eyes hooded and his coffee cup missing. I figured I'd find it on the back of the toilet come morning.

"Thanks. I've been outside since I finished chores at sev—sev—seven. I was drinking Jack to stay warm, and it got away from me." He grabbed the blanket off the back of the couch and wrapped himself in it before he sat down next to me.

"You didn't have to be out in the cold. That was a quarantine of your own making, no one else's."

"I wasn't exactly we—wel—welcome in either house."

"Also your own doing," I pointed out. I had to be careful. If I made Beau mad, he'd clam up and refuse to speak to me, just like the other day. I had to get him to talk without sending the message that his recent behavior was acceptable.

"Never said it wasn't," he shot back.

I held up my phone. "Everyone has texted me now. I assured Blaze and Heaven they could go to bed. Maybe you should, too. I won't let anyone bother you. Blaze said to take the morning off. He'll make sure the chores get done."

Beau rolled his eyes sarcastically, but it took some effort for him to get them back to the midline. "I'm sure he will, by making one of the other han—hands do them. I'm not going to neglect my duties and make someone else pa—pay for it. I'm not that kind of cow—cow—cowboy."

My head tipped when I realized what I thought was drunken slurring was a pronounced stutter now. The only time Beau ever stuttered was when he was upset or emotional. Then again, I'd never seen him this drunk before. Maybe that made his stutter worse too. "Okay, then I'll make sure you're up and out of here on time."

"Is that all you have to sa—sa—ay to me?"

"I don't know what to say to you anymore, Beau. I'm afraid that no matter what I say, it will be the wrong thing."

"You're going to stop being ma—my—my friend, too? Is that what you're sa—sa—saying?"

I shook my head at the man in front of me. "I don't recall ever saying that, Beau. Would people who don't want to be your friend be out in the cold searching for you late into the night?'

"Toots, Bla—Blaze could have found me at any time in the barn. He knows ma—my—" He froze for a moment and swallowed, taking a deep breath. "He knows my schedule." His words were slow and purposeful with that statement.

I tipped my head in acknowledgment. "Blaze was trying to give you space. When you didn't show up after three days, he got worried. Besides, we both know you weren't in the barn. You had the other ranch hands doing those chores. We might look dumb as a bullbat, but we aren't."

Beau didn't say anything for so long I was afraid he had fallen asleep. When he did speak, he spoke slowly. Whether it was because he was trying to stop the stutter or because he had sobered up a little bit, I didn't know. "Did Blaze ever tell you about the time I lived on his ranch without anyone knowing but him? I ate ah—apples and ka—rrots from the horse barn. It turns out every—everyone knew I wa—was there. I was eleven and thought we were sneaky."

"Blaze never told me that, though I'm not sure why he would. That said, being out in Texas in March is a whole lot different than being out alone in a Wisconsin winter."

"It was in July. I had run away from my fa—fos—ter family and right to Blaze's ranch. We'd been best friends since the third grade, and he was all—all—all I had left."

He was getting upset, so I rubbed his arm through the blanket to calm him. "Beau, relax, okay? I want to hear your story, but I can tell you're struggling. Just take a deep breath."

His inhale and exhale were apparent, though I suspected they were unconscious. "I ya——ya—use to have a stutter pra—pa—problem, did you know that?" I shook my head, and he nodded his up and down. There was more than a touch of shame in the motion. "I ga—gre—grew out of it, except if I—I am mad or sad or drunk. Sor—sorry."

"That must be hard, Beau. No need to apologize. I'd like to hear the rest of your story. I don't mind if you stutter. You can take as long as you need. I'm not going anywhere."

When he spoke again, he was calmer. He had grabbed hold of my arm and wasn't letting go. "I hid during the day, and at night, Blaze, he'd bring me food out to—ta—to the barn. Two weeks after I got there, his momma and daddy sa—sha—wed up. They let me stay in the house then as their foster son. They wanted to adopt me, but I wouldn't let the—the—em."

"Did you need adoptive parents? Why wouldn't you let them? You and Blaze are closer than any two brothers I know."

"My momma was dead and my daddy," he shook his head in disgust. "Well, he was a real son of a motherless ga—goat. I didn't even know the man. My momma made sure I never knew who he was. Ba—ba–ut, I heard stories. I da—do—not know if—ah—if any are true."

"I'm sorry about your mom, Beau," I said softly, unsure what part of this story I was supposed to be focusing on—his mother, his father, or living with Blaze. Something told me it was his mother. "What was your mom's name?"

"Samantha," he answered, nodding. "She la—la—oved that I had Blaze as a friend. He an—an I were like brothers. Amity and Ash raised us that way after she passed. We scrapped a lot, but we knew who loved us an—ah—and where they lived, if you know what I mean."

"I do," I agreed, deciding it was less about the story for him and more about just needing someone to talk to who wouldn't judge him.

"The McAwleys are good people, Da—Da—Dawn Lee," he said, his tongue struggling to keep up with his brain. "Sometimes, most times, I wish I had their last name. It would have made my life ba—ba—etter. Then I see my momma's face in my mind, and I ra—rem—mber that if they adopted me, my name would change. Did you know after someone dies, that ya—ya start to forget their face? I didn't believe my foster family when they told me that. I thought they were being jack—jackah—jerks, but they were right." He cleared his throat and stared down at the floor. "It will be twenty years in a few weeks. I have to look at pictures to ra—rah—remember her now. I wonder if she ever would have found someone to love like Blaze found Miss Heaven. I wonder if sha—if she would have done all those things she talked about doin'. I wonder a lot of things, but I won't ever know the answers."

"Beau, I'm sorry," I whispered, moving closer to him to offer comfort. Suddenly, the blurry picture from the last few months came into sharp focus. His reaction to Blaze's engagement, his usual easygoing manner flipping to *fly off the handle* in the blink of an eye, and his need to seclude himself from others. "I had no idea about any of this."

His shoulder went up and back down before he picked up my hand and inspected the fingers. "I'm sa—sa—orry 'bout leaving you at the café the other da—day," he whispered. "I ain't been myself lately. I feel ra—really bad about it. Miss Heaven told me you hurt yourself, and that made me feel even worse. When I don't know wa—wa—what to do with the way I been feelin', the—then I know it's better if I'm away from people.

When I feel like ta—this," he said, squeezing his fist to his chest and pounding it. "I hurt people. I don't know why baa—but it ain't on purpose, Dawn Lee."

I brushed the hair out of his eyes and tipped his chin up to meet my gaze. "Beau, we've been friends for a long time, right?" I asked, and he nodded, his brown eyes dark and half full of whiskey. "Then, if you can't be a jerk to your friends, who can you be a jerk to?"

Beau stared me down, but his head shook slightly. "Still ain't right. My momma raised me better than that. I—I—am old enough ta—to know better. Accept my apology?"

"It's already forgotten," I promised. "Maybe you could cut yourself a little slack, though. We're all terribly worried about you. We don't expect you to be happy-go-lucky all the time, and we don't want you running off. When you disappear, we worry about where you are and what you're doing. We'd rather you stayed on the ranch and be grouchier than a bison cow ready to calve than not be here at all, okay?"

Beau nodded once, and a smile tipped his lips. "You're startin' to sound Texan, Dawn Lee."

"I sure hope not, Beau Hanson," I answered, hugging him to me and rubbing his back. He was tired—bone-tired and emotionally tired. I could feel his fatigue soak into me as I held him. Beau was every kind of tired you could be, and to add insult to injury, he thought he was alone in what he was going through.

"We all care about you, Beau," I promised, my lips near his ear as I hugged him. He reeked of booze and bad decisions, but in the morning, he'd dust himself off and go on with life. That's what guys like Beau always do. "Everyone at Bison Ridge has been scared to death that one day you're going to leave and never come back."

When I leaned away from the hug, his gaze held mine and refused to let go. "Do you care about me, Dawn?"

I brushed my hand down his cheek, his five o'clock shadow more like a soft beard after so many days away from a razor. "I have since the day I met you, Beau. When you come into someone's life, you make it better just because you're you. I'm pretty sure that's how Blaze's family felt about you from day one, too."

Beau captured my hand against his cheek and searched my eyes for whatever it was he needed from this world at one a.m. on a Wednesday night. "I've cared about you since the day I met you, too," he whispered. He lowered his forehead to mine, and even sporting the smell of whiskey, he smelled of the quintessential cowboy made of fresh air, sunshine, and horses.

He stared down into my eyes until his lips lowered to mine. His were warm, soft, and hesitant. I didn't know this Beau. The Beau I know would have asked three times before he kissed a girl. This Beau was still out of his element, but he was taking a chance that I would accept him for who and what he was, all of him, no matter his condition.

Instinctively, I relaxed into his kiss. I had to. I couldn't use one side of my lips to say I would always be there for him and use the other side to push him away. Not when what he needed the most was acceptance, even of the parts he thought no one liked.

I liked everything about Beau Hanson, from his silly sayings, kindness, dedication to Bison Ridge, and the vulnerabilities he showed me tonight. Everyone thought Beau was a happy-go-lucky cowboy, but tonight I got to see that this cowboy was far more complicated than any of us thought.

I'd been dreaming about the day I got to kiss Beau Hanson for six years. I was starting to think it wouldn't happen, but the insight he gave me tonight told me why he was also so hesitant around me. He needed our friendship, which made his fear of losing me stronger than his courage to take a chance.

He didn't disappoint.

He tipped my head to align our lips at the perfect angle, and I fell into his chest, bracing my hands against his hard muscles and silently taking great pleasure in the way they trembled under my touch.

Beau buried his hands in the hair on the top of my head and moaned against my lips. The sound shook me to my core, and I gasped. When my lips fell open, he took full advantage and moved the kiss into territory that was even more unexpected. His tongue darted in to steal a taste of mine, and honestly, it was the most beautiful experience of my life. He was Jim Beam, coffee, and mouthwash from my bathroom vanity. He was sadness, resilience, and dedication to a craft few understood. He was heat, strength, and weakness on a cold winter night. I experienced all of Beau Hanson in one kiss, and it was everything I dreamed it would be and more. He was everything I needed but would never have.

When he ended the kiss, he rested his forehead back on mine. "I've wanted to do that for six years, Dawn Lee. It was worth waiting for."

"God, Beau. Same. What made you do it now?" I asked, my voice breathy and no louder than a whisper.

"I do—do——" he cleared his throat. "Do not know. I wanted to know what it was like to taste you, even if it was only once in your living room at one a.m. I wanted to know just in case I disappeared and never came back. At least I experienced a few moments of pleasure before I left this earth."

I gripped his face tightly and held him nose-to-nose. "You better not be planning on leaving this earth, Beau. I will call for help if I think that's the case."

His eyes closed, and his head shook in my hands. "Not what I meant, Dawn. See, my momma, she died in the blink of an eye, and so did Miss Callie. I work in a place that can take me just as fast, that's all. I should go to bed before I say or do something stupider. I'm a stupid man."

"You're not stupid, Beau," I whispered adamantly. "I think you're confused, scared, and lonely, but I don't think you're stupid. Not even the littlest bit. Do you hear me?"

His head nodded in my hands, and I stared into those sad brown eyes. What I saw there would have broken my heart if it wasn't already in two pieces. I pulled him up off the couch and turned the light off in the living room.

"Come on. It's time for bed."

He yawned and followed behind me like a lost puppy dog as I pulled him down the hall to my bedroom. I flipped the covers back on the bed and motioned for him to lay down. He unhooked his belt and stripped it off but thankfully left his jeans and t-shirt intact. He sighed with satisfaction as he settled into the mattress, and his eyes closed almost immediately. I clicked the light off by the side of the bed and paused beside him. I was enraptured by the vision of the man in the moonlight. His hair needed a cut, and the brown locks curling slightly around his ears gave him the look of a Hollywood cowboy. His beard had grown in soft and brown, but I knew the next time I saw him, he'd be cleanshaven again. I once suggested that he grow a beard to keep his face warm in the winter, but he informed me that beards made his face itch. Besides, he was convinced a woman loved nothing more than running her hand over the face of a cleanshaven cowboy in the moonlight. Unfortunately, I had to agree with him.

I'd dreamed of having Beau Hanson in my bed, and maybe he was tonight, but it wouldn't last. I could never have him. Not tonight. Probably not ever. There was still too much left unsaid between us. I would be the friend he needed tonight when his defenses were down and his mind was in turmoil. Come morning, when he dusted himself off and got back to the job of living, I'd let him go. I had to. The life I had to lead now would only hold him back.

I lowered myself to the mattress and swung my legs in, pulling the covers up over us and resting back on the pillows. I thought Beau was asleep until his hand snaked over and slipped into mine. He squeezed it once, and I wondered if life got any better than this. The truth was if I could spend every night with this man in my bed, it would get better, but for tonight, all I could do was pretend.

As I drifted off to sleep, the truth struck me with blinding clarity. We were both pretending, and neither one of us knew how to stop being so damn afraid and just be honest. Until we figured that out, a stolen kiss in the dark was all we could be.

Four

The sunlight streamed into the quiet room, and I bit back a moan of pain. My head was already pounding from the bourbon last night, and when I opened my eyes, it was only going to get worse.

The next moan that I let loose was out of frustration. If the sun was up, I missed chores. I couldn't force myself to get too worked up about it, though. Considering the softness and warmth lying across my chest, I was happy right where I was. It had been so many nights since I woke up warm in a soft bed that I never wanted to move. My eyes snapped open. I was warm and in a soft bed with a softer woman snuggled into me. Where was I?

I glanced down at my chest, and my breath hitched. The sweetness spread across me was wide awake and staring up at me. "Morning," Dawn whispered. "You missed chores."

"I'm dreaming, right?" I asked, my hand discreetly checking under the covers. I was relieved when my hand encountered my flannel shirt and jeans.

Dawn shook her head against my chest, and the feel of it told me I most certainly was not dreaming. Maybe I'd dreamt about waking up like this every day for the last six years, but this was real. I forced myself to replay the events of last night. I remembered drinking half a bottle of Jack and stumbling drunk through the snow until I found Heavenly Lane. Even as I was knocking on the door, I didn't know if I'd be welcome, but I had to see her, even if she tossed me out on my ear.

I rested my hand on my forehead and let out a breath. "What did I do last night?"

Dawn sat up and pulled the blanket up to her chest. "You don't remember?"

I laughed sardonically and broke eye contact with her. "Oh, I remember. That was more like an, oh my God, what did I do last night? Kind of question."

"Nothing you can't take back, if that's what you're worried about," Dawn assured me with a shrug that she wanted to be nonchalant. She failed. "I put you to bed in here last night because you were so distraught. I was worried that you'd fall down the stairs in the middle of the night or wander outside if I didn't keep an eye on you. Nothing else happened."

I sat up slowly and held my hand to my pounding temple. "Something else did happen, though. I distinctly remember kissing you."

"You were drunk."

"I wasn't that drunk," I insisted, trying to swallow around the cotton in my mouth.

Dawn glanced away, and I tipped my head, my slow, sore mind registering that something wasn't right. I took her face gently and swung her chin to face me. "Dawn, did you hurt your eye? It's all red here," I said, running my finger under her left eye and down her cheek. "Does it hurt?"

Fear instantly filled those chocolate eyes that I thought about all day long. When they turned to the color of black coffee, I knew the next thing she said would be a lie.

"No, it's fine. I must have gotten something in it. I should make some coffee. Do you want some coffee?"

The shudder that went through her was the honest answer to my question, though. There was something terribly wrong with her, and she thought I was too drunk to see it. Too dumb to understand? Too caught up in my own life to want to help? I didn't know which one it was, but I had to get to the bottom of it before I lost her for good.

My half-sober brain told me now was not the time to push her on it, so I threw the covers off my legs and sat on the edge of the bed. "I need to be getting back to the ranch. The chores will have to be done, even if I'm late."

Dawn took my arm, and I glanced down at it, noting her fingers weren't as swollen as they had been at the café. That was good. She was healing from whatever she'd done to injure them. "Blaze made sure Corbyn did the chores."

I ran a hand down my face and groaned. "Son of a motherless goat," I moaned. "When I show back up around that place, Blaze is probably going to fire me from his ranch and as his brother."

Her snort of laughter made my heart pump harder. I loved when she let her joy out into the world. I hadn't seen her joy for almost a year, and I was starting to worry it was gone for good. "You aren't that lucky."

My guffaw made her smile for the first time since we woke up, and my finger trailed down her cheek until my hand could hold her chin again. "Dawn Lee, you're exquisite in the light of the morning sun."

"At least now that I don't weigh two hundred pounds, right?" She asked the question with defensive snark, but she kept her gaze pinned on the bed.

I dipped my head down until she was forced to make eye contact with me again. "I never said that. Why would I say that when I had no idea how much you weighed, nor did I care? I didn't care then, and I don't care now."

"You're a liar, Beau Hanson."

"You're right, I am," I said, and the light in her eyes dimmed to near extinction. "What I mean is, I care about your weight loss because I'm worried that you're sick. I'm worried something is seriously wrong. I don't care how much you weigh as long as you're healthy." I blew out a breath in frustration. I had too much to drink last night and wasn't thinking well on my feet. I finally had an opening to find out what was going on with her, and I was stumbling around like a minutes old red dog. "I'm sorry, Dawn. My head is still messed up, but I was trying to say I'm worried about you. Please don't be upset with me."

Her hand touched my arm, and my heart calmed instantly. The simple slowing of my heart told me more than anything, but I didn't know what to do about it.

"I'm not upset. I'm sorry for being defensive. My head is kind of messed up this morning too. I'll make that coffee while you clean up," she said quietly. "Blaze and Heaven are waiting at the ranch to talk to you."

My eyes closed at the thought. "Can I just stay here with you?"

Dawn chuckled, and when I opened my eyes, she had her robe on and stood by the side of the bed. "Sorry, being an adult doesn't work that way, Beau."

I stood too and walked around the bed. "I know I have to apologize to Blaze and Miss Heaven, but I don't know how to apologize for something you can bet the farm on."

Dawn tipped her head, and I noticed she wore her confused expression. "Bet the farm on?"

"Something true."

She crossed her arms over her chest, but she grimaced when she did it. I would bet the farm that she didn't even know she did it with every movement.

"In a nutshell, you told Blaze he doesn't respect you and doesn't care about his ranch. Is that what you mean by the truth?"

"I never said he didn't care about his ranch. I said I'm running it while he plays. There's a difference. If that ain't the truth, then God's a possum. Same as when it comes to him not respecting me. He doesn't. We're the same damn age, and he acts like I'm his little brother."

"I can't deal with any more of your sayings before coffee, Beau. All I know is, you're going to have to talk to them whether you want to or not."

"I hate it when you're right."

Dawn smiled then, and it lightened the load on my shoulders a little bit. I loved her smile, but she hadn't worn it enough lately. "I'll get the coffee started. I have my chores to do too."

"Thanks, Dawn."

She walked to the bedroom door and paused. "But, Beau?"

"Yeah?"

"I'll give you a little piece of advice in a way you'll understand it best. There are two sides to every story. Remember that when you're talking to your best friend today."

She tapped the doorframe and walked out, leaving me to think about what she said and the way she said it. They couldn't make it plainer to me that no one was on my side. Not about how I was feeling or how the business was being run. I fell to the bed, my limbs heavy at the realization it was high time I packed my bags and found a place that appreciated my work. A place where my heart didn't break every time that pair of brown eyes refused to give me a chance.

When I arrived at the ranch, the barn was blissfully quiet other than the soft snuffles of the horses. I was never more grateful for a frigid morning before in my life. Once the chores were done, no one hung around the barn. Dawn offered me a ride, but I'd walked back instead, and I was glad I had. I wanted to clear my head of the bad decisions I'd made over the last few nights.

After the cold walk, my headache was gone, and I was ready to get a few hours of work under my belt. I planned to stay hidden away in the barn, so Blaze and Heaven didn't know I was here just yet. Sure, I was delaying the inevitable, but there was one last thing I had to do here before I could tell them goodbye and be on my way.

"Hey, Grover," I cooed to the horse, who hung his head over the stall door for a nose rub. "How's it going, buddy?" I asked while I rubbed his speckled snout. "You're a good boy, aren't you?" I gave him an apple, and he munched it, his lips flapping in response to my question. "You work hard to keep Miss Heaven safe, so I'm going to help you out a little bit now. You're getting old, boy. You gotta stop getting up and down to help your rider. I have a way to do that."

I lifted the saddle off the side of the barn stall and carried it into my workshop. While I worked, I played over the situation with Dawn in my mind. The stuff I said and the stories I confided in her last night haunted me today. I never talk about when my momma died or how. I didn't even talk to Blaze about it, and he knew her. I suppose the Jim Beam was the reason, but now that fly was out of the barn, and I couldn't get it back. I could already feel the awkwardness with Dawn this morning. Then again, that might have had more to do with me kissing her like a fool than anything. I hated that things were going to be awkward between us forever now.

Well, not forever, I guess. Not once I leave. The weird part was, I'd known Dawn for six years, and I'd never once mentioned my family. I was meticulously careful never to say a word. Blaze knew better than to mention it, so I never had to worry about him spilling the beans either. In the end, I had to worry about my own lips opening cans of worms that were better left closed.

"Doesn't matter, Beau," I said as I hefted the newly redesigned saddle back into my arms. "Once you leave this place, none of it matters."

That wasn't true. Not even a little bit. All of it mattered, and I suppose that was why a bottomless pit of pain and sorrow had opened inside me. Leaving was what I had to do, but it wasn't what I wanted to do.

I carried the saddle to the barn stall and hoisted it over Grover, then adjusted the billets. I was just completing the final check of the working parts on the saddle when someone cleared their throat. My hand froze, and I waited to see if it was one of the ranch hands or if Blaze had finally realized I was on the property.

"What are you doing with Grover?" asked a meek voice from behind me.

Miss Heaven.

I turned slowly and kept my hand on the gentle giant standing next to me. There, in the middle of the barn, was my best friend and his fiancée. He had a cup of coffee in each hand and held one out for me. "Thanks," I whispered, taking a sip of the warm brew.

Grover saw his favorite gal and flapped his lips in protest at being kept from her. I patted his neck. "It's fine, boy," I whispered to him until he settled down.

Miss Heaven pointed at her horse. "I would say that looks like my saddle, but I can't."

I nodded my head a couple of times. "It's your saddle. I was just making a few adjustments to it."

"Adjustments?" Blaze asked as they both descended on the stall.

To keep Grover from freaking out, I led him from the stall so he could nuzzle his nose into Heaven's body. She laughed, and the sound cut through the tension in the barn. Her laughter brought a smile to mine and Blaze's lips. She always had a way of doing that, even when you couldn't find a smile in a haystack.

I'd hurt these two people and couldn't find the words to apologize, but she was still here offering me grace rather than anger. My heart was broken knowing this was the end of Blaze and Beau, and nothing should make me smile, but yet, it was Heaven who made sure I was. I would be grateful to her for that as I rode away from the place I thought would always be home.

Heaven patted the horse's neck while she took in the changes to the saddle. "I've never seen anything like this, Beau."

I shook off my doom and gloom and flipped the left armrest up. Then, I walked around the horse and lengthened the right stirrup. "I've been making some modifications in the workshop."

"Modifications?" Blaze asked, and I nodded as I flipped the leather hand strap over the saddle horn. It seemed like he was going to repeat everything I said this morning.

"Things to make it easier for Miss Heaven to mount and dismount when she doesn't have the mounting stairs. I know Grover can get up and down on command, but the old guy is getting up there in age. My hope is the changes will keep him from getting arthritis in his joints. It will also protect Miss

Heaven better in the saddle when she's riding. I think, anyway. I'm not real smart, but I did do some research online."

Heaven had her head tipped to the side in confusion while I rambled. I thrust Grover's reins out to her. "I'll show you?" She accepted the reins and nodded. "I devised a system that will let you get up from ground level," I stepped into the extended stirrup and used the hand strap with my right hand, which is the only hand she could still use. "Once you're in the saddle, you flip this arm down off the extended back," I explained, flipping the armrest back down. "Then, you lay your left arm in the armrest and wrap your fingers around the handle. I made sure it's nice and padded, so it doesn't bother your fingers," I explained, demonstrating how she would do it. "Once you have that arm braced, you just pull this leather tab and re-ha—ha—ook your stirrup at the right level." I showed her how the strap looped through hooks at different levels to change the length if someone else was riding the horse. "The shin ba—braces are based on the idea of a ja—jumping saddle. They'll allow you to use your legs to balance on the horse instead of just your torso. You'll also be able to ba—brace against them if you hit a rough patch."

I was talking fast, so they couldn't jump in and interrupt me. I didn't want to hear that Heaven didn't like all the changes, even though I knew it was a real possibility. Riders have a religious reverence for their saddle, and I was messing with hers without permission.

Since they weren't saying anything, I jumped back in. "To g—ga—get down, you just do it all in reverse. I—I—I suggest you have someone spot you the first few times to be safe. You have to make sure the armrest is flipped uh—up before you mount or dismount so you can flip your leg over the saddle, of course. There is a quick-release button, so once your arm is out, you can pa—pu—push—push it with your knee on the underside."

I went through the motions to get back down. When I hit the ground, they were staring at me with their mouths slack. I patted Grover nervously and swallowed around the fear sticking in my throat.

"But—uh, don't worry," I stuttered, hating that when I talked fast, I couldn't break the impediment. Everyone always wondered why I spoke slowly. Well, they would wonder no more. "I didn't fix anything on permanently," I explained, forcing myself to slow down. "It all comes off with no damage to the saddle. I used the best bison leather I had so that it would hold up to the ah—el—elements. I—uh—I didn't think you'd mind, Ba—laze I think it matches okay, but if you don't, you won't hurt my feelings none if you don't use it."

Heaven threw her arm around me and hugged me as hard as she could with one arm. "I can't believe you did all of this for me, Beau," she whispered. "I had no idea you knew how to do something like this. You're incredibly talented."

I shrugged at her compliment and patted her back awkwardly. "I don't know so much about that, Miss Heaven. I just wanted to make sure you're safe when you're out riding between the ranches. I—I—I'm gonna be going on to a different place na—now, but I didn't want to worry about you being hurt again."

Blaze squeezed my shoulder in appreciation when she let me go. "I'm speechless, Beau. I didn't know anyone could make something like this."

"Well, I had to retrofit it to the saddle, so it was a custom thing, but I think it turned out okay. You can let me know if it needs any changes or adjustments before I leave, Miss Heaven."

Her finger came up into my chest again, and this time, her eyes held fear instead of excitement. "I'm dying to try this saddle, Beau, but your Texas cowboy butt better be right over there on that bale of hay when I return. Do we understand each other?"

I nodded once. "Yes, Miss Heaven."

"Good, and for God's sake, stop with the miss thing, would you? I know it's a show of respect for you Texans, but I'm about to be a Mrs., which is going to make it weird." Blaze and I both had to bite back a smile until she motioned for Blaze to spot her.

I hooked Grover's reins on the new hook I installed to keep him in place while she mounted using the new system. I wasn't surprised when she could pull herself up quickly but held my breath when she had to work the armrest from across her chest. I was afraid she'd fall out the other side, but I should have known better. She'd been riding horses since she was two, and for the last ten, she'd been doing it one-handed. She had herself situated faster than I had done it. She grabbed the reins from the hook and sighed. "Incredible," she whispered, sitting tall against the new backrest I'd added to help her stay upright. "Can I take him for a ride to test it out?"

Blaze patted her leg and nodded. "Just be careful, and don't try to get down until you're back here. If you need help, use the walkie." He grabbed one from the barn wall and clipped it to the saddle, where it always hung when she was out alone.

"I won't be gone long!" she promised, taking off like a shot once she was clear of the barn doors. Her laughter echoed through the still morning air, and both of us were grinning as we stared at the now-empty barn door.

"Well, you just made her year," he said, still not turning to look at me. "Maybe her decade. I don't know what to say."

I darted into my workshop, grabbed something off the bench, and carried it back out with me. "I made you something, too. I noticed yours was getting rough."

Blaze accepted the brown Stetson and ran his hand over the soft leather. "Beau, this is stunning. Bison leather?"

"Yep," I agreed. "It's just like your old one, but I made some changes to the way I tanned the leather. I hope that makes it more durable. I thought you should have a new one for your big day."

He ran his finger across the hatband and glanced up at me in surprise. I held up my hands in defense. "I didn't make the band. I asked the ladies who made your bolo tie to do it. After they finished, they shipped it out here. I knew you'd be wearing your tie for the wedding. I figured Wicapiwakan brought you good luck, so she should represent at the ceremony."

Last July, Blaze and Heaven had transported a sacred white bison calf and its mother to a Lakota reservation in South Dakota. Blaze's most prized possession was the hand-beaded white bison bolo tie the tribe had made for him. They told him if he wore it for special events, it would bring the spirit of Wicapiwakan to him and offer prosperity and peace. Now, he had a matching set for his wedding. I wouldn't be here for it, which felt like a punch to the gut, but at least Wicapiwakan would be.

He took off the old hat and set the new one on his head. "Fits like a dream. Thanks, Beau. You didn't have to do that, but I appreciate like hell that you did."

"It was your bison hide. The least I could do was make you a hat. I'm working on your coat. Sorry I didn't get it done in time for this season, but you'll have it next winter. I've been busy, and there is quite a process for preparing the bison hide to make clothing."

Blaze held his hand up to quiet me. "I'm not worried about it, Beau. I'll be grateful for it once it's done, but I'm in no rush. I'm glad you put the saddle modifications for Heaven ahead of it. You don't know the relief inside my chest right now knowing I don't have to worry about her every single second she's out on the horse."

I nodded and stared at the floor, brushing my foot through the hay. "I think I do. I remember the horror. I remember it all."

He clasped my shoulder again and nodded grimly, his lips in a thin line as we thought about the moment in the pasture that day. A bison bull had trampled his wife Callie and killed her. Heaven was hurt falling off Grover when she tried to rescue her. "I know you do. I'm guilty of forgetting I wasn't the only one affected by the events of that day. I'm reminded every time I look at Heaven, and now, every time I think about the things you said to me in that house."

"La—listen," I stuttered, biting my tongue to force myself to slow down. Whenever I got upset, I tripped over my tongue. "I shouldn't have said those things. I apologize for being that way, especially in front of Miss Heaven," I paused and cleared my throat. "In front of Heaven. It wasn't right of me to take out my frustration on both of you."

Blaze nodded while his shoulder shrugged, but his gaze remained trained on the floor until he finally shook his head. "While I would have preferred Heaven hadn't witnessed my fall from grace, you have nothing to apologize for."

I crossed my arms over my chest while I stared out the barn door. "In my opinion, it's better to keep my mouth shut and seem a fool than open it and remove all doubt, Blaze. I definitely removed all doubt a few days ago."

Blaze put his arm around me and directed me to a hay bale to sit. "See, that's where you're wrong. You didn't sound like a fool, but I sure as hell looked like one, and rightly so. After you left, Heaven told me she'd do what you should have done, and then she punched me in the gut."

I chortled, and the sound was easy and relaxed for the first time in weeks. "She has never been afraid to tell you what she thinks."

Blaze grinned and leaned back, crossing his boots at the ankles. "Nope, and she was right. I spent a good long time out on the ridge the last few days. Not having you out there with me, well, I didn't like it. I didn't like it at all."

"We haven't ridden the ridges together in at least a year." I snapped my jaw shut, so I didn't say the rest of what I was thinking, which was that he was too busy doing everything but what he should be doing.

"We haven't, which in hindsight is also my fault."

"Not sure why it mattered to you then, Blaze," I said, baffled. I might be a simple man, but I'd known this guy for years and usually didn't struggle to follow our conversations.

"I guess my point is, even though we hadn't done it in a long time, I knew we could, you know? I could jump on Rapunzel and yell for you to ride out with me, and you'd be right by my side. Over the last few days, I didn't even know where you were. I couldn't race you across the field to the first paddock and laugh while doing it. That was the moment I realized I'd rather be doing that than anything else."

That got a loud bark of laughter from me. "I think you'd rather be doing Miss Heaven, but the sentiment is nice."

Blaze shoved me in the shoulder, laughter in his voice when he told me not to be vulgar. "Truth is, Beau, I already knew something had to change and that something was me. I can't work you to death while I pretend like I'm carrying my weight around here."

I reached out and rubbed the nose of Cloudy Day, who had come over to investigate why I'd been ignoring him. "You don't have to carry your own weight around here, Blaze. You own the ranch, and it's your right to delegate the work. I was out of line implying anything else. Ultimately, that's the reason I've decided to move on to a different place in a different town. While I know that you don't have to carry the weight around here, I can't carry it all anymore. We grew up together, we got in trouble together, we scrapped together, we lost together, and we built this ranch together. It don't feel right doing it alone now. It just don't, and I can't." I snapped my jaw closed then and rubbed my face with my hands. I was still tired from my drunken bender last night, making the emotions harder to control this morning. I was glad I had gotten it all out without stuttering about. That didn't mean saying goodbye to my brother wasn't breaking my heart and bringing tears to my eyes.

Blaze squeezed my shoulder and shook his head. "You're not leaving, Beau. I know you think I don't understand how you're feeling, and I'm well aware that in some aspects of what you're dealing with right now, I don't. When it comes to the ranch, though, the last three days have shown me the same things you just told me. I also have to say that you're wrong. I don't own this place."

I leaned forward on my thighs and brushed off my hands. "What are you talking about, Blaze? Ash signed this place over to you months ago. Did he take it back?"

Blaze shook his head and leaned back on his elbow, content to take his time in explaining himself. "No, he didn't, but I will no longer own Bison Ridge Ranch just like Heaven will no longer own Heavenly Lane Dude Ranch upon our marriage."

"You're selling both places?" I asked, standing upright on my bootheels. "Cripes, now I do gotta find a new job. I gotta warn Dawn." I took off for the barn door like the hounds of hell were on my heels.

"Beauregard Hanson!" Blaze yelled, and I froze, turning back to face him. "We're not selling the ranches. Geez."

I tossed my arms out and grunted. "What the hell are you talking about then?"

Blaze pointed at the haybale until I sat again. I went back to rubbing Cloudy Day's nose to calm me down. "Heaven and I sat down and talked about it over the last few days, and we've decided no one is benefiting from things the way they are now. Not you and not Dawn or Tex. That can't continue, especially once we're married. Heavenly Lane will be in Dawn's and Tex's hands for the most part."

"That's true. I know Dawn is a little worried about how it will all work. She's already overwhelmed and stressed, which I don't think is good for her health."

"That's understandable," he agreed, rubbing his hands on his pants. "They are already doing most of the work. Part of that is because Heaven is there less, part is because her doctor said if she doesn't back off the work, her arm will always be painful, and part of it is, she wants to see what they can do when she's not micromanaging everything."

I tipped my head at him. "Miss Heaven's arm is that bad? I noticed she's always wearing a strap on it now."

His expression turned from love to guilt instantly, as it always did when we discussed Heaven's arm. It wasn't his fault, but he didn't see it that way. After she fell off the horse as a teenager, her shoulder and arm never grew again, but she could still use it. After she fell off Grover trying to save Callie from that bull, the nerves were damaged beyond repair.

"It's that bad," he whispered. "Or it was until I insisted that she see a doctor. Beau," he shook his head and ran his hands through his hair. "She's been in so much pain that even daily activities were torture. It turns out that it isn't uncommon with an injury like hers, but Heaven wouldn't know that because she refused to talk to a doctor. She has a plan now to treat her arm, and by following the guidelines of the doctors and therapists, it's improved rapidly over the winter."

"Will she always have to wear the strap now?"

Blaze nodded, adding a shoulder shrug at the end. "She will if she wants the pain to go away. Keeping the arm supported at the upper arm and wrist stops them from pulling on the tight muscles that want to spasm all the time. The therapists want to make her a specialized one that will distribute the weight of the arm evenly and make her steadier on her feet, but she's refusing."

"Why?" I asked in confusion. He rubbed his fingers together to indicate money, and I shook my head in frustration. "Why does she have to be so stubborn?"

Blaze chuckled, which was a relief to hear. I hated how much he blamed himself for her injury. "Someone spilled the stubborn jar on that girl when she was born, but I honestly love that about her. I don't know if money is the reason or if she feels like she's admitting defeat by having it made, but either way, once we are married, I will get my way."

"And your way is her getting the brace."

He clapped me on the shoulder with a laugh. "You know it, brother. The money excuse will be gone since she will be on my insurance. I'm hoping that the months of improvement she's seen wearing the shoulder support she has now will be the swaying factor. I'll try to convince her that she doesn't have to admit defeat, but a custom brace will help her get more done during the day, especially if we want to have a child. Any help with that would be appreciated."

I raised a brow. "Help with getting a brace made or help convincing Heaven to have a child?"

He laughed again and shook his head. "Getting the brace made. She already wants to have a baby. I don't need any help in that department."

"I didn't think so," I said, laughing with him. "Back to the ranches. What's going on, Blaze?"

"Well, we're going to discuss it with everyone once our lawyer gets back to us, so I'd appreciate it if you kept this between us for now."

I clapped my hands once. “That should be easy since I still don’t know what *this* is.”

“The two ranches will come together under the umbrella name Bison Ridge. Both ranches are already called that by the townspeople, so it’s a no-brainer. However, we will both retain the original name of our ranch for business purposes. Heaven will be the CEO of her ranch, but Tex and Dawn will get shares of the ranch as owners, too.”

My eyes widened in surprise. “Damn, son…”

“It’s time, and Heaven knows it. She wants to keep that ranch in the family for years to come, so this is the only way to keep it viable. The terms will be that if Tex or Dawn leave, they must sell their portion back to Heaven, but I don’t see that happening.”

I shook my head. “Me either. Those two are homesteaded on that ranch as much as I am on this one.”

“Which brings me to Bison Ridge,” he said, motioning at the barn. “Once the deal is signed, you and I will be equal partners in the ranch, with the same stipulation as hers. If you want to leave, you have to offer your shares back to me.”

I blinked twice and then one more time. “I think there’s a light or two burned out on your string, Blaze.”

He shook his head and held his hat in his hands. “I’m not crazy, Beau. What you said a few days ago was the most honest anyone has been with me in a long time. Even more so than Heaven. I wouldn’t have this ranch right now if it weren’t for you. You kept me going when I wanted to give up. You broke your back for years to keep our daddy from knowing how bad things were here. You were loyal and remained the kind of friend I wasn’t. That changes now. Now, we’re partners, like we should have always been. That’s why you aren’t going anywhere. Do you read me?”

I grabbed the back of my neck and held tight, my heart pounding in my chest. "I—I ain't real good at paperwork and business, Blaze. I ca—ca—an't talk to people like that."

He gave me the slow-down motion with his hand like he used to do when we were kids. I moved my jaw a different way and puffed up my chest, two other techniques to stop the stutter once it started.

"You're wrong about not being good at business, Beau. You've kept this business alive for years. I know you don't like paperwork or talking to people, so I'll take care of all those things. You'll take care of the hands and the animals, but you won't be doing all the grunt work. You'll be hiring, firing, and training the others to work with the bison and the horses. That will give you time to do more work in the workshop."

"Hiring and firing?"

His nod was immediate. "You'll be ranch foreman, which you are now, but now you'll be getting paid for it. You won't have to do all the chores either. We'll also be providing Heavenly Lane Dude Ranch with bison for their guests, so there will be more hides, which means more leather for your work. I'd like to see you grow your hobby into a business. You're crazy talented with leatherwork, which has taken me by surprise. Now that I see your passion, I want you to reap the rewards of your years of hard work. I want you to have time to make custom hats like these," he explained, tipping his hat. "I think it could be a great little side business for you. We'll certainly never run out of leather."

My mouth was open, but I couldn't force words out. Was he serious right now? "Wha—your daddy is okay with this?" I stuttered, my mind going a million miles a minute.

"I own the ranch now, Beau, but he did give me his blessing to make you a full partner. In fact, he said he'd thump me all the way from Dublin if I didn't. He's coming up for the wedding. You can ask him then if you don't believe me now."

My head was shaking back and forth in disbelief. If what he was saying was true, I finally had a reason to stay here. I finally had a reason to dig in and make something of this life. I'd been entrenched on this land for as long as Blaze had, but I was never more than the grunt work to keep it alive. My heart pounded at the thought that maybe I could make something of myself in this place after all.

Blaze tipped his head. "Beau, are you okay?"

I stood, my legs shaky and my mouth dry as cotton. "I—can I have a minute?"

The door to the barn was open, and I ran for it, stepping outside the door and leaning over on my thighs while my stomach heaved. I regretted the Jim Beam I'd drank last night, but I regretted, even more, the things I said to them. Worse yet, the things I said that no one else heard. The words I said in anger rang loudly in my head, and the shame of them made my stomach roil again.

The hand I knew like the back of my own came down on my shoulder while his other hand planted itself on my chest. "It's okay, Beau. We have to forget about the stuff in the past, both distant and not so distant, and remember that we're family first and foremost, right?"

I nodded, my head still hanging toward the dirt. I swiped my hand over my mouth and took a shuddering breath. "I'm still real ashamed of my behavior, Blaze. Real ashamed. Toward you, Heaven, and Dawn Lee."

I stood up, and my bones sagged from exhaustion and spent emotion. Blaze kept his arm around my shoulder and walked me into the house, motioning for me to sit while he got me a glass of water. Before he handed it to me, he held it up. "See that?"

I shook my head slightly. "See what? It's clear water."

Blaze handed me the glass, and I drank some down, being careful, so I didn't heave it back out. "It is, and that's going to be us starting today. From here on, our water is made clear with honesty and forgiveness. We've filtered out everything else that muddied it for so long. Does that make sense, Beau?"

I stared at the glass for the longest time before I could meet his gaze. "That's the most sense you've made in years, Blaze. Some of my water is still muddied, but I'm going to work harder at filtering that out, too."

Blaze clasped my shoulder and nodded. "I think that's a solid idea. The best place to start is with the one person who accepts all of you even when you don't think she should."

He lifted a brow, and I nodded once, his message received.

Five

"Dawn! Dawn!"

I ran for the back door and threw it open, surprised to see Heaven and Grover at the back of the house. I jogged down the stairs and grabbed Grover's reins. "Heaven, what are you doing here?" I paused when my mind registered what it was seeing. "Girl, what's with that saddle?"

Heaven wore a grin from ear to ear when she answered. "Cool, right? The saddle is Beau's handiwork. Watch!"

Heaven made all kinds of precise actions to the saddle and then motioned me over. "Spot me. This is the first time I've gotten down from the saddle, and Blaze made me promise to have help."

I stood ready to grab her if she started to fall, but she was able to get down on her own, her smile widening when she did, if a wider smile was even possible. "I don't understand what I just saw," I said, completely flabbergasted.

Heaven showed me all Beau's changes to the saddle and how it worked to keep her safe. She was always one wrong move from falling off Grover, and we all worried about her safety when she was riding. We couldn't tell her that she couldn't ride anymore, that would destroy her, but we did want her to be safe. Beau was the one to find the solution to the problem, which didn't surprise me in the least. He spends a lot of time in his head, and I had a feeling this was the result of a lot of thinking.

"You should have been me about thirty minutes ago. Beau decided I should be able to mount and dismount without mounting stairs or making Grover lie down. Dawn, he made this system just for me. He even made it to match my saddle. I rode over here and was stable for the first time in years. It was just mind-blowing."

I rubbed her back while she gathered herself. Tears fell down her cheeks, from what I imagined was happiness and gratefulness. "Why don't you put Grover in the barn, and we'll have some coffee?"

Heaven led the horse to the barn and let him into his stall, leaving the saddle on since she wasn't staying for long. When she came into the kitchen, she sat down at the table while I got coffee. "It's nice to see you so excited about riding again. I know riding has become more difficult for you over the last few years."

"I guess you weren't the only one to notice."

I set my cup down on the table and leaned my chin on my palm. "I can't believe Beau made all of that, though. I know he's handy and an excellent leatherworker, but that involves more than a little bit of design and engineering work."

Heaven set her cup down, too. "All Beau said was that he wanted me to be safe when I was riding, and he thought he had a way to do that. He was right, but I can't wrap my mind around it yet. The braces he added to the saddle for my legs make all the difference. Balance has been hard for me, but those changed the game."

"I'm happy for you, Heaven. Maybe we can go riding for fun now."

"I would say absolutely, but those fingers don't look up to fun," she said, taking my hand from the table.

I slid it away from her and hid it on my lap. "Don't be silly. It's fine."

"I don't think it is, Dawn. Why is your eye beet red? Did you hurt it?"

"Did Beau find you guys to talk before he showed you the saddle?" I asked, completely ignoring her questions the same way I had ignored Beau's this morning.

She shook her head, her eyes roving over me in a way that said she knew I was lying to her. "No, Blaze and I waited in the house after you texted, but he never showed. Finally, we walked out to the barn and found him there working on the saddle. We never did get around to talking because he already had Grover saddled up." She checked the clock. "I've been gone long enough now that I suppose they have gotten down to business. It's okay that I'm not there. Blaze had some things to say to him that should stay between them. I wasn't offended by what Beau said to us. He was right in everything he said that day. After he left, I punched Blaze in the gut and told him to get his head out of his Wranglers before he lost his best friend."

I chuckled, but I was nodding. "Beau will never leave Bison Ridge, but he will carry hostility if this isn't cleared up, and that's not good for anyone."

Heaven took a sip of coffee before she answered. "I don't know about that. After Beau showed us the saddle, he explained he wanted to ensure I was safe after he left. Said he was going to find a different job in a different place because he couldn't keep doing this here."

I stood before I realized it, my hands shaking. "No! Beau can't leave Bison Ridge. What is going on? I have to stop him!"

I ran to the door and grabbed my coat then tried to stuff my feet into my boots. I tipped, falling and landing on the hard floor, clutching my sore hand and holding it to my chest. "Oh, God," I moaned, rolling back and forth in pain a few times while I sucked in air. When I opened my eyes, Heaven was kneeling next to me, her hand on my shoulder.

"Dawn, stay down," she ordered, taking my boot off again and hanging up my coat. Once I could breathe again, I sat up and dropped my hand, wishing like hell she hadn't just witnessed that. "Are you okay?"

"Yeah, I'm fine," I promised, pushing myself up to standing again.

"Take it slow," she insisted, grabbing my elbow and helping me to sit in the kitchen chair again. I wrapped my sore hand around the mug while she rubbed my shoulder. "Would an ice pack help that, or would heat be better?"

I shook my head mutely, and she sighed heavily, sitting down in the chair opposite me and grabbing her mug. "If you had let me finish, I would have said that he promised not to leave without hearing Blaze out. I know Beau is upset right now, but he and Blaze will work it out. They always do."

I took a sip of coffee and willed my heart to stop pounding in my chest. "That better be true. If you get home and things aren't better, I want to know immediately."

Heaven made the sign of the cross followed by the girl scout pledge. I laughed and shook my head at her antics. I wished everything didn't hurt like hell, but I was going to smile if it killed me. "I have to tell you that Cece is an amazing cook. She does some prep here but, for the most part, does all the cooking at the bunkhouse. I wanted to run some changes by you, though. I have one of the applicants we didn't hire for Cece's job, who is still interested in working here. Landry would make a great housekeeper, which would help me get the bunks turned over faster on check-out day. She's neat, meticulous, and fast. I also thought we could use her as a substitute cook for when Cece needs time off. She loves working with small animals, too. We might be able to utilize her in several different areas as a floater."

Heaven was nodding along. “Hire her for part-time until summer, and then hopefully, we can advance that.”

I pointed at her. “Right, that's what I was thinking, too. I also thought I should order another full set of bedding for the bunkhouse. It means we can turn the bunks over without worrying about washing the laundry to complete the task.”

“That also makes sense. Do it.”

I breathed out a sigh of relief. I was trying to make things move smoothly since this was new to all of us. “I'll get on it today. Cece is moving in this weekend once Tex is free to help her load the truck. She'll be in one of the upstairs bedrooms temporarily. Then she’ll move into mine down here after you’re married. I’m going to take your room.” I didn’t want to tell her it was so I could use her accessible bathroom. I was already using it when she wasn’t here, and it did make a difference in how safe I felt in the shower.

Heaven finished her coffee and leaned back in her chair. “I'm glad. I want to move over to Bison Ridge full-time, but I don't like leaving you here alone.”

“Soon?” I asked, surprised. “I thought you were waiting for the wedding.”

“The wedding isn’t that far away. I’d like to be moved over there completely beforehand because, after the wedding, everything is going to get super busy with bison calving season and the grand opening here.”

“True,” I agreed. “I don’t like the idea of living here alone, either. Tex is way out at the back of the property and wouldn’t know if there was a problem before it was too late. I inadvertently invited Beau to move in the other day, though.”

“What?” she asked in shock, leaning forward and staring me down. “How do you inadvertently invite a guy to move in with you?”

I refused to make eye contact because I already knew what look would be in hers. “Beau told me he didn't want to be at Bison Ridge once you got married. I had been thinking about it a lot because I suspected that was part of the reason he was sleeping up on the ridge or in the barn. Without really thinking about it, I just said that maybe he should move into this house since we have plenty of empty rooms.”

“What did he say?”

I fidgeted with my coffee cup without answering, knowing she'd see right through me. I wasn't surprised when she gasped.

“That's what he got mad about at the café the other day.”

“It seems so. I don't understand it, either. Beau had just finished telling me he didn't want to stay at Bison Ridge. I thought it was a good solution.”

She nodded, biting her lip to hide a smile. “It would be if the boy didn't have a crush on you the same size Caleb has on Texas.”

I shook my head but didn’t make eye contact. “I don't think so, Heaven.”

“Explain why he stalked off and left you stranded in town then?”

I tapped the table with frustration. “Okay, first of all, Beau didn’t strand me in town. I don't need a man to get me from one place to the next.”

Heaven held up her hand to hush me. “Which I realize, I just meant that the Beau we know wouldn't just up and walk out rudely without making sure you were safe.”

“I agree with you there. I suppose it didn’t help matters that I mentioned how life was changing now, even more so than when Blaze married Callie. He’s so transparent when it comes to his emotions, and he doesn’t realize it. It’s plainer than the nose on my face that he’s mourning the loss of what he and Blaze used to have together at Bison Ridge. Change is hard. I understand that better than anyone. Anyway, he apologized last night when he came over."

"I knew he would."

"He also kissed me." I slapped my hand over my mouth and grimaced. Dammit, Dawn! You weren't going to tell her!

I swear they could hear her squeal two counties over, and she slapped her hand down on the table. "Oh my God, next time, lead with that!" She must have noticed the look on my face because she took a deep breath before speaking again. "What did you do?"

"Kissed him back?"

"Why did you make that a question?" Her brow was in the air, and I sighed, leaning back in my chair to try and find a comfortable position.

"Because I don't know if it was the right thing to do, if he really wanted to kiss me or was just drunk, or if he even liked it. He had just finished telling me about his family and how he met Blaze. I think he was seeking comfort from someone who understood his pain. Again, he was incredibly drunk, so it might have been that."

"I assure you, he kissed you because he wanted to. The booze just lowered his firewall of good manners enough to let him go for it."

"Could be," I agreed noncommittally. "I wanted to know if I imagined the feelings coursing between us ever since we met, so I kissed him back."

She gave me the out with it motion with her hand. "And? Did you imagine it?"

"Absolutely not," I whispered, hating to admit she was right. "That doesn't mean we can be more than friends, though."

She posed like a psychiatrist and eyed me. "Tell me why."

I tossed up one hand. "Isn't it obvious?"

"I wish it were, actually," she said, her brows doing a strange dance until they paused somewhere near her nose.

"We've known each other six years, Heaven. He never once made a move on me. Now that I'm seventy-five pounds lighter, he's suddenly interested in more than friendship? Feels a little suspect."

Heaven shook her head, her gaze roaming up and down me. It was filled with worry and fear. "You've lost seventy-five pounds? Dawn, I've been worried, but now I'm beside myself with it."

"You missed the point, Heaven," I grunted, smacking myself in the forehead.

She shook her head as she leaned over the table. "I didn't miss the point. I just don't think the fact that he finally kissed you had anything to do with how much you weigh."

I tipped my head to the side in disbelief. "You don't think it's highly suspicious that he stayed hands-off until I looked like a completely different person? Then suddenly, he can't wait to put his lips on mine?"

"No, because Beau's in a bad place right now. His life is changing, and he's scared. You have always been a constant for him. You've always been there when he needed someone to dump on, be it his pain or anger. After the week he's had, he probably decided he had to know if one thing in his life was real."

"He was drunk," I insisted. "We're probably reading too much into it."

"I don't think we are. Beau was drunk, but that just meant his inhibitions were finally gone."

"Well, whatever the case, it won't happen again. I can't let it happen again. He's already messed up enough. He doesn't need me dumping more on him."

Her head tipped and curiosity filled her eyes. “What would you be dumping on him?”

My chin trembled when I sighed. I couldn’t keep carrying this burden alone any longer. If anyone would understand, it was Heaven. I brought my hand out from under the table and held it up.

“There’s a problem here. A serious one, right?” Heaven asked, standing, and walking around the table.

I nodded, unable to give her an answer with words.

“The weight loss and your eye are part of it?”

I nodded again as the first sob escaped my lips. Heaven put her arm around me and guided me up and out of the chair, leading me to sit on the couch where she hugged me with all the caring and love I needed at that moment. She didn’t make me talk about it or explain it to her. She just let me be sad in a place I always felt safe and offered me the comfort I needed now more than ever.

We’d had nothing but problems at the ranch for the last week. I’d had holes in fences, winter damage to buildings, and bison on the loose. Even Blaze was out helping to get everything under control. He was getting married in two weeks on this ranch, and his daddy wasn’t going to show up to see the place falling apart. Not if I had anything to say about it. I’d work morning until night if I had to. The ranch had to be in tip-top shape when the McAwleys rolled into town. It had been years since Ash and Amity had come to Wisconsin. I was going to make sure they noticed the improvements we'd made since they were here last.

Every rancher knows there will be problems with equipment and buildings, and Blaze's daddy is no different, but he will expect the place to look respectable. It would look respectable, even if it killed me. I owed them so much more than respectable. I owed them my life. I guess that was why I put up with so much from Blaze over the years. I was just so damn grateful for the opportunities they gave me that I never wanted to disappoint Ash, even if his own son did.

I wasn't dumb when it came to life. I was raised by a single momma and had spent a lot of time alone, even when she was alive. I know if Ash and Amity hadn't taken me in, who knows where I'd be or what I'd be doing. They shielded me from a lot of horribleness that I could have experienced in the foster system and beyond. They made me one of their own without asking for anything in return. This was one of those times when I wished I hadn't been so stubborn at fourteen. I wish I had agreed to let them adopt me, so I had their last name. I wanted to be part of the family in name, and by the time I was seventeen, I had come to regret my decision. I didn't want to say anything then because everyone was happy to respect my wishes and let me remain my mother's child.

I wiped my brow on my shirt sleeve and braced the pitchfork in the hay bale next to me. I had to stop thinking about the past and the mistakes I made back then. It just made me feel like even more of a failure in the eyes of Ash and Amity. The only thing I could do was show them the lessons they taught me all those years ago were what had helped me make this ranch successful. I could start by making sure this barn was in tip-top shape when they arrived.

The barn here at Bison Ridge held sixteen horses, eight on each side. Each stall had a door that opened to the outside and allowed fresh air inside. We'd redone the barn about six years ago, and it was beautiful with light oak wood stall doors and black wrought iron stall bars. We had a functional tack room on one end, and a few years ago, we added an addition that holds all our seasonal equipment like lawn mowers, snow blowers, and the UTVs. Since the barn was our backup location for Blaze and Miss Heaven's wedding ceremony, I had to make sure it was spic and span. If it rained, we'd be using the tack room for their vows, and I didn't want to scramble to get it all done right before the wedding. Besides, when Mr. McAwley arrived, it better be so clean you could eat off the floor.

We had a small barn by the house where we kept Rapunzel and Cloudy Day. Last fall, Blaze had added another stall in that barn for Grover, so Miss Heaven had a place to keep him when she was here. That was also where my workshop was. It was the small tack room, but it was big enough for what I needed right now. If I got more hides like Blaze was talking about, though, I'd need a more extensive workshop.

"I've never seen it gleam like this before," a voice said from the open door. "The sun glints off the wood."

"Hey, Miss Heaven. Thanks, it's taken a lot of work, but I think the barn is finally ready if we need it for the ceremony."

"More likely, you're worried about what the senior McAwley will say about the place when he flies in."

I shrugged and leaned against a stall, taking a drink of water from my bottle. It was barely April, but the days were warm, especially when you were working hard. "It's been exactly six years since he was here the last time, Heaven. I want him to see the improvements we've made since then."

Heaven walked up to me and sat on a haybale, handing me a cold Dr. Pepper. "It would be hard not to notice, and most of that is because of you. I'm inviting you, Dawn, and Tex to have dinner with us tonight. Cece is going to do steak and potatoes with chocolate cake. After we eat, we have some things to discuss."

I nodded while I swallowed half the can of Dr. Pepper in one swig. "I'm available, but I already know what's going on. Blaze cut me in on it the other day. I don't want to get in the way of you explaining things to Dawn and Tex, Miss Heaven. I'll stay back here and hold down the fort."

"I know," she agreed. "Blaze told me he cut you in on it. That's fine. Regardless, I want you there. You're as much a part of this family as anyone else. Considering you'll be co-owner of Bison Ridge, I think you should be there. I know Dawn is going to need some reassurance. Something tells me she will accept them better from you than me."

I cocked a brow and lowered the can from my lips. "I don't think that's true, Miss Heaven."

She held up her hand. "I'm begging you, Beau. Stop calling me Miss Heaven. Heaven is fine. It's what everyone else calls me."

I grinned and tipped my hat backward on my head. "I know, but you'll always be Miss Heaven to me. Maybe after you get married, I'll learn to drop it. It's a respect thing. No disrespect is ever meant. I was raised to be a proper gentleman; unlike that hick you're marryin'."

She snorted and almost choked on her Dr. Pepper. "Hey, now!" she exclaimed, but laughter filled her words. "He used to call me Miss Heaven, too. I just finally convinced him not to. Don't sidetrack me, though, boy. It is true that Dawn listens to and respects your opinions. You've worked on a ranch a lot longer than she has, so you understand the intricacies that go into running a business like this. If you tell her she should jump on the deal, she will."

I lowered myself to a bale of hay and leaned over my thighs. "I'm not sure why Dawn would need me to tell her to do that.

You're offering her a chance to own part of the business she's poured her heart and soul into for the last half a decade. I can't believe she won't jump at the chance."

Heaven swallowed her soda slowly as though she had to search for the right words to say. "Dawn is having a hard time of it right now. I don't want her to do something rash in the short term when circumstances can easily change for the better down the road."

The can slid out from between my fingers and hit the barn floor. "What are you saying? Is she sick? That's what her weight loss is about, right? I'm afraid she's going to snap if I touch her too hard. She's got little chicken bones now." I thought about how swollen her hands were when I took her to the pharmacy a few weeks ago. "Dammit, I've been so wrapped up in myself I didn't put two and two together. Her hand, right?"

Heaven didn't answer. She just tipped her head and averted her eyes to her can.

"Miss Heaven, so help me God, if you don't tell me what's going on right this minute, I'm going to drive over there and tell her you did!"

"No!" she hollered, jumping up and almost tipping over. I grabbed her and righted her, but she was angry, ripping her arm from my hand. "Don't threaten me, Beau Hanson!"

I stood to my full height and took her hand. "I'm sorry. I didn't mean to upset you. I wasn't threatening you. I've been worried, but now I'm scared. I want to know what's going on. Is she dyin'?"

Heaven's hand squeezed mine for comfort. "No, she's not dying. She's scared and worried and in pain, though. I don't want to lose her as a friend or have her leave the ranch. She needs us right now, even if she pretends like she doesn't. It's not my right to tell you what's wrong with her or how she feels about it. I won't hurt her or break her confidence by doing that. I will admit to you that she's afraid to tell you about it."

I held both hands out to my sides. "Why? Does she think I'm going to judge her or what? We've been friends for years. If she thinks I can't see she has a problem, then there's a porch light on, but no one is home. I've seen it. I just haven't pushed her about it because she clams up every time I do." I groaned and hung my head.

"What?" she asked, confused.

"I shoulda been lookin' after her." I pounded my fist into the side of the barn, shaking out the pain in my knuckles from the collision with the wood. "I should have pushed her!"

Heaven grabbed my upper arm and held it tightly. "Beau, I'm not telling you this to make you feel guilty. I'm telling you this because she needs a friend right now. She acts strong and brave, but she's weak and scared. Weak in body, I should clarify. She will never show weakness, but she's scared for her future, and she's afraid no one is ever going to love her now."

"How does Dawn being sick equate to no one ever loving her?" I was so confused I wondered if I'd been drinking and didn't remember hitting the bottle. "Just tell me, is she eventually going to die, Miss Heaven?"

"Eventually," she said, smirking, "when she's eighty or ninety, at least physically. Emotionally, she's already dying on the vine, Beau."

"You're her friend, and you know the truth. Is she ignoring your advice or something?"

"No, she's trying to downplay it because," she motioned at her arm, "she thinks my problems are so much worse, so she shouldn't complain."

I swiped at the dust on my jeans to avoid making eye contact with her. "I hate it when people do that. My momma used to do that. She had this friend who was in a wheelchair after a car accident broke her back. Momma would always say, well, I have lupus, but I'm still walking, so it's not so bad. The thing is, it was bad sometimes. I think she did it to make me feel better, but I still always felt bad." I snapped my lips shut to keep from saying more. I could see in Heaven's eyes that she was about to launch into a whole load of questions.

"That's the first time you've ever told me a story about your mom. I think you should do that more often, Beau. It sounds like she was a great lady. She raised you, so I know she was. What was her name?"

"Samantha," I said wistfully. "She was beautiful. She died almost twenty years ago now. She raised me until I was ten, but then Blaze's momma took over. I have a whole book of stories about her, did you know that?"

Heaven shook her head, but she didn't let go of my arm. "I didn't know, but that's sweet, Beau."

I shrugged, embarrassed to be discussing this with her out of the blue. I was out of my element and secretly ashamed that I didn't talk about my momma more. I probably should, but it was still too painful even after all these years. "I suppose now that I'm a thirty-year-old man, protecting a book that I wrote as a child makes me sound like one. I started right after she died because my foster family told me I'd eventually fa—fa—forget her. I didn't want that to happen, so I had a secret notebook where I wrote down stories about her every na—night. When I moved in with Blaze, I didn't have to keep it a secret anymore. I haven't looked at that notebook in ya—ears, but it's comforting to know I have it." I paused and cleared my throat of the stutter, concentrating on holding my jaw the right way. I was upset, so I knew the stutter would only get worse if I didn't. "I keep it at the bank so it can't ever get wet or burned up in a fire. I want to be able to read those stories about her to my kids."

"I seriously love that idea. My daddy hasn't been gone for very many years, but I am starting to forget some of the funny things he used to say or do. Maybe I should start a notebook, too. If you wanted to, you could type those stories up, and then you wouldn't have to worry about the physical notebook being damaged."

I shook my head, hooking my thumbs in my belt loops. "I can't work a computer for nothing, Miss Heaven. You know that."

"I do know that, but do you know who is fantastic at the computer?" I shook my head to the negative. "Dawn." She winked, turned, and walked toward the door. "I'll see you tonight for dinner, Beau. Be prepared to stay late. Dawn might need to talk."

Heaven disappeared through the door and left me standing there alone.

Be prepared to stay late.

I was prepared to stay forever, but I couldn't find a way to tell Dawn that. A little voice told me if I could find a way, I just might find redemption on this cold, unforgiving ridge after all.

Six

I stacked the dishes in the dishwasher, my mind a jumbled mess. I was caught in a haze, and I didn't know which way was up. All my focus was on one thing: becoming part-owner of a dude ranch in the middle of northern Wisconsin. Yesterday, I was worried the ranch would fall apart after Heaven got married. Today, I found out that I'd be running it. Heaven wants me to take over her position as the guest services manager. For now, she will continue to do the bookwork, but once I'm ready, she wants me to learn that, too. Heaven will continue to hold thirty-four percent of the shares in the ranch, while Tex and I both own thirty-three. She wants less to do with the day-to-day operations once she gets married, and I can't blame her, considering they also have Bison Ridge to run. It still feels like she's putting a lot of trust in me to keep her family's legacy alive when I know nothing about dude ranches.

I lowered myself to a seat at the table and stared at the dishwasher as it started the wash cycle. "I can't believe this is happening."

"Hard to take it all in, isn't it?" Tex asked from the doorway. "A year ago, we didn't think this cattle ranch was going to be here, much less be converting it to a dude ranch and becoming full partners." He made the mind-blown motion with his hands as he pushed off the door and walked into the kitchen.

I cleared my throat before I spoke to ensure my voice didn't sound as unsure as I felt about the situation. "Are you going to sign on the dotted line?"

"Well, of course, Miss Dawn. I'd be crazy not to. I get to keep doing what I love, but now I'll own rights to the place. I never wanted to leave Heavenly Lane, and now I don't have to. I've never been prouder in my whole life."

I smiled at the man in front of me. He was young at barely twenty-four, but he'd put his heart and soul into this land for the last six years. "I can tell by the way your chest is all puffed out, Tex. You do most of the work here, and you deserve to have a piece of it."

"You do the rest of the work, Miss Dawn. I don't know why you aren't equally as proud. We turned this place around for Miss Heaven. She knows it, too. That's why she's rewarding us for it. Simple as."

I couldn't meet his gaze when I nodded. It wasn't his fault I was torn up and unsure about the extent of my future here. "You're absolutely right. I am proud, but I don't know that Heaven should be giving up so much of her rights to this place, you know? Heavenly Lane has always been her daddy's land and her granddaddy's before that. It feels wrong to me to take something that isn't mine."

He nodded pensively and tapped the table while he thought about it. "I guess you're right, but Heaven does protect herself in the deal. We must sell our shares back to her if we want out, so she retains ownership anyway. She's also got the controlling interest, so she's not going to lose her daddy's ranch no matter what. We also can't make decisions without the full board voting, so it's not like anyone can get power-hungry and try to make changes without full approval. From what I can see, they've put enough fail-safes in place that Miss Heaven and Blaze will always be protected. This land was her daddy's, that's true. Over the last year, though, she made it her own. She saw that things had to change, and she couldn't keep doing what her daddy and granddaddy did without a lot of success. Maybe Heaven turned the ranch on its ear, but she made it hers. Now, she's making it ours. I think that's pretty cool. I'll take part-ownership for what it is, but I won't change how I do things around here. I love working with the guests and the animals. I'm not going to sit at a desk and bark orders. That's not who I am."

I squeezed his shoulder with a heartfelt grin on my lips. "That thought never crossed my mind, Tex," I said, chuckling. "I'm torn about taking the ownership rights from Heaven, but at the same time, I'm thinking about ways I can add to the guests' experience if I'm doing nothing but the guest service job. That's exciting since my background is in hospitality."

"There are a lot of things we could change and implement if you have someone else doing the grunt work, Miss Dawn. I thought maybe you could offer retreats for those church groups and such since this house is so big. They could come and do all that team-building and personal introspection stuff. You could organize trail rides for them and campfires."

I tipped my head to the left in surprise. "Tex, that's a brilliant idea. I bet if we offered something like that, we'd have the upstairs booked every week. I'm going to talk to Heaven about it. I'm giving you credit for it, though."

"I'm glad you like the idea, Miss Dawn. I suppose there are all kinds of things you could do using that train of thought. I hope you stay and accept Miss Heaven's offer. I don't think nothing would be the same around here without you."

"I second that statement," another voice said from the doorway. I glanced up to see Beau lounging on the frame.

"Hey, Beau," I greeted him before I pointed at Tex. "We were just talking about the ranch."

Tex tapped the table and stood. "I gotta be getting on anyway. I have chores to finish before I turn in. There's a new group of guys coming this weekend, so I better rest up."

He pushed in his chair then turned to Beau. "Please, convince her to accept Miss Heaven's deal?" he asked. The desperation was loud and clear in his words. "I don't want to do this without Dawn working here. The two of us, we've put too much into this place to give it all up now. If it weren't for her, we wouldn't be standing here. She kept us going when Miss Heaven couldn't. I think that's more than a good enough reason for her to accept this reward now."

Beau nodded once but no words passed between them before Tex patted me on the shoulder and walked out the door.

I rubbed my temple without making eye contact with the guy I couldn't stop thinking about every single minute of the day. I hadn't seen him much in the last few weeks since the kiss, which was probably for the best, even if it left my heart in more pain than anything my body could dish out. There was something about a broken heart that was three times as painful as a broken bone. "You can go, Beau. I'm sure you have work to do at the ranch. I'll be fine."

"Nope, my work is done. I was thinking about starting a fire or going for a walk on the ridge. Do you want to join me?"

I glanced out the door before I answered. "It's dark already."

"I like the darkness. I can hide in it, and no one can find me. That's the most relaxing part of my day."

I lifted a brow. "The darkness also likes to hide bears and wolves."

"I walk loudly and carry a big gun," he volleyed.

"I guess we could go for a walk. I could stand to work off that steak," I finally said, my head shaking at his determination.

"First, you would have to eat some of it," he murmured.

"I ate, Beau," I insisted. "I just don't eat a lot at one sitting. Besides, you know how I feel about bison meat." I did an involuntary shiver, and he chuckled as he walked the rest of the way into the kitchen.

"I do know how you feel, but I think your aversion to it has more to do with the fact that you always thought Blaze was gonna take this ranch, and you refused to like anything Blaze McAwley had a part in."

I patted his chest on my way to my room. "You might be right. I love bison meat, even more than I love beef. The thing is, I'm not a camp deserter. I learned the hard way about the pitfalls of that. There, my secret is out. I'm going to change my clothes. I'll meet you at the barn."

I was almost to the end of the hallway when he spoke. "Maybe one secret is out, but something tells me you have more secrets than a porcupine has quills."

I heard him, but I refused to turn and acknowledge it. He could think whatever he wanted to think. He wasn't getting my real secrets out of me now or ever.

The ridge was always peaceful in its harmony. The occasional call of an owl, the gruff grunts of the bison, and the whisper of our feet in the grass as the snow melted was the melody. We walked along the fence toward the lower pasture that used to be Heavenly Lane's land. When Heaven sold it to Blaze last year, that made it part of Bison Ridge, but in the end, none of it mattered. In a few more weeks, all of this was Bison

Ridge, and we'd move the cows and red dogs down to the lower pasture closer to the watering hole.

Heaven only keeps about a hundred head of cattle now, primarily for her guests to learn to work with while they are at the dude ranch. With Heaven's physical limitations, she could never manage a big enough herd after her daddy died to keep the ranch in the black. When Heaven flipped this place into a guest ranch, she had found more success than any of the three generations before her. For that, I think she deserved the success and happiness she was experiencing now. Heaven had poured more than her fair share of pain and heartache into this place. More than anyone should have to. I was glad she had Blaze now, even if it seemed to everyone else that I wasn't.

"You're quiet," Dawn said, leaning into me a bit to shake me from my thoughts.

"I was just thinking about Miss Heaven and her daddy. A lot has changed since he passed."

Dawn's head bobbed in the moonlight. The beam rested across her beautiful face making her glow like a goddess. She was a goddess, in my opinion. I just wished she was my goddess. "I would venture to say for the better."

"For Heavenly Lane Dude Ranch, and Miss Heaven, yes. I don't know about for you."

"Definitely for you," she said without missing a beat.

Dawn Lee was good at never allowing the spotlight to stay on her. This whole venture to convince her to talk was more challenging than I thought, and I already knew it would be challenging. I put my arm around her shoulder and tucked her in close to my side. I wanted to direct her down toward the lower pasture. I had a plan, and I wanted her to stick with me until we got there.

"Blaze told me I would be getting the partnership in the ranch that day when I went back to apologize to them," I admitted, hoping to get her to open up.

"I texted them that you were on your way back, but Heaven said you didn't even go inside. They decided to hunt you down in the barn and found you messing with her saddle."

"I can still see the look on her face when she saw me in the barn by her horse," I said with a chuckle. "She was ready to read me the riot act until she noticed Grover. Her anger turned to tears of happiness on a dime. It was glorious."

"It was glorious to make your friend cry?" Dawn asked with a lilt to her voice.

"No, the look on her face when she realized what I'd done to the saddle was glorious. Sorry, that did sound rude," I sighed and shook my head at myself.

Dawn shoulder-bumped me and then tipped her head up to gaze at me. "I know what you meant, Beau. She came racing into the yard, screaming my name at the top of her lungs. I ran out thinking she was hurt or something. When she showed me all the changes you made to the saddle, I was flabbergasted. I'd never seen anything like it. You have a real talent with leather, Beau."

I tipped my head uncomfortably, never sure how to accept a compliment like that. I figured out long ago that I got that from my momma. She was the same way. Blaze always said I was too humble, but I don't think that's a thing. I'm not a bragger. Never have been, and never will be.

"That's what Blaze said, too. He wants me to spend more time doing my leatherworking once I'm a partner in the ranch. He doesn't want me doing the grunt work anymore, at least not full-time. I'll be training the guys to work with the bison as well as hiring and training new hands, but I won't be doing chores every morning and night like I have all these years."

"Sounds like reason enough to sign on the dotted line to me," she said, nodding.

I led her down through the trees and stopped in the pasture's clearing. She turned in a circle out of surprise while I gathered some twigs and got the kindling burning in the fire pit. Once it had caught, I laid longer logs over it in a teepee fashion until the fire was crackling intensely bright and offering warmth to the air around us.

"This is where you were those nights you were missing?" she asked, gazing around the space. "You'd never see a fire down here from up on the ridge."

"I didn't want anyone to notice it, so I always kept it small. You'd see this fire from up on the ridge," I assured her, motioning at it. I held up my finger and grabbed my flashlight, finding my waterproof bag right where I left it in a tree. I pulled out several blankets and carried them back to the log I used to rest my back on. I laid one down on the ground and helped her sit, then covered her with the other one before I joined her.

"Wow, Beau, were you always a boy scout?" she asked, straightening the blanket out so I could throw it over my legs, too.

I was the furthest thing from a boy scout growing up, but I wasn't going to tell her that. "Would a boy scout bring this?" I asked, reaching in my coat and pulling out a small bottle of Jack Daniels. I lifted a brow and screwed off the cap, taking a healthy gulp before handing it to her. She took a long swig herself and gave it back to me, coughing a bit when she swallowed. "I don't know any boy scouts who carry Jack around in their pockets," she agreed once she'd cleared her throat.

"I think they would have kicked me out of the boy scouts," I said, my laughter echoing around the pasture. "Besides, I worked hard on the McAwley's ranch. I learned everything I needed to know from Mr. McAwley. Man, I can't wait to see Blaze's momma and dad again."

Dawn leaned over onto my shoulder, and I put my arm around her so she could get more comfortable. "I would venture a guess that at this point, they're your mom and dad, too. At least in the sense that they love you like a son. I know no one can replace your mom." She was stumbling about trying to fix what she thought she'd said wrong.

"I know what you mean, Dawn. You're right, though. Blaze's mom came through for me when she didn't have to. She's my second momma in my eyes. Senior was the father I never had and was never gonna have. He taught me how to respect myself, my friends and, most importantly, how to respect women. I could have gotten along far worse if they hadn't helped me through my teenage years. Sometimes, I still didn't know nothing from nothing, but at least the discipline I got for it fit the crime."

"Nothing from nothing?" she asked, her laughter making my chest shake.

"Yeah, down south, that means I was dumb. I did dumb stuff a lot. I was tryin' to fit in. Sometimes I succeeded, and sometimes I failed miserably, but Blaze's daddy was always there to remind me I could try again or help me see what I had to do to fix the situation. He'd been raising boys for a long time by the time it was just us left on the ranch. He had plenty of experience with rough and tumble, wild boys."

Dawn patted my chest and left it against my jacket, either for warmth or comfort. I didn't know which. I didn't much care. Having her this close to me was as comforting to me as to her. "If my opinion matters, I think he's going to be impressed with the way those two rough and tumble, wild boys have succeeded in this state. You've built something from nothing. Not just anyone can say that."

"You can," I promised, laying my lips on her forehead for some reason. Whether I wanted to comfort her or me, I also couldn't say, but the warmth of her skin soaked into my lips, and I didn't want to move them.

Dawn shifted to get more comfortable, and I held her closer to me until she was spread across my lap, facing the fire. I rubbed her neck and pulled the blanket up over her a little bit higher. It felt strangely intimate and more than just best friends sitting by the fire, but I wouldn't change it for the world. Dawn had relaxed for the first time in too long, and I wanted to keep her that way.

"I haven't built anything, Beau. Sure, I've helped Heaven keep the place going, but the grit on the back of her neck did that, not mine."

I shook my head vehemently in the firelight. "Not true. You did the work after Heaven was injured again on the ridge when she couldn't do it herself. You could have walked away, but you didn't. You hung in there. I know you weren't getting paid a quarter of what you were worth, Dawn."

"You don't walk away from your friends when they need you, Beau," she whispered, her words practically drowned out by the crackle of the fire.

"I know, but that doesn't make anything I said less truthful. My point is, you worked hard for years to get where you are with the ranch. Why on earth would you want to walk away now?"

Dawn tossed her hand up and let it fall to her hip. "I don't want to walk away now, but I'm not sure how to feel about Heaven just giving us a piece of the property. I don't know how her daddy would feel about that either."

Duane Lane had passed away five years ago after contracting an illness from the cattle he loved to raise. Right before he died, he begged Heaven to make sure, no matter what, that she held onto the ranch. It had been in the family for three generations, and he gave up everything for it, including Miss Heaven's momma when she couldn't stick around and live that kind of life. Miss Heaven had promised him she would do her best, but the medical bills his illness created nearly broke that promise before she could think about keeping it. Against all odds, she managed to recover and not lose the ranch to the bank. That only happened because Dawn and Tex worked for nothing but room and board for nearly a year.

I ran my fingers through the hair on the top of Dawn's head, glad the season of hats was gone so I could play with her silky tresses again. "Duane would be thrilled to know the ranch was still firmly in his daughter's grasp. He wouldn't quibble about her business decisions as long as it stayed in the family. Tex is right, too. Miss Heaven has put plenty of safeguards in place to protect the ranch if one of you decides it's time to leave. She wants you to have a piece of something that you've worked for, Dawn. Miss Heaven wants you to feel the pride of being a landowner and a business owner. Everything changes when you're working for something that you own. Suddenly, all those late nights and extra shifts are worth it. You get to be the one who benefits from your good ideas when you implement something that brings in more guests or money. Those are the benefits of having a piece of the pie. Not to mention, your duties are going to be a lot less, which will make things easier for you."

Dawn sat up instantly and stared at me with fire flaming in her eyes. "What did Heaven tell you?"

I held up my hands in the don't shoot position. "Nothing, darlin'," I promised, helping Dawn to get comfortable again. "I just meant I can't quite figure out why you'd want to keep killing yourself when you've been handed the power to delegate work? If you take ownership of the ranch, you can focus on the work you *want* to do instead of what you *have* to do. There's a big difference." I blew out a breath and shook my head. "Am I even making any sense?"

"You're saying that I've already put in the hard work, so not signing on the dotted line to reap the rewards is just plain stupid."

I rubbed her arm to keep her warm but chuckled at her breakdown of the situation. I was thrilled when she didn't pull away from me instantly like she usually does. "That's exactly what I'm saying. Besides, the way Heaven has it set up if you decide to leave any time after you sign on the dotted line, she has to buy you out. You could flip your part of the place and walk away with a hefty payday in a matter of a month."

Dawn gasped and flipped over to glare up at me. "I would never do that to Heaven! What kind of person do you think I am?"

I laid my finger against her lips until she hushed. "I'm not saying you ever would. I'm saying there is no risk of taking what's due to you. The only way to go wrong in this deal is not to sign those papers."

My finger fell away, and she heaved out a sigh. "I never thought of it that way, but you're right. But also, I'm going to point that out to Heaven. She's going to want to fix that clause."

"I doubt it," I said, my gaze glued to hers. "Heaven wrote it that way because she trusts you and Tex. She knows if you sign the paperwork, you're not going to screw her over. It's going to be so you can continue to run that ranch together. No other reason."

Dawn nodded slowly, the alcohol finally hitting her bloodstream and helping her relax. "You're absolutely right there. I would sign that paperwork for no other reason, and she knows it."

"That said, she also knows that life changes. If you or Tex decide to move on for whatever reason, you still deserve your reward for keeping the ranch going. At that point, the reward becomes monetary when she buys you out. Blaze and Miss Heaven are fully aware that clause is in the contract, just like it's in my contract. The terms of the sale and the price you'd get for your share are also there. Miss Heaven has protected herself and you. You can't go wrong becoming part owner in Heavenly Lane, Dawn."

"I haven't seen the contract, but if what you say is true, then there's no reason for me not to sign."

I gave her a finger gun and winked. "So, that's decided?"

Dawn nodded, a smile tugging her lips upward. "That's decided. Don't get me wrong, Beau. I never wanted to turn her down. She just took me so much by surprise that all I could think about was how this would negatively impact her."

I leaned back against the log and rubbed her shoulder to keep her relaxed. I craved physical contact with Dawn, and I wanted her warmth against me every opportunity I got. Now that I'd had a taste of her, I wanted all of her. I didn't want to scare her away, though. "She knows, which is why she asked me to come tonight. I already knew about the partnership with Blaze, so the rest didn't apply to me, but she wanted me to be here in case you had questions that you didn't want to ask one of them."

She tipped her head to the side to make eye contact. "Wait. If she asked you to be here tonight just in case I had questions, and you knew the answers, then you had to have known what she was going to tell us."

My eyes widened, and I blew out a breath, banging myself on the forehead several times with the palm of my hand. "Stupid, stupid, stupid. I wasn't supposed to say anything. Dammit," I groaned. "You're so beautiful, and when I'm staring into your gorgeous brown eyes, I forget what I'm even sayin'."

Dawn closed her eyes and swallowed before she responded. "I'm not upset. I understand what Heaven was trying to do. It's okay if she told you what she had planned. I suppose she knew I was going to be hesitant, so I can't blame her for that either."

"Blaze spilled the beans when he told me about our partnership last week, Da—"

"Wait, you've known for a week and didn't say anything?"

I laid my head back on the log and banged it over and over. "Why am I such an idiot?" I moaned, the sound echoing sad and melancholy through the pasture.

Dawn's laughter zipped across and over it, filling the sky with bursts of light and my heart with an emotion that I didn't want to define. If I thought too long or hard about it, I might suspect it was love.

"I'm teasing you, Beau. Man, you're so easy to rile up. I don't care when you found out. I know that you would never break a promise to a friend. I have no doubt that they both made you promise not to tell us."

I smiled down at her, happy to see the twinkle back in her eye as the fire crackled behind her. "They did, and I never would break a promise. You can tell me anything, and I promise I won't ever tell another soul."

"I don't have anything to tell you," she said too quickly and too easily. "But thanks."

"I may not be a well-educated man, Dawn Briar Lee, but I don't need a degree to see that was a lie," I drawled, my brow up in the air. "A huge one that I think you've been practicing for a long time."

Slowly, Dawn rolled back over to face the fire. Putting her back to me was her way of flipping me off, I had no doubt, but I couldn't let her go on thinking no one cared about her. We all cared about her, most especially me.

I leaned over, rubbing her shoulder until I could make eye contact with her again. There were tears on her cheeks, and she was biting her tongue to keep the sob from breaking loose.

"Darlin'," I whispered, pulling her up and into me. "I don't know what's wrong, but it sure is breaking my heart to see you so torn up about it. I can promise you that I don't have the answers to the questions you keep asking yourself. What I do have are strong arms I can wrap around you when you need a hug, okay?" I whispered, my lips near her ear as I held her. "You don't have to go through whatever this is alone. We're all friends here, and friends stand by each other. Friends hold each other up when they hit a rough patch."

Dawn clung to me but didn't say a word. The sobs she held inside shook her chest, and all I could do was kiss her temple and hope she could feel how much I cared about her when I kept my arms around her. I held her, letting my warmth comfort her, while the silence lingered between us. I was at a loss for what to say for the longest time until something she'd said before ran through my mind. "I was thinking about what you said in the café last month."

"About what?" she asked, sitting up and discreetly wiping her face.

"Your offer to let me move into the house at Heavenly Lane."

"I didn't mean to upset you by the suggestion," Dawn said immediately, holding her hand up to me. Her fingers looked red and swollen again. That scared me. I took her palm and massaged it, being careful of her fingers that had to hurt worse than anything I'd ever done to myself.

"I know you didn't, Dawn Lee. To be honest, the more I thought about it, the more I could see that maybe you're right. Maybe moving into the farmhouse isn't a bad idea. It would give Blaze and Heaven the main house to themselves, which they deserve, and keeps you from being alone at Heavenly Lane once Heaven moves out."

Dawn ran her hand down my chest while I held her other hand loosely. "You're always welcome at Heavenly Lane, Beau. Heaven has already moved to Bison Ridge full-time, but she's worried about me living there alone, too. Cece was supposed to move in but can't get out of her lease right now."

I trailed a finger down her cheek until it reached her chin, where I tipped it up. "I can take a room upstairs."

She nodded for a long time before she answered. "You could, but there are three rooms downstairs and four upstairs. I like Tex's idea of holding small retreat weekends for women's groups, and I want to explore that more. If I do, I might need those upstairs rooms for the business. You're welcome to my old room or the smaller one at the end of the hall. I've already moved into Heaven's old room."

I tickled her side carefully in response. "Oh, sure, suddenly, you own the place and get the room with a bathroom!"

"Hey," she squealed with laughter, "I earned that bathroom!"

I held her face in my hands and brought her nose to mine. "You sure have, Dawn. You've earned all the rewards coming to you now."

"Are you one of them, Beau?" she whisper-asked.

"Do you want me to be?" I answered with my lips almost on hers.

"It scares me how much I do."

"Don't be afraid, Dawn. Maybe we can fix each other," I whispered before my lips came down on hers to keep her from saying something I didn't want to hear.

She tasted of Jack Daniels and the right decisions. She tasted of a time long past dawn when the sunlight had faded, and the stars sang in the sky. She tasted of the future, hope, and redemption.

When she leaned into me, and a soft moan filled her throat, desire coursed through me. Her lips fell open, and she allowed my tongue to waltz in and dance with hers. She was velvet, sin, and heaven. She was the only thing that made my crazy world sane, yet she made me crazy with want, need, and desire. She brought out the protector in me. I would die for her right here on this ridge if it meant she never suffered again.

A moan fell from my lips and straight into her mouth, absorbed and accepted as payment for the pleasure given when she didn't have to offer me anything. Her tongue was soft, wet, and pushing back against mine in a way that made my Wranglers instantly tight at the thought of how it would feel to have her tongue running the length of me. A louder, longer moan forced its way from my chest and filled the air when she tipped her head to the side, digging deeper for whatever she needed from me.

This was where I wanted to be all night long. I wanted to kiss her forever in the darkness, taking my breath from her. I wanted to forget everything but the promise of a future with her that blocks out the loneliness I'd carried forever. I wanted her.

An electric shock of surprise went through me at the thought. My lips fell away from hers, and our chests heaved in harmony while I held Dawn's gaze. My hands cradled her face tenderly, but they trembled from the emotions coursing through me.

I want her.

I want her to be mine.

I want her to be mine forever.

Oh my god, when did this happen? When did I fall in love with my best friend?

Dawn's hands gripped my wrists and hung there, her eyes searching mine for whatever it was she needed from me. The fear in her eyes told me she needed trust. She needed understanding and passion. Most of all, she needed love. Love from someone that would offer her all those things without judgment.

My thumb stroked her cheek while I lowered my forehead to hers. "Let me take you out this weekend? We'll have a burger at The Wise Anchor and do a little line dancing?"

Her gaze dropped to my lips and refused to meet my eyes. "I don't feel up to dancing, but thanks anyway. You go and have a good time."

I raised a brow against hers until she lifted her gaze back to mine. "That defeats the purpose, gorgeous. I don't want to go if you aren't going to be with me. How about dinner at The Wise Anchor, a short horseback ride along the ridge, and a blazing campfire to end the night? That way, if you get tired, you're close to home."

Dawn stared me down for so long I was afraid she was going to say no and break my heart. I'd wanted to take her out on an actual date for years, but I was always too afraid to change the dynamic between us. The idea of losing her as my best friend was too much to think about over the last year. My other best friend was getting married again, and I would need her. The idea that if Dawn and I became more than best friends and things went wrong, then working together would be awkward. What had changed over the last few months, I didn't know. That's not true. I knew what had changed. Me. My heart had finally convinced my brain to be quiet and stop thinking so damn much. Dawn's hesitation made me wonder if this was nothing but a fool's errand and I should leave things alone.

"That sounds like a nice evening out," she finally agreed, and I released a sigh of relief.

"I think so, too." I stroked her cheek for several minutes before I spoke again. "You know that I'm always going to be here for you, right? Anything you need, Dawn, at any time. I'll always find a way to get it for you."

Her gaze immediately dropped to the ground again rather than hold mine. She let out a ragged sigh before she spoke. “I’d like to believe that, Beau, but my track record with people sticking around is about one for hundreds in my lifetime.”

“Who’s the one?” I asked, my head tipped to the side.

“Heaven. She’s the only one who ever stayed. No one in my family wanted anything to do with me, so I walked away.”

“Walked away from what?” Dawn never talked about her family, but I just assumed they lived in a different state, and she didn’t see them often.

“My family is Jehovah’s Witness, Beau. They live in Wyoming, or at least they used to. I haven’t seen them since high school. I don’t want anything to do with them, even if they showed up on my doorstep. Things were bad growing up. I didn’t have a choice, I had to leave, but now I’m truly alone in this world other than the people on these two ranches. I can’t risk doing anything to get kicked out.”

I held her head to my chest and kissed the top of her head. “Shh, you don’t have to worry about that, darlin’. You’re so loved here. Miss Heaven was near tears at the idea you didn’t want to stay on the ranch, and Tex was practically begging you to stay.”

“What about you, Beau?” She asked the question in a tone of voice that told me it took a lot of courage for her to utter those words.

“You’re my best friend, Dawn, but lately, the way I feel is changing. I can share things with you that I never share with anyone else. I can’t really explain it much more than that right now. Just relax and remember that we’re all here for you, even though the landscape at Heavenly Lane is changing. Sometimes, you get to pick your family. We aren’t that different in that arena. We both had to make a new family from love, not blood, and I think we’ve both hit the lottery. Don’t you?”

Dawn nodded against my chest, but her breath was heavy when she spoke. "Now you understand why I'm always so careful not to raise any conflict. Without this place, I'm nothing."

I rocked her gently against me while I rested my cheek on the top of her head. "No, darlin'. Without you, we're nothing. I'm going to make it my mission to show you the difference."

Dawn lifted her head to search my eyes for whatever she needed in this dark, uncertain world. "I hope you can, Beau."

I lowered my lips toward hers and paused, staring down at her kissable sweetness. "Darlin', I can do anything I put my mind to," I promised, and then I captured her lips again to help her take the first step.

Seven

The trip into Duluth wasn't more than an hour, but my entire body ached from sitting immobile for so long. My body constantly ached, but if I was moving around, at least my joints didn't stiffen up. I wanted to stay at the ranch, but Heaven didn't give me a choice in the matter. Her wedding was next weekend, which meant I *had* to find a dress today.

I stretched my neck and back inside the fitting room while I eyed the dress hanging on the hook. We'd been searching for a maid of honor dress since January, but we couldn't find anything that looked remotely good on me. Then again, maybe it was me. I didn't like anything I tried on and avoided looking in the mirror as much as possible. While I should have taken pride in my new figure, I was embarrassed and ashamed of it instead. I leaned against the dressing room door and closed my eyes, willing the tears to stay away. I was not going to cry over the situations in my life that I couldn't control when my best friend was waiting outside to see this dress.

Knuckles rapped on the closed door. "Do you have it on yet?"

I cleared my throat before I spoke. "No, I'm getting there," I promised, pushing off the door and stripping my shirt off, then my boots and pants. "I don't think this is going to be what you're looking for, Heaven. The dress is the exact opposite of a traditional maid of honor gown."

There was silence while I pulled the dress on over my head and smoothed it down across my hips. I slid my feet back into my boots since I'd be wearing boots with the dress anyway. Heaven and Blaze were getting married on a ranch, so there was no way I was wearing heels. Not that I could right now if I tried.

I unlocked the door and pulled it open. Her gaze took me in, and Heaven's mouth dropped open. "Dawn, this is—"

"Bad," I said, looking down at the lace dress. "I warned you."

Heaven shook her head back and forth for at least ten seconds before she spoke. "No, it's stunning. It's so … you. Those other dresses were pretty, but this just screams Dawn Lee. Look at this," she said, holding the lace sleeve out. "Delicate, beautiful, simple, and badass, all in one dress."

I tried to hold in my laughter, but it came out in a choked snort. "It's red," I pointed out. "You want your maid of honor wearing a red dress?"

She lifted one brow. "It's rose red, and I'm carrying red roses in my bouquet. I think it's perfect. Oh, but wait!" she said, holding up her finger and dashing away. I stood in the doorway, unsure of what she was doing.

While I waited for Heaven, I turned and stared at myself in the mirror, working to see the dress from her eyes. My mind's eye wandered to what look would be on Beau's face when he saw me in it for the first time. Would he smile? Would he kiss me on the cheek and tell me I was gorgeous? Would he frown because he hated it? I didn't think it mattered what I wore anymore. He always told me I was gorgeous. According to him, he was also going to prove to me that I make his world better. Okay, so technically, he said I made everyone's world better, but

I think he was really talking about his world. At least that's what his lips told me when they were on mine.

"I'm back," she said, running into the dressing room with hangers hooked on her fingers.

I held them up and glanced between my hands. "A denim jacket and a leather fringe vest?"

Heaven nodded, jumping up and down once. "Put them on. I want to see which looks better!"

"What did Blaze put in your coffee this morning?" I teased, hanging the two hangers on the hook before slipping my arms into the denim jacket.

"It was what came before the coffee," she said, wiggling her brows.

I groaned and dumped my head into my hand. "I should know better. I walked right into that one."

Heaven was bent over laughing, her shoulder shaking. "You should, after all this time. I'm about to get married, after all." She clapped her hand on her thigh. "Okay, back to the dress. Turn," she said, motioning with her hand until I did. When I faced the mirror again, I frowned.

"It covers up the sleeves," I said. "That's the best part of the dress."

"Agreed. Try the vest."

I took the coat off and threw the vest on, straightening it so it hung evenly across my breasts. I turned left then right and tugged on the front a bit. When I turned back to face Heaven, she had tears in her eyes.

"It's perfect, Dawn. Now I know why the other dresses didn't work. This one was waiting for you."

I hugged her then, slightly embarrassed by her show of emotion. "I like it too. You know that's a miracle. Plus, I can wear it again for something since it's not so formal."

Heaven was grinning when she leaned back. "I agree. There's the added benefit that Beau is going to lose his boots when he sees you in it!"

That got a smile out of me. I shook my finger at Heaven. "You're naughty, and that's why I love you. Oh, Beau!" I exclaimed suddenly, and she tipped her head when I handed her the vest.

"What about Beau? He's already got his outfit. He's wearing a western tuxedo shirt, bolo tie, his dress Wranglers, of course, and a Stetson—"

"Of course, I would expect nothing else from that quintessential cowboy," I said, laughing with her. "What I meant was, I have a vest just like that. Beau made it for me last year, remember?"

Heaven held the vest up again and eyed it before she threw her head back and laughed. "I knew it looked familiar when I saw it out there! Okay, so we don't need the vest, just the dress?"

"I think so. I'll wear the vest Beau made me and my boots with the red roses on the side. Do you remember that pair? I save them for special occasions."

Her grin widened when she hung the vest back on the hanger. "I do remember those now! You haven't worn them in years. They'll rock with this dress. You're set! Let's check out and get lunch. I don't want to go back to the ranch yet. We drove all the way here, so we might as well play a little."

I pulled the dress over my head and handed it to her. She didn't take it from my hand. Instead, she ran her finger down my side. "I knew you'd lost weight, but Dawn, I can see your ribs. Are you eating anything?"

I grabbed my shirt and pulled it on to avoid having to look at her when I lied. "I eat all the time. My medication can bother my stomach, so I don't always eat a lot."

Heaven left the dress off the hanger and hung it over her arm. "Maybe, but you weren't being treated this winter."

I pulled my pants on and stepped back into my boots. After I grabbed my jacket and purse from the chair, I opened the door for her. "Let it go, Heaven. I can't change it right now, okay?"

We walked in silence to the checkout, where she insisted on purchasing the dress for me. I objected but couldn't do it too loudly and embarrass her in front of the associate. I held the door for her, and she scooted through, beeping the lock open on the new truck Blaze had bought her this winter when hers finally bought the farm. He'd had it outfitted with a unique steering wheel spinner knob that also had her turn signals, headlights, and windshield wiper controls built into it. The truck was much more comfortable for her to drive, and we all felt better knowing she was safe on the road now.

"Thank you for buying the dress, Heaven," I said when we were seat belted in and headed down the road. "I don't think that's the job of the bride, though."

Heaven shrugged and stared straight ahead. "Maybe not, but you've carried my butt more times than I care to count. Besides, the dress was less than fifty bucks. It wasn't a big deal. Should we get some lunch?"

I lowered a brow to my nose. "Are you going to harp on me about how much I do or don't eat if I agree?"

She shook her head and pursed her lips. "You're a grown-up and can do whatever you see fit, Dawn."

I sighed and dropped my chin to my chest. "I'm sorry if I upset you. God, you don't know how much I wish I had an appetite, but I don't. I do the best I can, and the doctor is monitoring my weight now, okay? He's making me supplement what I eat with those nutritional drink things for extra calories, too."

"Okay," she said softly. "I didn't mean to upset you either. I'm just worried about a lot of things. Your health is at the top of my list."

I squeezed her shoulder and nodded. "Let's go get some lunch. Maybe I can put some of those worries to rest, okay?"

She headed back toward the bridge on a sunny afternoon, and I stared out the window at the magnificence of Lake Superior. Visible for as far as the eye could see, you could certainly get lost on any part of it and disappear forever, never to be seen again. There were days I wanted to start over in a new place and forget about my problems in Wellspring, but those problems would just follow me wherever I went. There was no escaping my worries, but if I could make Heaven feel better about hers, then that was my job today. I didn't see my happiness written in the stars, so it might be my lot in life to make sure everyone else found theirs.

I thought back to Thursday night when Beau had his lips on mine as the stars twinkled above us, and it made me wonder if a person could write their own happy ending. The look in Beau's sienna eyes as they gazed into mine told me that was what I wanted more than anything else in this world.

The wind blew off the lake to ruffle the hair on top of my head. I made sure the food wrappings were inside the takeout bag and then tucked it under a log, so it didn't blow away. Heaven was down by the water, picking up rocks and trying not to get wet from the brush of the waves on the sand. The beach at Wisconsin Point was one of my favorite places to be in the spring. There was never anyone around, the sand was warm from the spring sunshine, and the peaceful sounds of the birds and the lake always lowered my heart rate and helped me relax. It had been a long winter. I loved coming here to find a little peace with nature, and I was grateful for the chance to visit before heading back home.

"I forgot how wonderful this place is," Heaven said, sitting beside me on a piece of driftwood. "It's always so soul cleansing. Whenever I sit here and stare at the water, I forget about all my responsibilities at home. Weird how that works, isn't it?"

I leaned over on my thighs and rested my forearms there. "Yeah, it definitely does that."

Heaven tipped her head at me and held my hand with her tiny one. "Are you leaving us, Dawn? I'll understand if you are, but it's going to kill me."

I snapped my head around to stare at her. "No! I'm not leaving. What makes you think that?"

"Your reaction to the offer to own part of the ranch, for starters," she answered immediately.

My gaze darted back to the lake to avoid her eyes. "You took me by surprise, and I didn't know how to react. I don't want you to do something you'll regret down the road with your daddy's ranch. You've hung onto it with all your might for so many years. You don't have to give us a partnership in it. You don't. You can promote us and pay us more without giving us a slice of the pie."

"I'm aware of that," she said, nodding with me. "The thing is, I don't want to do that. I want you and Tex to own part of the land you've essentially homesteaded."

"We didn't homestead anything. You owned the property, not the government."

Heaven made the so-so motion with her hand. "While that's true, you have worked the land for more than five years. That's the rest of the definition. I want you both to stay and work the ranch because I trust you. By giving you each a part of the controlling ownership that assures me that you have something to stay for."

I nodded while I stared out over the breaking waves in the midday sun. "Beau helped me see why you were doing it. He explained to me the things I don't see, but everyone else does. When he laid it out the way he did, I stopped feeling like I was stealing something from you and started feeling like I was contributing to a family. A family I've never had before. I'm going to sign the paperwork after you're married."

Heaven's chin fell to her chest, and she sighed. "Oh, thank God," she whispered, turning her head to the sky. "Like, thank God, and thank you, Beau. I was worried you were going to leave. Like leave-leave forever. I know I left, but I'm always just a ridge ride away."

"I don't begrudge you finally marrying your one true love, Heaven. I'd be mad if you stayed back for me. I do want you to consider changing one thing about the contract, though." I turned to hold her gaze while I filled her in on what Beau told me about flipping the rights back to her to get cash immediately. "The way it stands now, you could be out big bucks if you don't."

"I see your point, but I'm not worried. Neither of you would do that. If it makes you feel better, I'll talk to the lawyer about adding a clause of six months or a year. Does that help?"

I held both hands up in defense. "You don't have to make me feel better. I want you to protect yourself. I do think you need to at least address it with the lawyer. I know neither Tex nor I would ever plan to do it, but things happen. I don't want you to get hurt in the process."

Heaven nodded once. "Done. As long as you plan to stay, I'll do anything I have to do to keep you here."

"You know I'd never leave Heavenly Lane by choice. I'm excited to take over as the guest services manager. Tex had a great idea the other night that I'd like to run by you. Of course, if you'd rather I wait and talk about it with everyone, I'll understand."

She waved her hand at her throat. "Not necessary yet. I still own the ranch, so I'm still making the decisions. I want to hear what it is."

"Okay, well, Tex said maybe we should use the bedrooms upstairs for church groups to come on the weekends for a retreat. I started thinking about it and realized companies might want the same thing. We have four rooms that we could rent out for the weekends. I could plan activities and team-building options they could do at the ranch. It's a gamble, but if we do it right, it could be a lot of fun."

Heaven was grinning when I finished speaking and jumped up, hugging me gently. "It's not a gamble. It's a home run! Those rooms are sitting empty right now, we have enough horses, and we're already buying food for the rest of the guests. There's no initial investment required beyond maybe some games or things for the groups to do if it were raining. Everything we take in from renting the rooms is income. I love the idea. Let's sit down after the wedding and get a plan laid out and the advertising in place. As long as you think you can handle the added work."

"By then, it won't be a problem. I've got Landry hired on to take over my chores in the barn and to prepare the bunkhouse each week. Tex hired a new ranch hand, Tobi, to help him with the horses. I know he plans to hire several more. With everyone in place, I'll have plenty of time to concentrate on the house.

Beau is moving in, but I don't think that should impact it much. He'll mostly only be there to sleep."

Heaven reared back and stared at me. "Whoa, slow down, cowgirl. Beau is moving into the house on Heavenly Lane? When did this happen?"

I checked my watch. "It's probably happening right now. I'm in your room now to have the private bathroom, and Beau's taking over my old room. That leaves the third and smaller bedroom downstairs if Cece needs to stay over. At least until she gets out of her lease in town. Beau and I decided on it Thursday night."

"Were you going to tell us?" she asked, her voice high pitched and aggravated. "I'm sure Blaze would like to know that his friend of twenty years is moving out!"

I held my hand out to calm her. "This just came up. I would guess Beau has told Blaze by now."

"I would guess not!" she exclaimed, holding up her phone. "Blaze would text me the moment he heard if that were the case."

My gaze went back to the lake. "I'm not responsible for what Beau does and doesn't do, Heaven. He's a big boy. I wasn't intentionally keeping it a secret. I just thought you'd know once he told Blaze. If Beau hasn't done that yet, then I apologize, but he hasn't made it a secret that he doesn't want to crimp the newlyweds' style."

"Which I don't even understand," she said with exasperation. "Beau lived there the entire time Blaze was married to Callie. What's the big deal?"

I stretched my legs out in the sand, my time on the driftwood starting to ramp up my pain, but I didn't want her to know, so I bit back the grimace. "The big deal is that this time, everyone can see you are who Blaze should have married the first time. You and Blaze have such a different dynamic than he and Callie did. They were friends, but you two are friends and lovers. There is always a deep flow of passion when you're together. Beau said if a guy like him can see the level of deep, soul-changing love that you have, then you should be able to make a home without a third wheel hanging around all the time."

Heaven scratched her temple and eyed me from behind her hand. "He seriously said that?" I nodded, and she let out a sigh. "He's not wrong. We both know that, but I feel terrible that he thinks we don't want him there. We'd put up a small cottage for him before we asked him to leave the property."

"Which he knows," I agreed. "But since Heavenly Lane has space, he would do just as well to live there for now. He worries about me being there alone now that Tex lives on the back of the property."

"You know I feel the same way. Not that you can't handle yourself, but I'd feel better if you weren't alone in that big house."

"Win-win, then, right?" I asked. "I'll have someone else rattling around in the old place, so you won't have to worry about me. You deserve time alone as much as any newly married couple, regardless of where you live and work."

Her head nodded once, and she smiled. "Okay, it's settled then. I'm still going to make Beau tell Blaze, though. He needs to be the one to explain his reasons to his friend. Blaze doesn't want anything but for him to be happy."

I shielded the sun from my eyes with my hand. "And he's not, so I'm hoping that a change of scenery will help him find the happiness that he's lost."

"Does it help that the new scenery is you?" she asked, tongue in cheek.

I snapped my head around to look at her. "This is strictly platonic, Heaven. He's not moving in for *that* reason."

"I don't doubt what you say is true right now, but the question is, would you consider *that* if it came up?"

I blew out a sigh and pulled my feet back up under me so I could lean on my knees. "Beau kissed me again Thursday night by the fire."

Her facial expression never changed when she spoke. "I'd squeal, but you'd tell me not to."

I snorted and shook my head. She was right. I would. I wasn't that girl.

"What did you do this time?" she asked, stripping wood off a stick.

"I kissed him back out of desire instead of curiosity this time," I answered, my head bobbing a few times. "He's a great guy, but—"

"But?" she asked. "You just said you kissed Beau out of desire."

"I did. I could definitely feel his desire, too, if you know what I mean."

She bit back a giggle and threw the stick into the sand. "But?"

"But … I don't know. I keep coming back to why now? Is it because his best friend is getting married and he's finding himself at a crossroads? Is it because my appearance has changed so much that now he finds me attractive as more than a friend? Is it because the anniversary of his mom's death is almost here? Is it because he's tired of being alone?"

Heaven blew out a breath and shook her head once. "That's a lot of heavy stuff to be packed into one but."

"I know, right?" I moaned, dropping my head into my hand. "We know so much about each other, but sometimes I think we don't know anything important about each other. We've both tiptoed around our past and our families for our own reasons. I don't know that I can open up about mine the way he has about his. At least the little bit he's told me."

"He doesn't know anything about your family?"

I gave her the so-so hand motion back. "I told Beau that they live in Wyoming, but I want nothing to do with them."

"Maybe you should start there then," she suggested. "Start where your life changed and go forward. You're right, you both know a lot about each other, but there's always something new to learn. I just don't want to see you throw away a chance to be with a wonderful guy because you're afraid."

"It takes a fool to know a fool," I muttered, rolling my eyes.

Heaven chuckled and punched me lightly on the arm. "Fair, but I did finally learn to trust Blaze. Maybe you need to start by trusting yourself."

"Trusting myself?" I asked, confused. "You mean trusting Beau."

"No," Heaven said, pulling me up and walking with me up the wooden plank walkway to the truck. "I mean trusting yourself. I couldn't trust Blaze until I trusted myself. Trusted my feelings is what I'm trying to say. You need to trust what's in here," she said, patting my chest, "before you believe what's up here." She tapped my temple and let her hand drop to her side again.

We finished the walk to the truck in silence, and the ride back was equally as quiet while I thought about what Heaven said. Trust yourself. To your own self be true.

I knew one thing for sure, that was way easier said than done.

Eight

I slid a bin of boots into the back of the truck and turned for another one when I spotted the man I was trying to avoid standing on the porch. He had his hat in his hand and his eyes taking in the scene before him.

"Going somewhere?" he drawled, that Texas accent still strong even after all these years. Not that I had a lot to say on the matter. Mine was just as strong.

Time to face the music.

I knew I would have to, but I didn't know how to tell him I was leaving.

"I—I," I cleared my throat and tapped my fingers on my thigh. It was an old trick I'd learned to break the stutter. If I tapped a rhythm on my leg while I spoke, it made me focus on something else. "I'm moving over to Heavenly Lane ta—to—ah—day."

His brow went up, and he walked down the stairs and sat on the top one. "You don't say? You don't have to leave, Beau. We aren't kicking you out."

I jumped up on the tailgate and let my legs swing under me while I stared out over the ridge that was now my home. "I know you ain't, Blaze. I never said you were. I'm not comfortable here anymore. An—and before you get all ry—riled up a—about Heaven, let me finish."

He motioned at me to continue. "I'm listening, but, Beau?"

"Yeah?"

"Take your time. I'm not upset. You don't have to defend yourself. Just let it come," Blaze said, motioning with his hand the way he always did when he wanted to remind me to take my time. I think the motion was an old Native American sign for 'it's all good,' loosely translated, of course.

I set my hat down on the tailgate and leaned over, curling my fingers around the edge of it. "This ain't about Heaven."

"I know," he said, nodding as he leaned over his thighs with his forearms. "It's about you, and that's okay."

"That's okay?" I asked, surprised that he led with that.

"You only live once, Beau. Sometimes you have to choose yourself, and that's okay."

I ran my hand through my hair and blew out a breath, still avoiding eye contact with him. "See, it's like this, Blaze. You're my brother, and we've lived together a whole lot of years. Even after you married Callie, it was like nothing changed. This time, everything has changed."

"You think so?"

"Why do you think I've been avoiding the house? It's not because I'm mad or annoyed that Heaven is here. I'm not. Bison Ridge is where she belongs. There is a draw between you and her that I can feel in the air. I guess that's the only way I can explain it."

"I don't understand, Beau," he admitted, but I could tell he was trying.

"It's like when she's not here the ranch holds its breath until she comes back. I guess, lookin' back now, I can see the ranch had been holding its breath for all those years she wasn't here. Now that she is here, it doesn't want to let her go. The house is brighter, sunnier, warmer, and happier when she's here. I know that sounds dumb as a post, but it's the truth."

"Like the dark curtains have been pulled back, and the sun can stream in again."

I pointed at him. "Just like that, yeah. In light of that, I think y'all need to have the house to yourselves. That draw between you has been denied for too many years. Now that you're together, I want you to start your life just the two of you. The way it should be."

He nodded a few times and stared out at the small barn where we kept our favorite horses. "I respect that, Beau. I also appreciate the hell out of you for thinking of it. I know it's probably time we don't live in the same house after what? Twenty years?"

"Thereabouts," I agreed. "It's time, Blaze. You've got your life together. Now I need to do the same."

His chuckle was all Texan, and it brought a smile to my lips. "I don't know about having my life together, Beau. I just got my head out of my backside long enough to see that Heaven was the only thing that could put me back together. I would suggest building you a foreman's cottage somewhere on the property, but I think you're moving in the right direction to find your way back together, so I'm not going to."

"You been drinking, son?" I asked, trying to make sense of what he'd just said.

He shook his head as he stared up over the ridge. "No, what I mean is, you're moving to Heavenly Lane to live now. Seems like that's the place you're being drawn to, and I understand that you need to go."

"No," I said, shaking my head immediately. "I'm not going to work for Heavenly Lane. I'll be back for Cloudy Day as soon as Dawn can give me a ride over to get him. I'll be working here every day, just like always, Blaze."

He held up his hand to hush me. "I wasn't talking about work, Beau. I was talking about the draw. Your draw. Your sunshine when you pull the curtains back. She needs you to be there for her. Now is the time to make that move."

I cocked my head to the side. "You know something I don't know, boy? Spill it."

He held up his hands in defense. "All I'm saying is, keep following your heart and stop listening to your head so much. It took me too long to learn that lesson. I don't want you to miss out on more years with someone who you're meant to be with because your priorities are in the wrong place."

I nodded, swallowing around the lump in my throat a couple of times. "I hear ya, boss, but tha—tha— ain't why I'm moving there. Not at all. I ha—have my own ra—room." I wanted to get him off Dawn quickly before he made me admit things I didn't want to say out loud. "I'm glad you're not upset that I'm leaving. I was wa—wa—worried."

"I wish you had just come and talked to me about it. Were you ever going to?"

I shrugged my shoulder in a way that said, 'probably not.' "Change is ha—ha—hard."

He stood up and walked over to the truck, hopping up beside me. "Change is hard, and we've sure had a lot of changes lately. This is the end of an era. I'm struggling with it as much as you are."

The laughter that escaped my lips was unamused. "Doubtful."

"It might feel that way to you, but that doesn't mean it's not true, Beau. I have a lot of brothers, but you're the only one I've ever really known. We might not share blood, but we sure as hell have been through everything else together the last twenty years. So while it might feel like I'm the one on the winning end of this hand, I'm not, okay? I'm just …" He put his hands up as though that was all he had. "I'm not."

I clasped his shoulder and kept my hand there, wanting him to know that I felt the same way. "I'm not leaving you here to do this alone, Blaze. I'm just sleeping somewhere else. You know I'll be in the barn before you are even out of your lazybones bed and still be riding the ridge when you climb back in it every night. That's the way it's been and the way it will continue to be."

His laughter could probably be heard at Heavenly Lane. "Maybe that's the way it has always been, but I've got bets riding on Dawn Briar Lee flipping that idea on its head. I sure as hell hope she does anyway. You need a woman like her, both to keep you in line and to give you a place to rest your tired heart. That's all I want for you, as your brother and your friend."

There was so much I wanted to say, but I didn't have the words, and I knew if I tried, I'd do nothing but stutter until I gave up.

He jumped down off the tailgate and pointed to the house. "Come on. Let's have one last beer for the road."

He jogged up the stairs, and I followed behind him, the scene hitting me hard in the heart. It had always been about Blaze leading the way since the first day I met him. I followed him wherever he went, learned from his mistakes, and made notes of his accomplishments. Today, as I followed him into the kitchen and clinked a long neck bottle with him, I told myself I hadn't learned from his mistakes. If I had, I would have gone after the woman I wanted years ago.

I was done waiting.

This was where Blaze and I parted ways. It was time for me to be the leader.

"How do you like it?" a sweet voice asked from the doorway, and I turned, once again taken aback by her beauty. Dawn wore a women's flannel shirt and a broken-in pair of Wranglers that made my own tight at the zipper. She had a belt around her waist that accentuated her hips and a long necklace that rested between her breasts to draw the eye. Did it ever draw my eye. I wanted to touch her, hold her, and kiss her.

I put my hand to my chest. "I'd answer your question, darlin', but that outfit is stealing my words."

Dawn glanced down at herself for a second. "This old thing?" She winked to tell me she was kidding, and then she walked the rest of the way into the room and leaned against the wall. I wanted to run my fingers through her freshly washed hair while my tongue teased hers in a wet kiss of desire. My pants started to tighten more, so I pushed those thoughts back. We hadn't even left for dinner yet, and I was already in trouble with my libido. I better learn to control it better now that I lived here, or I would walk around half hard for her twenty-four seven.

I walked to her and kissed her cheek, forcing myself not to take her lips and own her right up against the wall of my room. "Nothing is old when you're wearing it," I promised. "I'm almost ready. Just gotta find my boots."

When I opened the closet door, her chuckle from behind me was instantaneous. "Why am I not surprised that your boots and hats were the first things you organized. Did you need a separate trailer just for them?"

I bit back a bark of laughter, so she didn't get a big head about her comedy routine. "Darlin', a man ain't nothing without boots and a hat for every occasion."

"And here, I always thought that was a woman's thing. Matching their shoes and hats, I mean. Do you have a handbag picked out for the evening?"

I stood to my full height and shut the closet door. "My, my, someone is full of themselves tonight," I teased, grabbing Dawn around the waist and kissing her lips this time. It was chaste and fast, but I could sense she yearned for more the same way I did. "I'll have you know that my wallet matches all my hats and boots."

Dawn rested her forehead on my shoulder while she laughed. "Good to know. Did you get everything moved today or do you have more to pick up?" She glanced around my room and back to me. "There isn't much here."

I walked to the door and shut the light off, then ushered her out of the room. "I'm a man of few needs."

I helped her on with her coat, and we headed out the door. What I said was the truth. I was a man of few needs. What I didn't say was that I was also a man of few possessions. It was never more apparent than when I packed up my stuff, only to realize everything I had at Bison Ridge was Blaze's other than my bed, chair, and clothing. Pathetic but true. Maybe that just meant I was satisfied with my life and didn't need many material things to remain that way. As long as I had my horse, boots, and hats, I was a happy man.

"When did you finally tell Blaze that you were moving out?" she asked. "You did tell him, right?"

I rolled my eyes to the sky in response. "Of course, I did. I told Blaze when he caught me packing my boots in the truck."

Dawn shook her head and bit back a smile. "Guess I lost. I bet Heaven that you wouldn't even tell him."

I scrunched up my nose as we walked. "I'm not a fan of confrontation. He was cool about it, though. Honestly, I think he was even a little bit relieved. We've lived together for a lot of years. It's time we both find a new way forward."

She squeezed my hand in solidarity and nodded. "I figured that might be the case. I know Heaven was relieved when I told her it was okay to move there permanently. These changes are new for all of us, Beau. Hey, aren't we going to dinner?"

We had walked halfway up the ridge already during our conversation, and I winked at her in the moonlight. "I know I promised dinner out, but I also know you were out all day. Perhaps you'd prefer to enjoy a famous Beau's Hobo Dinner while sitting by a campfire instead?"

Dawn didn't break stride or turn back toward the house. "Does that hobo dinner have bison in it?"

"Do bison have horns?" I asked teasingly. "It's not just any bison, though. It's prime-cut bison steak. Besides, I know you love it."

She shoulder-bumped me and then rested her head on my shoulder for a heartbeat. "I'm more than happy to stay here and have a relaxing night. I'm a little worn out after spending the day in town with Heaven. I did find a dress, though. Heaven was relieved, so it was a good day."

I put my arm around her and kissed her temple as we approached the lower pasture where the fire was already burning. "I bet it's gorgeous. My eyes are going to be glued to you the entire time we're standing up there."

"Depends on if you like lace," she said flippantly.

I groaned long and low in my throat. "I like anything you're wearing, darlin'," I promised, "but lace might be my undoing."

"I guess we'll just have to wait and see then." Her words were flirty, but the tone of her voice was downright sexy. I swallowed back the moan and begged my lower half to behave.

She pointed at the campfire that was burning low and slow. "A little confident, weren't ya?"

I laughed and ushered her onto the soft blankets that covered the ground. I wanted to keep her warm, so I had a waterproof pad under the blankets to protect her from the cold earth, as well as pillows for reclining. She might think I was an obtuse man who didn't notice anything, but I noticed everything when it came to her. Dawn often struggled to get up if she'd been sitting too long or if it was cold outside. I wanted to spend the night with her, but I didn't want her to be in pain because of it.

"I asked Tex to start the fire so the coals would burn down. He would have put it out if we had decided to go into town. All I have left to do is put the food on the fire. We can have a drink while it's cooking and enjoy the bright, beautiful stars and the call of the owls."

She lowered herself to the blankets and patted the thickness with her hand. "You went all out. The mattress is super comfy."

I grinned as I put the hobo dinners on the fire and grabbed a bottle of red wine from the cooler. "I'm glad you think so. I wanted to make sure you were comfortable. I know you get sore sometimes." The look on her face told me I better change the subject immediately. "Wine?" I asked, holding up the bottle.

"You're drinking wine? How fancy."

I sat next to her and handed her the bottle. "We'll put fancy in quotation marks because you're going to have to drink it out of a plastic cup."

Dawn chuckled and filled the two cups I held out. She set the bottle to the side and took her cup, tapping it against mine. "To finding a new way forward."

I raised my cup and drank the wine down in one gulp. I was nervous being out here with Dawn, and I'd wanted to toss back a couple of shots of whiskey before we left. I didn't just in case she wanted to go into town because driving drunk doesn't look good on anyone. She refilled my cup, and I sipped it slower this time while we talked.

"It's always so beautiful in the spring on Bison Ridge," she sighed. "Lake Superior was beautiful today with the sun shining down on us and the waves brushing the sand, but there's nothing quite like the stars here."

I leaned back on my elbow to hold her eye. "I think you're the most beautiful thing on Bison Ridge."

"You always were a smooth talker, Beau Hanson," she said after she finished her wine. She refilled her cup while I shook my head in frustration.

"I've never been a smooth talker, Dawn. If anything, I'm just the opposite. I only say what I mean. When I say you're the most beautiful thing out here, I mean it."

"Really? You mean it?" she asked sarcastically. "Funny how you never mentioned a thing about my beauty until I'd lost seventy-five pounds. Suddenly, I'm the most beautiful thing on Bison Ridge." Her eyes rolled with sarcasm while she lifted the glass to her lips.

I held her arm in place until she was forced to make eye contact with me again. "You were serious about losing seventy-five pounds? When you said that at the café, I thought you were being sarcastic." The slight shake of her head answered my question. Knowing she had lost that much weight scared me. "Dawn, I was worried about you before, but now I'm terrified. That's a lot of weight to lose in six months."

"Well, don't worry about it," she snapped, shaking off my hand and finishing the wine in her glass. "You missed the point, anyway. How long until dinner is done? I'm hungry."

I shook my head as I stared into her eyes. "I didn't miss the point, darlin'. I've had a crush on you for so many years that I've lost track. You have always been beautiful. Do you understand me?" I asked, tipping her chin up to force the eye contact she had gotten ridiculously good at avoiding. "I never acted on my crush because I was afraid to ruin our friendship. I needed you in my corner. You were the only one who understood me in this place. Not even Blaze understands me the way you do, and he's known me forever."

"So suddenly, I'm half the person I used to be, and voila, it's time to risk our friendship?"

I finished the wine in my glass and set it to the side before I hugged my knees. "No, that's not it at all, Dawn. I've tried to pretend that I'm happy just being your friend, but I'm miserable. This feeling in the pit of my stomach started when Blaze and Heaven finally got together. At first, I was angry. I was angry that he got to throw caution to the wind and risk everything to be with the woman he loved. Hell, just to take her out on a date was more than I could work up the courage to do. It made me bitter and angry at everything and everyone. I don't want to feel that way anymore. I want to feel the way I do whenever we're together."

"How is that?" she asked so quietly I barely heard her over the snap of the fire.

"Happy. Content. Excited about life. I'd rather feel those things over anger and discontent any day, wouldn't you?'

Dawn tipped her head in a half-nod and refilled her glass. At this rate, she was going to be falling down drunk before I pulled dinner off the fire.

"Can we circle back to the part about you losing so much weight? I've been concerned, and so has Heaven. We're worried you're sick and trying to push through just to keep things running at the ranch."

"I'm not sick," she said, swallowing the wine. I could already see it was going to her head as she relaxed back into the pillows. "Well, I am a little sick, but then aren't we all?"

"Dawn," I said with a tone of warning in my voice. "I'm not kidding around here. What's going on with you?"

She stared into the cup of wine, and it tremored slightly. "I don't know that I want to tell you. I don't want to risk you planting me back in the friendzone. As much as changing our relationship scares me, so does keeping it the same."

I scooted forward and took her hand, holding it to my chest. "Darlin', you can tell me. I know you think I'm an obtuse cowboy who doesn't notice anything, but that couldn't be further from the truth. I notice everything that goes along with the job I do here. I've seen the weight loss, the depression, the pain, and the swollen fingers. Put it all together for me, please."

Dawn refused to make eye contact and stared into the fire, her lips trembling until she took a deep breath and let it back out. "I suppose there has been some depression over the winter, but that wasn't the main reason I was losing weight. When I was a kid, I had what was called polyarthritis."

"How is that different from regular arthritis?" I asked, unsure what the term meant but wanting her to tell me every last secret she had so I could make her feel better.

"It means the arthritis was in more than five joints at the same time. Then, as if that weren't bad enough, I developed enthesitis arthritis."

"What is that in English, Dawn?" I asked. "I'm not real smart about this kind of stuff, but I want to understand. Please."

She stared at our hands joined together for the longest time before she spoke. "Your entheses are the spot where your ligaments or tendons connect to the bone. There are one hundred different places you can get enthesitis. Boys usually get that part of the disease, but I was one of the unlucky girls who also had it. It affected my hips, spine, and knees."

"You had juvenile arthritis?"

"Yes, that's the umbrella term," she agreed, but I could see she was struggling to funnel all the technical information she understood into something more straightforward for me.

I ran my finger under her eye. "Is that why your eye was red, too?"

Dawn nodded and glanced away. "That's another kind of inflammation that can occur with this kind of arthritis. The arthritis I have now circles back around to the disease process I had as a child. I suffered for years with it, and now I have a lot of damage to my joints because my parents didn't get me the proper treatment."

I sat in silence and gazed at her, working to keep my anger at her parents in check. "Why didn't they get you treatment? Jehovah's Witnesses don't have a problem with doctors, right?"

She shook her head and gazed down at her hands. "No, they don't. As long as you don't take a blood transfusion, you can have any medical procedure you need. They tend to stick with doctors of their own kind, though. The doctor they kept taking me to preferred to treat me with herbal supplements over actual medication to treat my inflammatory disease."

I bit back the cuss word that wanted to fall from my lips. "I'm sorry, darlin'. That wasn't fair to you. I can't imagine the pain you must have been in."

Dawn shrugged, but I noticed the tears in her eyes. I decided not to acknowledge them and embarrass her any further. "It was hard," she agreed. "We owned a ranch, so the work was physically demanding. Some days I couldn't even move, and that made my parents even angrier. They insisted the supplements I was getting were enough to get rid of the pain, so they insisted I do my chores like everyone else. Since we were homeschooled, which consisted of reading a book when we weren't doing chores, I couldn't get help from outside sources. When I turned seventeen, I'd finally had enough."

"And that's when you left?" I asked, remembering what she told me about her family.

"I did. I ran, Beau. Only not actually because I was in too much pain. I took a bus to Minnesota and found a job as a guest manager for a large hotel. With that job, I had some basic benefits and was able to get treatment for my arthritis after living in pain for almost ten years. Once it was treated, the symptoms slowly subsided, which is typical with juvenile arthritis. After I was feeling better, I moved on from that job and found the ad for Heavenly Lane. When I stepped onto the soil here, it was just like I was home. That's the only way I can describe it, Beau," she whispered, lifting her head to the sky. "I was so happy when Heaven and Duane hired me the same day as my interview. I had missed working with the animals, but more than that, I'd missed being part of a family and not feeling so alone all the time. The arthritis had been gone for about seven years, and I never expected it to come back."

"But then it did," I said softly, rubbing her thigh.

"Then it did," she agreed with a nod. "When the pain returned last fall, I just thought it was because I was doing too much work from picking up Heaven's slack. Then it got worse instead of better, which scared me even more. The doctors are still testing and waiting to see how things develop, but the working diagnosis is psoriatic arthritis."

"Do you have psoriasis? I've never noticed any problems with your skin. It's always soft and glowing."

She wouldn't make eye contact with me, and I allowed it for now. Telling me about her past with her parents and her current health problems wasn't easy for her. That much was obvious. I wouldn't make it harder on her than it had to be. I cared about her too much. All I wanted to do was hold her, comfort her, and protect her.

"I don't have skin problems, and most people don't know you can get psoriatic arthritis without having psoriasis. My family history and my childhood history of arthritis make me more likely to have it. Either way, the doctors started me on a new anti-rheumatic medication to help relieve some of the symptoms. That's why I had to go to the pharmacy that day when you saw me in town."

I hung my head with shame, the acid churning in my gut. "I'm so sorry, Dawn," I whispered, rubbing the palm of her hand. "I was a real jackass doing what I did to you."

"It's already forgotten, Beau. I'm not upset about it. I was just explaining why I was there. Over this past winter, the pain became unbearable. I couldn't take it anymore and finally had to see the doctor."

"That's why you lost weight?"

She rested her chin on her knees and stared at the fire. "To a degree, yeah. The pain sapped my strength to the point I never had an appetite. I was depressed from dealing with the pain, knowing that the arthritis was back, and all the changes at Heavenly Lane, too. Arthritis can cause weight loss, so that was thrown in there, as well."

"It was a perfect storm, is what you're saying," I said, kissing her knuckles gently, so I didn't hurt her.

"Complicated by my inability to face any of it. I wanted to pretend like none of it was happening. The first time I got sick, my own flesh and blood didn't want anything to do with me. I was inconveniencing them, and all they wanted was for it to go away, so their life wasn't so hard."

I couldn't stop the growling groan that escaped my lips. "I have no respect for those people. They may have created you, Dawn Lee, but you're nothing like them."

"I know," she said, a smile on her face again, even if it was small. "That was the driving force behind who I became.

Everything I did was the exact opposite of what they would do. I figured as long as I kept that idea in the forefront of my mind, I'd always be in the right. It has worked for me so far."

"At least until this past fall when you decided to torture yourself again and not get treatment." I lowered my brow at her, and she sighed heavily.

"I was afraid, Beau. Afraid of losing the family I'd created at Heavenly Lane. At the same time, I was lonely, which sounds absolutely daft, but this is us being honest, right?" she asked, finally lifting her gaze to mine.

I nodded, working hard to keep a smile on my face when I wanted to do nothing more than take her in my arms and comfort her. "Honesty is always hard. Once the truth is spoken, then you do feel a lot better. I promise you, darlin'."

Dawn nodded, biting her lower lip. I wanted to moan at how sexy she was, but I bit it back so I didn't distract her from the honesty we were sharing.

"I've always cherished our friendship, Beau. It's been the last few years that I've wanted more. I told myself that was crazy because I'm not the kind of girl Beau Hanson looks twice at, at least as anything more than a friend. I wasn't delusional. I noticed the type of women you dated. They were the exact opposite of who I am."

I shook my head in confusion. "Dawn, I haven't dated since this beautiful, brown-eyed beauty started workin' at the neighboring ranch."

Her head snapped up, and her eyes flamed with anger from across the blanket. "I'm not obtuse, Beau!" she exclaimed, shoving me in the shoulder. It only made her angrier that it didn't even budge me.

"I don't know what you think you've seen, but it hasn't been me dating anyone," I whispered, rubbing her arm up and down to calm her.

"What about all those women you keep dancing with at The Wise Anchor."

"Well, darlin', dancin', and datin' are two different things. I don't necessarily want to dance, but my momma's manners are always ringing in my ears. I dance when a woman asks me to dance, but that doesn't mean I date them. It also doesn't mean I bring them home with me or anything else you imagine in that beautiful head of yours."

Her mouth opened and closed twice before she got words out. "Why not date them, though? They're beautiful women."

"The answer is simple. Those women aren't you. You've probably never noticed, but no matter where I am on that dance floor, my eyes are always searching for or locked onto you. I could be dancing with Hollywood's hottest actress, and I wouldn't know it. I only have eyes for you, Dawn Lee. It's been killing me to keep you in the friend zone, but I didn't think you'd be interested in a guy like me. I don't have much to offer a woman. I'm just a misplaced cowboy who doesn't have a lot under his hat."

Her hand slipped up the side of my face until her thumb was stroking the skin at my temple. "You're wrong, Beau," she whispered into the stillness of the night. "What you have to offer is exactly what I need. I know you think you aren't that smart—"

"I'm not," I assured her. "I barely made it through school. I never could sit still in class long enough to learn a thing."

Dawn shook her head and laid her finger against my lips. "You were a kid who had gone through a lot at a young age. When you were on the ranch, the work and the animals kept your mind busy. It was understandable that being forced to sit inside a classroom all day made it even harder to put the thoughts of your mother aside so you could learn."

"School was a struggle," I agreed. "I preferred working on the ranch and ridin' horses. I didn't think about my momma all the time then."

"I'm sorry," she whispered, her thumb stroking my lips now. "Just know that I think you're a genius in the things that matter. You can run a ranch better than Blaze can. You have a soft touch with the horses that has saved more than one life, and you have an incredible talent for leatherwork. You undervalue yourself because you've always lived in Blaze's shadow. Now that you're going to own half of this place," she said, holding her hands out, "you have to stop doing that."

I took her hand and held it to my chest. "I can say the same thing to you, babe. Maybe here tonight, we should both vow to hold each other accountable."

"To what?" she asked, her head tipped to the side.

"To let the negative thoughts and feelings we have about ourselves go and concentrate on the positive ones. To let ourselves believe we deserve the same kind of happiness that Blaze and Heaven have. To stop pretending that we don't want something out of a belief that it's for the greater good of the ranches."

"What do you want, Beau?" Dawn asked, her voice breathy and soft.

"You," I answered, my head starting a slow descent toward her lips. "I want you, Dawn Lee. I don't care what anyone else thinks. I want you."

The kiss heated immediately when my lips landed on hers. Dawn moaned against them until my tongue convinced hers to open so we could tangle them together in a dance of honesty and trust. She was everything I wanted and the only thing I wanted. If I couldn't have her, I might shrivel up on this ridge and disappear into the earth.

"God," I moaned, my lips still on hers, "I need you just to breathe now."

She didn't say a word, just straddled me, buried her hands in my hair, and went back to kissing me like I was oxygen, and she was a dying woman.

Nine

"That was superb, Beau," I said as I leaned back against the pillows and pulled the soft wool blanket up around me. The excellent food and sweet wine had finally relaxed me enough to make me sleepy. I stared up at the beautiful sky full of twinkling stars while Beau cleaned up dinner and stoked the fire.

I'd spent the entirety of dinner trying to put right in my head what he'd said. Did he want me and no one else? How could he still want me when I had already told him the truth about my health?

"I'm always going to have arthritis and need treatment," I blurted out, the wine in my system making it hard to be anything but honest.

Beau finished his work with the fire and then sat next to me, his hand tenderly stroking my thigh. "I figured that out already, Dawn. I didn't think it was just going to go away, even if you wish it would."

"I don't want to saddle someone else with that kind of life, Beau. Especially someone who loves the outdoors, riding, and being active as much as you do. There could come a point in time where I can't do those things anymore."

He tipped my chin up until I made eye contact with him. "Didn't we just vow not to let negativity get in our way anymore?"

"We did, but this isn't negativity, Beau. What I'm saying now is the truth. I'm being honest about what my future holds. You said that sometimes honesty hurts, and I can tell you, it does."

He smiled his famous Texas cowboy smile and stroked my jawline with his thumb. "Darlin', I was raised by a woman with an autoimmune disease. I'm aware of the implications and complications. We can weather them together as long as we trust each other."

My eyes darted to the blanket as Heaven's words ran through my mind. We know a lot about each other, but not the important stuff. Now was a chance to learn something about Beau that I didn't know. "Did she die from lupus, Beau?" I asked, my voice soft and caring.

His thumb faltered on my jaw for a moment before it started its rhythmic stroking again. "No, Momma died at the hands of a coward. We don't know who killed her. He escaped and has never been found. It was a home invasion gone wrong, and she died a horrible death while I was having fun at Blaze's ranch. I'll never forgive myself for not being there to help her."

My gaze sought his again, and the pain and anger in them were raging, even this many years later. "Beau, if you were there, your fate would have been sealed, too. Your momma wouldn't have wanted that. She would have wanted you safe."

His eyes fluttered closed, and his Adam's apple bobbed a couple of times before he spoke. "La—la—gically, my brain knows that. My heart," he shook his head and moved his jaw around a couple of times. "The—that still struggles. Momma was so wonderful, and then just like that," he said, snapping his fingers, "she was ga—gone. I know I couldn't have helped her, but I tha—tha—ink it's the idea that I—I—I could have done something. Ah——ah—anything, you know?"

I nodded, my heart breaking for this man who, twenty years later, still carried guilt for something he never had any control over. "I understand, Beau. The situations you found yourself in as a kid shaped the man you are today."

"Yes," he whispered as he trailed his finger down my cheek. "Ba—but I could say the same thing about you."

"Right or wrong," I agreed. "I just want to stop feeling alone when surrounded by people. I want to stop feeling like the weight of everything around us is on my shoulders. I know it is to a degree, but I guess what I'm saying is, I want to start enjoying life again. The problem is, I've spent so long not enjoying life but pretending that I was, that I don't know how to stop. God, I've had too much wine. I sound like an idiot."

"You're not an idiot, Dawn Lee. I know what you're trying to say, so let me teach you," Beau whispered, his lips coming down to tease mine into a frenzy again. He tasted of sweet wine, and the sensation of his tongue stroking mine was overwhelming.

I wanted to learn from him. I wanted to absorb everything Beau had to teach me, but something told me he had just as much to learn. He needed me as much as I needed him. Our strengths complemented each other's weaknesses. We could find commonality in that if nothing else.

My head fell back against the pillows, and he followed me down, his warm body laying across me gently to share his warmth. His tongue stroked mine into overdrive while I moaned softly, the darkness of the night swallowing it like a secret held nowhere but this pasture. His hands buried themselves in the hair at the top of my head, and it was his turn to moan. His lips came off mine long enough to hold my gaze. "You have no idea how long I've wanted to do that. The sensation of your hair running through my fingers while I kissed you was more than I even dared to dream about."

"You've always wanted to run your hands through my hair?" I asked, my fingers finding their way into his soft locks, too.

"It's tortured me for years," he growled, then his lips were back on mine. His fingers tightened against my locks, holding me in the place he wanted so he could kiss and suck my tongue into submission. He wanted me. The hardness pressed against my thigh was tangible evidence of that. I raised my thigh and pushed back against his bulging zipper, his moan so loud I swore they'd hear it in town.

His hand slid from my hair and trailed down my side to cup the outside of my breast. He pulled my lower lip through his teeth and tugged gently before releasing it. "We have to stop, Dawn," he moaned, his thumb still stroking the outside of my breast. "If we don't stop, I'm not going to be able to. I don't want to ruin what we have going on here."

I took his face in my hands and held his gaze. "Why would you ruin it? Are you that bad at taking a roll in the hay?"

Beau barked with laughter and rested his forehead on mine to suck in a breath. "I don't think so. At least I don't think I would be if I were rolling in the hay with you. The truth is, I don't want to ruin what we could be by jumping the gun too early."

"We've known each other for five years, Beau."

"Are you trying to talk me into this?" he asked jokingly.

I was shaking my head before he finished the question. "I wouldn't try to talk anyone into sleeping with me. That's just rude to say." I pushed at his chest so I could get up, but he wouldn't budge.

"I didn't mean it like that. You have to be able to feel how much I want you, Dawn."

"I can, and that's why I'm confused. I've wanted you for years, Beau."

His lips found mine again as his finger trailed down my cheek. "I wish I hadn't waited years to kiss you."

"Why the hesitation then? Am I a terrible kisser?"

Beau lifted his head from where he was kissing his way along my collarbone. "No, you aren't a terrible kisser. I lose myself in your kiss every time our lips connect. I'm afraid to hurt you, though. We aren't exactly on a cushy mattress at the Hilton."

I stroked his cheek with my finger, the bristle of his five o'clock shadow rough against my skin. "I don't need the Hilton. I just need you." He opened his mouth, but I put my finger to his lips. "Beau, you won't hurt me, but if you'd rather wait, then put that fire out and take me home. There's a comfy mattress waiting there."

He growled and attacked my lips, his hand working his way under my shirt to caress my breast through my bra.

"As God as my witness, Dawn, if I have you once, eternity will never be long enough."

I lifted a brow in the air. "Prove it."

Before I blinked, he had my shirt gone. He knelt between my legs, his finger bumping across my ribs, a frown on his lips. "Dawn, this ain't right. This ain't right at all. I shouldn't be able to count your ribs, baby. I'm scared for you."

I held his hand against my side to stop his fingers from running up and down my ribs. I loved the sensation, but he would have to stop if I were going to form a sentence. I pulled the blanket up to cover myself and stared up at the star-filled sky.

"It's okay, Beau. Let's just go home," I whispered. "This was a mistake."

And I knew it would be. I knew once Beau saw all the parts of my body that I could hide with my clothes, he'd realize I wasn't as attractive as he'd made me out to be in his mind. It still hurt to live through the agonizing moments of rejection for something outside of my control.

Beau lowered himself to the blanket and stretched out the length of me. His nose was almost touching mine when he spoke. "Dawn, I don't ra—ra—member saying this was a mistake. I can be wa—worried about you," he paused and cleared his throat while his fingers pulled the blanket back down so he could stroke my side. "And still want to be with you. You are glorious in the firelight, don't ever mistake my concern for my desire."

He started kissing his way down my chest and along the ridge of each breast. His tongue dipped into the center, and he inhaled deeply through his nose before he nipped at the swell of my breasts. "Do you see the difference now?"

I squeaked from surprise but thrust my chest into the air. "I think so," I said on a moan that fell from my lips.

He tenderly grasped my face and tipped it to face him in the firelight. "I don't want to hurt you, but now, I'm worried I will. You have to be honest with me as we go, okay? As long as you do that, no mistakes will be made."

I had barely nodded, and my bra disappeared, the chill of the night air peaking my nipples into mountains, and he licked his lips before he suckled one to tease and taunt. The sound that vibrated low in his throat made me wet instantly. I ground my pelvis against him, hungry for him physically but desperate for him emotionally. It had been years since I'd felt cherished and loved. Connected and part of a partnership that was about mutual trust and satisfaction.

He lavished my breasts with attention for far too long, so I grabbed his shirt and brought him to my lips for a quick tangle of tongues.

"You have too many clothes on, Beau Hanson."

"And you're kind of bossy, Dawn Lee."

I fumbled with the buttons on his shirt while his fingers worked over my nipples, making it hard to concentrate on my task. "Beau," I groaned, my frustration almost boiling over. "I can't get this damn shirt unbuttoned."

"Darlin', you're also impatient," he said, giving me his famous get 'em chuckle. He knelt, unhooking each button painfully slow, knowing how much I wanted him the whole time. It was a dirty little reverse striptease that I was suddenly all about. Transfixed by his rough hands working at the tiny mother of pearl buttons, I moaned when my eyes traveled to the bottom button. The silhouette of his manhood waited for me just below it, and the thought of nipping and sucking him the way he did me made my mouth water.

Beau stripped the material down and off his arms, and I came face-to-face with his t-shirt. I groaned, but he laughed a sexy as hell bedroom laugh that I wanted to hear for the rest of my life. "Patience, my beauty," he drawled. Before I blinked, his t-shirt was gone, giving my fingers permission to bury themselves in the hair on his chest. His muscles flexed under my fingers, and his lips sought mine again. Distracted by what his lips were doing, I didn't notice his fingers working my jeans down until the cool air stroked my thigh and sent a shiver through me. My lips still on his, I kicked my boots off, and then he stripped me of the denim, leaving me to sit before him in nothing but a pair of lace panties.

Beau fell back on his butt when he took in the whole picture, and his gaze swept the length of me. "Dawn, you're gorgeous. You take my breath away." His eyes closed, and he took a deep breath. "I need a minute. I've dreamed of this day, but never did I dream this."

I wrapped my arm around his neck and tried to pull him back over me. "Just don't look too closely."

He laid me back and straddled my ankles with his hands gently braced on my thighs. "I'm going to do more than look. I'm going to kiss every part of you," he promised, starting at my shins. "I'm going to keep kissing my way up your beautiful legs to those panties. Once I'm there, I'm going to take them off with my teeth."

His words died off, and he did as he promised. He kissed his way across every bony protuberance of my knee, giving each side equal loving attention. "I want to be the one to soothe the pain in these knees, Dawn, please," he begged between kisses.

I twined my fingers in his locks until he lifted his lips to hold my gaze. "Being with you soothes all of my pain, Beau. Every last ache is covered by the balm of your," I paused, unsure what word to use, so I swallowed and went with the only word I could right now, "touch. I need you to touch me, Beau."

"That's all I want to do," he promised, his lips moving north and kissing along my thigh to where the lace sat, blocking his view. He used his teeth to tug back and forth at the sides until the lace was gone and he'd revealed his prize. The moan that rolled from his chest vibrated through me. Before I finished the thought, his tongue parted me, lapping upward in one stroke.

"Oh my God, Dawn, you're sweeter than honey," he sighed, his fingers squeezing my hip before he dipped his head for another taste. I squirmed under him, my hands burying themselves in his hair just to have something to hang on to while his tongue gave nothing but sweet torture.

"You still have too many clothes on, Beau," I hissed as his tongue took a longer, wetter, more precise tour of the triangle between my legs.

He looked up and made eye contact for a brief moment before he rose up and slowly unbuckled his belt. The silky burgundy boxers he wore under his jeans took me by surprise when he lowered his zipper.

"You are a mystery, Beau Hanson," I breathed out when his pants and boots were gone.

He knelt before me in those silk boxers. "I'm not, Dawn Lee. I'm just a guy who happens to want the beautiful woman in front of him. If she wants him, she'll have to show him how much." He glanced down at his boxers and back to my eyes several times.

"This cowgirl happens to know exactly how to show a cowboy how much she wants him," I whispered, then hooked my fingers in his waistband. I took my time pulling them down a little at a time on each side, the same way he'd removed my panties.

It took me longer to work the silky material over the evidence of his desire, but when he bobbed free into the night air, the moan that escaped my lips left no mystery about how I was feeling about it. About him. About what we were doing. Tentatively, I stroked his velvety flesh with my finger, pausing at his sharp intake of breath when I brushed across his tip.

"I'm not very experienced, Beau," I whispered, wishing my voice didn't sound scared to death.

Beau tipped my chin up and kissed me, giving me time to get used to the feel of him in my hand. "We can take it slow, darlin'," he promised, brushing a kiss across my brow. "I know we're going to be beautiful together as long as you trust me."

I gazed up at him, his rigid need still in my hand. "I do trust you, Beau Hanson."

To prove it, I lowered my lips to his tip, giving him a sneak peek of what it would be like inside me. Warm, wet, and tight. He gasped when my tongue traced his edge, and then he had my face in his hands and his lips on mine in a frantic kiss of desire. His hips thrust against my hand rhythmically, showing me how to love him to take away my fear. Our moans of pleasure and desire rocketed around the open pasture and into the starry sky, where they burst open and carried through the atmosphere. His hips froze when the kiss ended abruptly.

"I don't have any protection," he groaned, his forehead coming to rest on mine.

"We're covered," I promised. "As long as you trust me."

Beau leaned me back against the pillows and hovered over me, his lips taking mine again as he pushed my legs apart and settled between them. His kiss carried me up onto a tightrope of sensation, and then he was parting me, his tip slipping inside my heat on a moan. "Dawn, oh, Dawn." His words were a sigh of coming home.

"Beau!" I cried, lifting my hips to take more of him.

"Do you feel how much I trust you?" he whispered, his hips struggling to remain still when he wanted to thrust into me harder and deeper.

"Yes! I trust you, too, Beau," I cried as he pulled out and pushed forward again, burying himself inside me. He was velvet and steel. He was forgiveness and a new life. He was home, and he was my home. It was a feeling I could cherish for the rest of my life.

"Dawn," he moaned, his legs shaking as he held onto the little bit of control he had left. "You're incredible. It's never been like this before. Oh, God," he moaned, his hips bucking against me again. His forehead came down to rest on mine so he could gaze into my eyes. "I can't, Dawn. I can't explain it."

I caressed his cheek tenderly while I gazed into the unfathomable depths of his coffee brown eyes. "We don't need to, Beau," I promised when I lifted my hips to meet his. "Right now, all we need to do is fly. Should we fly up into the sky together?" I whisper-asked, feeling the tension building inside him. The words barely left my lips before his hips took over and carried us both up into the night to dance among the stars.

As soon as the back door opened, a brisk wind accompanied my best friend inside. The wind reminded me that it might be April, but it was still Wisconsin. I turned from the stove to see Heaven standing there, her hair windswept around her face and her cheeks ruddy.

"Chilly out?" I asked, chuckling as I stirred a pot of soup.

"It's brisk, especially on the back of Grover. I'm relatively sure Mr. and Mrs. McAwley are going to hate us for picking April as the month to get married."

I shut the burner off and pulled the pot off the stove. "It wasn't like you could wait until June. The bison will be calving by then. You didn't have many choices."

Heaven sat, and I scooped out two bowls of soup, setting one in front of her then sliding into my seat. "Thanks," she said, digging into my homemade chicken and wild rice soup. It was always her favorite, and it made me smile to make her happy.

"When do they arrive?" I asked between bites.

"Later today. Ash and Amity are flying into Duluth and driving from there. I should be at the ranch, but I needed to escape for a few minutes. Blaze is a bit intense right now."

I snorted and washed my soup down with a swallow of hot coffee. "Beau mentioned that last night. He said, and I quote, *the dude needs to chill the F out. He's going to give himself an aneurysm.*"

Heaven almost choked on her soup but couldn't stop the laughter from escaping. She pointed her spoon at me while she swallowed, then she lifted an eyebrow. "I noticed you and Beau have been rather," she waved her spoon around in the air, "happy the last few days. Ever since, oh, I don't know, perhaps since you spent Saturday night in the pasture."

I lowered my spoon and rolled my eyes at her words because she'd expect that reaction. What she wouldn't expect was the bomb I was about to drop. "We didn't spend the night out in the pasture. We made a fire, talked, ate Beau's famous hobos, and made love before we returned to the house to sleep."

"Shut the front door!" she yelled, jumping straight up from her chair, and almost spilling the rest of her soup. "Why didn't you tell me?" she demanded, stomping her foot. "Oh my God, I can't believe you two finally gave it up and realized you're perfect for each other! Did you tell him about your arthritis? How did he say I love you?"

Her enthusiasm was a lot to handle on a day like today. Whatever look was on my face had her plopping back into the chair and taking my hand.

"He didn't say I love you?"

I barely shook my head as an answer. "Neither of us said I love you. You don't have to declare your love for each other to have sex," I said, withdrawing my hand from hers so I could finish my soup.

Heaven frowned. It looked like I'd stolen the wind from her sails. "You don't, but it's so obvious to everyone else, so I thought for sure …"

She thought for sure that we saw it, too. It wasn't that I couldn't see it. At least I knew I was in love with Beau Hanson. Since the day I met him, I had been, but that didn't mean it was wise to declare that aloud if he wasn't ready to hear it.

"I have to be careful," I finally answered. "The twentieth anniversary of his mom's death is today, and Beau is struggling with it. I just thought it was wise to give him what he needs right now and not upset the apple cart in the process."

"But you do love him?" Heaven asked, her spoon balanced in the bottom of her bowl.

"You said it was obvious."

"I said it was obvious to everyone else, but that doesn't mean it's obvious to the two of you."

"It's obvious to me that I love him. I can't speak for him, though. I won't push him to feel something he doesn't. That never works out for either party."

Heaven nodded in agreement and took the spoon from my hand. When I glanced up, she was staring me down. "What about the autoimmune disorder situation?"

Heaven was aware his mother had lupus before she died. Even though she didn't die from the disease, Beau experienced how difficult living with someone with the condition is.

"I explained to him about my arthritis and how I'm getting treatment for it now. He told me we would weather the complications together as long as we continued to trust and be honest with each other."

Heaven smiled, her eyes filling with relief. "Totally sounds like the Beau Hanson that I know."

"At least the one we knew before last fall, right?" I asked, knowing exactly what she meant.

She tipped her head in agreement. "I will take the blame for that one."

I waved my finger at her in anger. "No, you don't get to do that. You and Blaze getting together might have been the catalyst, but you were not the cause. He's been unhappy for a long time."

"No, he's been lonely for a long time," Heaven corrected, a small smile tilting her lips upward. "Things are looking up for Beau now, though. He's a partner in the ranch he's put his blood, sweat, and tears into and has a new place to live with someone who cares about him."

I waved my hands wildly. "No, we aren't like living together living together," I insisted. "Beau has his room, and I've got mine."

She laughed with abandon. "Tell me, how often are you in those rooms together alone?"

"That's none of your business," I said haughtily.

Heaven burst out laughing, bending over at the waist in a dramatic flair of ridiculousness. When she sat up, she was grinning. "I'm thrilled for you, Dawn. I am. I'm having fun with you, but secretly my insides are all mushy."

"It's not a secret if you come right out and tell me."

Heaven chuckled and gave me a finger gun. "True enough, but I want you to know that Blaze and I will do anything to keep that smile on both of your faces. In fact, I came to deliver an invitation to dinner tonight. We're eating with Blaze's parents at the ranch."

I waved my hand at my neck in the cut motion. "Tonight is a special time for family, Heaven. It's been years since Blaze has seen his parents."

"Beau is going to be there," she said before I could take a breath.

"Beau is family," I reminded her. "He's as much their son as Blaze is. I think he's terribly torn up about how things went down there when he was a teenager, too. He probably wants to sit and visit with them tonight without extra people around. Especially taking the anniversary of his mom's death into account. He needs them more than me right now."

Heaven cocked her head in confusion. "What do you mean when he was a teenager?"

"I don't think I should answer that question. It feels wrong to talk about Beau when he isn't here," I answered, biting my lip in regret.

"Blaze told me his parents wanted to adopt Beau."

"Did he tell you why they didn't?" I asked, pushing the soup away from me.

She made the so-so hand in the air. "That it was Beau who didn't want to do it."

I didn't want to talk about this behind Beau's back, but at the same time, I knew I had to. There would be no peace from this woman until I explained the situation. "He wanted to, but if he agreed to the adoption, then he had to give up his mom's last name. He probably could have hyphenated his name, but he was a kid and didn't understand its intricacies. Anyway, in his mind, the Hanson name was all he had left of his mom. Now, all these years later, he understands how untrue that is."

Heaven leaned back in the chair and eyed me. "He's approaching this anniversary of her death from a lot of different directions, isn't he?"

"North, south, east, and west," I agreed. "It's one of the reasons I'm letting him direct things between us. I'm afraid if I push too hard in one direction, he'll run to the other."

"Understandable," she agreed, blowing out a breath. "You really don't want to come tonight?"

"I want to come, but only if *he* asks me to come. I know you asked me to come, and if he and I weren't," I motioned around and finally dropped my hand in frustration, "what we are, I would come to support you. Since he's family to the McAwleys, I feel like I should let Beau come to me and ask. Does that make sense?"

Heaven smiled an encouraging smile and took my hand. "It does. Remember, I've met them before. I'm not some fragile flower who can't hold her own with the soon-to-be in-laws. At the same time, I don't want you to feel left out or hurt if Beau doesn't ask you to come tonight."

I shook my head immediately. "No, it's an either-way situation for me."

"Either way?" she asked, confused.

"I'm fine with it either way. If he needs me there for support, I'll be there. If he wants to enjoy the evening without the added stress of introducing me to them, then I will also support him in that way."

"He's a lucky guy, Dawn," she said with a wink.

"He knows it," Beau said from the doorway.

My eyes widened at Heaven, and she winked again before she stood and threw her coat around her shoulders. "I better get back to the ranch and help Blaze. Thanks for the soup." She hugged me, patted my back with a *talk later* whispered in my ear, and then she was gone.

Ten

When I walked the rest of the way into the kitchen, Dawn turned to me with a smile planted firmly on her face. I could tell she didn't feel it. "Hi," I said, kissing her lips. She tasted of salty, cheesy soup and buttery bread that made me hungry … for her. "You're gorgeous as ever, darlin'."

Dawn kissed me back before she answered. "I'm wearing old jeans and a ratty flannel shirt, Beau. Thanks, though," she answered, winking. "Soup?"

I rubbed my hands together and walked to the stove, ladling some into a bowl. "I'd love some. It's chilly out there today." I stopped talking long enough to eat the soup while she cleaned up their bowls. I set mine in the sink when I was done and washed it down with a drink of water. "I love your wild rice soup. It's almost as good as the bison steaks Cece's doing on the grill tonight."

"Almost as good?" she asked, hip checking me. "Why is Cece cooking?"

I shrugged and leaned against the counter. "Blaze asked her to so we could sit with the folks and not be distracted. I would have rather done the grilling, but I know Cece will do just fine."

Dawn leaned into my side and put her arm around my waist. "She will do better than just fine. She's a professional. My question is, why would you have rather done the cooking? Don't you want to spend time with Ash and Amity?"

"I do, but I also want Blaze and Heaven to have plenty of time with them," I said, not meeting her eyes. Whenever she could stare into them, she always saw what my words didn't say.

Her hand tenderly stroked my chest before she spoke. "Beau, you live with me now, which means they will have a lot of alone time with Blaze and Heaven. I know you are kind of nervous about seeing them again, but you shouldn't be. They love you."

Apparently, after making love to me a dozen times, she doesn't even have to look in my eyes to know the truth. "I know you're right. I'm struggling with their arrival today on the anniversary of Momma's death. I don't know how to feel, and it's chewing me up something fierce. Will you come with me to dinner?"

Dawn let her arm fall from around my waist and gazed up at me. "Are you sure? Did you hear Heaven and me talking, and that's why you asked? I don't want to be in the way or make anything awkward for you with Mr. and Mrs. McAwley."

I took her hand and brushed a kiss across her knuckles before I answered. "You won't make anything awkward. I want you to meet them, and I want them to get to know you. You don't have to come, but the invitation stands. I know that's why Heaven was here, right? She was inviting you?"

She nodded and pointed over her shoulder at the door. "I told her I wasn't going tonight …"

"Unless I asked you to come, right?" She shrugged, but it held a degree of guilty agreement to it. "I wasn't over at the ranch for the last four hours trying to decide if I wanted you to come if that's what you think. I was working and was just now able to sneak away. I want you there, and it has nothing to do with what I overheard between you and Heaven. Please."

"I'm more than ready to come and meet the infamous Ash and Amity McAwley," Dawn finally said, a smile on her face. "I even made …" She held up her finger and walked to the fridge, opening the door, and motioning inside.

The spread inside the fridge made my mouth water with one glance. "Oh, mercy me," I moaned. "Dawn's famous Wisconsin cream puffs."

I reached for one, but she smacked my hand away. I barely got my head out of the way before she closed the door. "Not until dinner!" she exclaimed firmly.

I grabbed her around the waist and kissed her neck, suckling lightly until she shivered. "What were you going to do if I didn't ask you to dinner?"

"Eat them all myself," she moaned, another shiver darting through her when my tongue trailed its way up her neck.

"I doubt that. I bet you were going to give the cream puffs to Heaven and not even save me one."

"I might have, but I did save extra cream. I figured you could have a Dawn puff once you got back tonight."

I buried my nose in her neck, my hardness pressing into her thigh to make his presence known. "Woman, you're going to make me come like a pubescent boy at just the thought."

Dawn laughed, but the sound was so naughty I nearly did. I swung her up into my arms, and she squealed until I silenced her with my lips while I carried her to my room. I slammed the door shut with my boot heel and tossed her on the bed carefully, following her down so I didn't have to break contact with her lips. My fingers were anxious and desperately tugged at the old worn buttons on her shirt until I could cup the warm flesh of her breasts, her sweet body driving me to the breaking point.

She moaned into my mouth, and the sound engulfed me, filling my head with fire only sliding into her center would extinguish. Our tongues, lips, and hands collided as we undressed each other until we were naked and panting.

"God, Dawn, every time. How can it be like this every time?" I asked into her ear before I had even buried myself inside her.

"Make love to me, Beau," she begged, her nails clawing at my back until I thrust upward, filling her completely.

"Dawn," I hissed as she lifted her hips and swallowed me whole again. She settled herself against my pelvis and braced her hands on my chest until she was sitting upright on me. My thumbs brushed her nipples, drawing out a shudder before she scooted back another inch, changing the depth and position just enough to drag a cry from my lips that was from somewhere deep within my soul. I held her hand on my chest, my body trembling and my heart beating in a way it never had before.

"I think I love you, Dawn Lee!" I cried when she started to come around me. Her cries were in sync with the waves of her body until we were both trembling and panting. When she relaxed against me, she gave me access to that soft hair on the top of her head.

I kissed it and rubbed my cheek in her locks, then buried my nose there until she groaned. "Not bad for a nooner, eh?" she asked, her usual Midwestern accent husky and sated. It sounded the same as mine, and I knew what emotion was clogging mine.

Love.

The word sent a shiver down my spine, and I wrapped my arms around her tightly. "That was pretty damn good for any time of the day, darlin'," I whispered. "I already want to do it again, but I'm holding out for that Dawn puff later."

She chuckled at the thought, which broke the mood. She sat up and hurried to the end of the bed while my gaze trailed her naked body down and back up until I met her eyes. Hers were brimming with tears, and I didn't know what to do.

Dawn grabbed her clothes and pulled her shirt around to cover her creamy breasts I loved to suckle. "I suppose we better finish today's duties before dinner tonight." She cleared her throat and stood, inching toward the door. "Are you going back to the ranch?"

I nodded with my gaze still locked onto hers. "I have a meeting with a potential leather client at two. My first paying client with any luck," I said, crossing my fingers. "By the time I'm done, Ash and Amity will be arrivin'."

Her shoulders slumped as she walked back to the bed and kissed my lips. "Beau, that's awesome. I'm so proud of you. A paying leather client."

I picked up her hand carefully, so I didn't hurt it, and held it to my chest. "Potential but thank you. Just don't be disappointed if they don't order anything."

Her smile filled me with light in a way I hadn't been for a long time. "Beau, I've never been disappointed in you before. I'm not going to start now."

I returned the smile and caressed her cheek with my finger. "Dinner is at seven. I'll come home, change, and pick you up?"

"I'll be ready," she promised as she walked to the door.

"Dawn?" She paused but didn't turn around. "Did I hurt you? I noticed your hand is all swollen again."

She shook her head but still refused to turn. "You didn't hurt me, Beau. I'm just … confused. I'll see you at seven."

She walked out the door then, the vision of her sweet backside one that would stay with me for the rest of the day. I glanced down at my naked body, my need for her already growing again. If there was one thing I was suddenly and acutely aware of, it was that Dawn Lee had ruined me for all other women. I had loved that woman since day one, but that emotion had changed from abstract to concrete in a way I never expected the first time I kissed her. I thought back to the words that fell from my lips a few moments ago and wondered if she had heard them. She didn't say anything, but she was flying into the sky on the wings of an orgasm. Maybe she didn't hear me after all. The image of the tears in her eyes told me she had. Was she crying because I said them, or was she crying because she couldn't say them back?

I sighed, sat up, threw my feet over the bed, and ran my hands down my face. I never claimed to understand women. I did know that I had just changed the rules of the game, and there was no going back. Dawn would either have to accept it or leave the game.

The barn was cold, silent, and gloomy when I walked in to ensure the animals had enough feed and warm bedding to tide them over during this cold snap. We're a guest ranch now, and the guests are supposed to be responsible for the care of the small animals, but I always check on them just in case the chore was forgotten. Besides, nothing brightens your day like playing with baby goats. Princess Bubblegum, one of our newest babies, hopped up to me with much enthusiasm. I bent down and lifted her from the cage, laughing at her pure joy to be held in someone's arms.

"Hello, baby," I cooed, her soft fur tickling my chin. "Are you staying warm enough in your sweater?" The argyle wool wrapped around her reminded me of something your grandpa would wear on a chilly afternoon while sitting by the fire.

The rest of the gang, Jake, Finn, and Earl of Lemongrab, all clamored over for attention as well. I laughed happily, hugging them and giving them all equal attention. When Heaven first started her small menagerie of pets, she decided to name them after cartoon characters. Her horse's name is Grover, and she always found it funny to come up with a name that fit the animal. Like our hen named Camilla and the love of her life, our rooster named Big Bird. Our latest collection of baby goats was named after the show Adventure Time since their mother's name is Marceline the Vampire Queen.

I shooed the babes back into their pen and brushed off my shirt, glad the hyperventilating that I'd been suffering from the last hour had finally eased.

Beau loves me?

No. Beau said he thinks he loves me. I plopped down onto a hay bale and put my head in my hands, the tears I'd been holding back dripping onto my jeans.

A tiny hand came down on my back, making me jump, and I quickly swiped at the tears on my face. "What are you crying about?" Heaven asked, sitting down next to me on the hay bale.

"Hey, Heaven," I said, clearing my throat of the tears. "I didn't hear Grover."

"I brought the truck over. I'm too cold from riding over at lunch, but Beau asked me to check on you."

She sat rubbing my back but didn't demand answers to the questions she didn't need to ask. Heaven was the kind of friend who understood when you were upset and needed to talk and when you were upset and didn't know how to talk.

"Beau asked you to check on me?" I finally asked, swiping at my nose with the sleeve of my shirt. "He didn't leave that long ago."

"He has a client about a saddle system for their disabled child, or he would have come over himself."

More likely, he had no idea what to say any more than I did.

"I knew he had a client, but I didn't know it was for another saddle system. How did they hear about it?"

Heaven patted my back once and then motioned at her left arm and shoulder. "I've been telling everyone I know about it! I even posted a picture of me in the saddle on one of my forums. The only other systems out there require you to order a whole new saddle, which is usually cost-prohibitive, especially for kids. Since Beau can retrofit the parts to the saddle they already have, it saves the client money. If the client is a child, the parts can transfer to bigger saddles as they grow. That isn't available in the industry right now, so it's a gamechanger."

"You're saying he might end up overrun with orders."

Heaven tossed her head back and laughed, her body shaking at the idea. "Lord, I hope so. That boy has so much talent and no confidence about any of it. It would be great to see him succeed to the point he doesn't need that ranch anymore."

"You don't want him to be part of the ranch anymore?" I asked, confused. "Blaze just signed over half of the rights to him."

Heaven slashed her hand through the air. "No, that's not what I meant at all. Beau is that ranch. Bison Ridge only exists because of him. We all know it. What I meant was, he doesn't need to work on the ranch anymore. He can be a partner but still focus on his leatherwork for the most part."

"Oh, right," I nodded, staring at my folded hands again. "Beau would probably like that, too. He loves the ranch and the animals, but he lives for the leather shop."

"I have to say, Dawn Lee, you are an expert at diversion, but you still haven't answered my opening question of what are you crying about."

I blew out a breath and stared at the open barn door and the pasture beyond. You could just make out the herd of bison grazing on the pasture grass, their giant, brown bodies swaying as they walked. The animals were majestic creatures from yesteryear that Blaze and Beau worked to corral. I couldn't say they raised them because you don't raise a wild animal as much as you contain them. They might be majestic, but they were also dangerous and deadly when they didn't want to be controlled.

"I'm just confused." I side-eyed her and could see that Beau hadn't told her why she needed to check on me. "He kind of told me he loved me. I think? I didn't know what to do, so I didn't say anything back. Now, I don't know if that was the right way or the wrong way to react."

Heaven cocked her head. "How did he kind of tell you he loves you? Either he did, or he didn't."

I laughed then, shaking my head at the woman next to me. "You don't know Beau Hanson very well if you think that's true. He's the master at always halfway committing to people. I understand why, but it's hard to know where to walk through that landmine sometimes."

"His mother's death messed him up as a kid."

I nodded and shrugged. "Rightly so. Considering today's date, Beau's even more unsettled. That's not his fault, and I understand why he's feeling this way. I was trying to distract him from it earlier and offer him a short moment in time when it didn't consume his thoughts, but I just made it worse."

"What did he say exactly? It had to have been in just the last couple of hours."

My cheeks flushed pink, and I swallowed, embarrassed to have to tell her exactly how it happened. When I finished the story, she was nodding her head while biting her lip.

"I agree, that's awkward. Throwing the word *think* in there makes you wonder if he said it in the ecstasy of the moment or if he was saying a commonly used teasing phrase."

I held my hand out to her in an *I know* motion. "Which is why I didn't say anything back. I think Beau saw the tears welling in my eyes, though. I wasn't upset or anything. I was confused and didn't know how to respond. I didn't want to screw up whatever this was between us. If I said I know I love you, and he was teasing about thinking he loved me, then I blew the whole thing, you know?"

Heaven put her arm around me and hugged me to her side. "I do know. It's a hard road to walk with Beau sometimes. He's worth it, though. Even when he breaks your heart and makes you cry, you're making progress. You're making him feel things again that he has kept tucked away for a lot of years. I would imagine that has to terrify him."

I nodded, wiping the rest of the tears from my eyes. "I know, which is why I'm not upset that Beau said it. I'm not even upset, truth be told. I know I'm crying, but not out of anger or being hurt. I'm just—I don't know."

Heaven rubbed my back and winked, her lips wearing a smile again. "You're crying out of frustration, which is an earned feeling. Especially since you know you love him, right? You don't even have to think about it?"

"Yeah," I agreed. "Mostly that."

"And you know what you have to do, and that's making this even harder."

I nodded, rubbing the sore finger on my left hand. "I can't push Beau. I know that. I can't make him feel something he doesn't."

"I don't think it's that, Dawn. He's feeling it. What you can't make him do is verbalize it until he's ready. It's hard. Blaze was the same way. It was for different reasons, but the result was the same," she explained with wistfulness in her voice.

"Patience," I said, sitting up and stretching out my back. "I have to be patient with him, and I am, when we're together. I let myself feel everything else when he's not here."

"I'm proud of you, Dawn. You're taking a hard situation for him and making it a little bit easier. I think tomorrow when he can see that there is a future past this big anniversary today, the turmoil inside him will ease a little bit."

I nodded and stood, grabbing her hand, and pulling her up off the hay bale, too. "I know that's true, and I'm holding onto it with determination. Beau invited me to dinner tonight, so that's a start, right?"

Heaven held up until I turned back to her. "He did? That's great! That means he's not afraid to introduce you to Ash and Amity!"

I made the so-so hand in the spring sunshine as we walked out of the barn. "Part of that is true. The other part is that I don't know how he's going to introduce me, and that makes me nervous."

Heaven looked me up and down and then checked her watch. "We have an hour before I need to be back at the ranch. Follow me. I have a plan that will guarantee he won't have a problem introducing you to them as more than a friend."

This time, she took my hand and dragged me back into the house, our laughter echoing through the hills of Bison Ridge.

Eleven

"Almost ready?" I called down the hallway toward Dawn's room. I didn't want to be late for dinner, but when I arrived to change my clothes, she wasn't ready yet.

"Just putting my boots on," she called back. "I'll meet you in the living room."

I grabbed her coat off the rack by the door and paced around the room. When Ash and Amity arrived a few hours ago, I spent time visiting with them before dinner. It felt good to hug Amity and shake Ash's hand after so many years. That didn't mean I wasn't nervous about dinner. I had no idea how I was going to introduce Dawn to them. Was she a friend? Was she my girlfriend? Was she a friend with benefits? I had no idea what the correct answer was. To be honest, any of them could be the wrong one in her eyes. I could ask Dawn how she wanted to be introduced, but that forced a conversation I wasn't ready to have. What if she wanted more or less out of the relationship than I did? Then what would I say?

My mind's eye went back to those tears in her eyes earlier today. I could blow this whole thing up if I picked the wrong title when I introduced her. Maybe she would introduce herself if I were lucky. Yes, that was an easy out. We'd arrive at the ranch, and I'd have to grab something from the workshop, sending her in to meet the folks without me.

Coward.

There was that voice reminding me that I wasn't being the kind of man my momma would expect of me.

I was a coward, though. That wasn't new information. I was positive that everyone who knew me already knew that word fit me better than a broken-in pair of Wranglers. I heard the clunk of her boot heels as they came down the hallway, and I turned just as she stepped through the doorway. I fell to one knee with her coat clutched to my chest while my eyes feasted on the beauty before me. She had taken my breath away so hard that I forced a deep inhale so I didn't pass out from the spots dancing in front of my eyes.

Her red western shirt sported mother of pearl snaps down the front, the top two open, allowing me a peek of her cleavage. There were lace cut-outs everywhere, teasing me with just the hint of her beautiful alabaster skin that made me instantly hard. Her jeans were tight, new, and hugged all the places I loved the most. Even her silver Heavenly Lane belt buckle that was bigger than my hand didn't distract from the image of what lay underneath. She wore the leather bison Stetson I'd made her this past summer with a red hatband to finish the look.

"Beau? Are you okay?" she asked, stepping forward to grab my shoulder.

The look in those beautiful brown eyes when I gazed up at her was my undoing. I grabbed her, kissing her so hard our teeth almost collided from the force. I pulled her down on top of me and dipped my tongue in to taste her. She tasted of Jim Beam, which told me she was as nervous about this as I was. I moaned, my hands knocking the hat off her head to bury themselves in her hair. Her chest heaved against mine until I released her so we could both suck in air again.

"I guess you showed me," she said, sitting up and straightening her shirt.

"No, you showed me. Holy hell, Dawn. This outfit. You're built like a Coke bottle, and you sure as hell can ride any horse in my string."

Dawn tipped her head to the side for a moment. "Beau Hanson, you sure have a way with the ladies." She shook her head with laughter on her lips. "I think those were compliments anyway. We better go," she said, pushing herself up off the floor and checking her lipstick in the mirror by the door.

I groaned again and rubbed the front of my jeans, the pressure against my zipper making them tight and uncomfortable.

Dawn spun around to face me. "You okay?"

I shook my head back and forth slowly. "Not even the least little bit. There's hardly any back to that shirt, darlin', and those jeans cupping your backside—I'm drowning in want. All my mind can think about is hearing the snaps on that shirt popping open tonight before I cover you in cream and lick you clean."

When I stood up, she pointed at my pants. "It seems I have indeed caused a problem. Unfortunately, we don't have time to do anything about it now, do we?"

I rubbed the front of my pants again, the pain almost too much to bear, especially with her teasing. She motioned me over with a crook of her finger, so I went to her, and the next thing I knew, she had my pants unzipped and my bulging need between her lips.

"Dawn!" I exclaimed as she sucked me deep into her throat. My legs shook instantly at being buried in her warmth again. Her tongue traced my tip and then stroked me up and down, her gaze holding mine the entire time.

Oh my God, this woman. She was going to be the very end of me and the immediate beginning. She was going to be my whole life if I could put aside the fear that I harbored about losing her from my life when I least expected it. My hips shook from the power it took not to thrust into her and hurt her, but at the same time, find that release I hadn't asked for but desperately needed.

My fingers slid through her hair, the silkiness erotic against my skin as she swallowed me whole, her hand wrapped around me to add extra pressure until I couldn't keep it together. I couldn't hold back the waves breaking over me, and I came with a guttural moan of pleasure, disbelief, and love. The strongest emotion I had as I stared into the eyes of this beautiful woman was love. I still didn't know what to do with that, but admitting the truth was the first step.

I ran my fingers through her hair again and let out a ragged sigh. "You are more than I deserve, gorgeous. Please, don't ever leave me."

Dawn winked and straightened her blouse while I fixed my pants and worked to bring my breathing and heart rate back under control. "I'm harder to get rid of than fleas on a farm dog, darlin'," she said before sashaying to the kitchen for her cream puffs.

The McAwleys were nothing like I expected them to be. Led to believe that Ash was a tall, lanky, weathered grizzly bear, I was greeted instead with a warm hug from a tall, lean, sweet man who was far more loving to everyone than I expected him to be. Amity, while husky and athletic in pictures, was friendly and engaging in person. She had story after story to tell about Blaze and Beau growing up together. Ash and Amity had a whole houseful of boys, and now they had five grandsons. Amity was begging Heaven for a granddaughter, but all Blaze and Heaven did was laugh. I just hoped she wasn't going to look at me anytime soon.

Beau had noncommittedly introduced me as Dawn Lee, and everyone accepted it without blinking an eye. I suspected that Heaven and Blaze had filled them in on Beau's inability to commit to the situation.

"I haven't seen Beau smile and laugh this much in just about ever," Amity said, walking into the kitchen carrying the empty platter that once held bison steaks. "I'm surprised he's doing so well considering the date."

I accepted the platter from her and plunged it into the hot, soapy water. "Beau's working through it," I agreed without saying more.

Amity lifted a bowl from the drainer and dried it with a flour sack towel. We had sent Cece home after dinner since she had a long day of cooking at the ranch tomorrow. "I bet you have something to do with it."

"Beau and I have been friends for years, Mrs. McAwley," I jumped in before she could say more.

She set the bowl down and put her hand on her hip. "Please, it's Amity. As for the number of years you've been friends, I didn't say anything about that. I said, I bet you had something to do with him doing as well as he is right now."

I shrugged and set the platter in the drainer before pulling the plug on the sink. "While I'm here to support Beau and let him feel whatever he needs to feel where it's safe, I think maturity is what's behind the situation. With age and experience, he's learned how to process his emotions better. He's also come to realize that while his mother might fade from his memory, he will never forget her as long as he keeps her memory alive in his heart."

Amity hmm'd her agreement until the platter was dry and put away. "We tried to teach him that as a child. Did you know that he has a whole book of stories he wrote down about her after her death?"

I crossed my arms over my chest as I leaned against the counter. "Beau told me, yeah. He said it was at the bank in a safety deposit box. I offered to make a digital copy for him, but he didn't jump on the idea, so I didn't push him about it. I don't think he's ready to share it with anyone yet, and I understand that. When and if he asks me to do it, then I'll help him with it."

"In other words, you're letting him lead the relationship, and his nosy foster mom should keep her giant Texas nose out of your business."

"No!" I jumped in, waving my hands. "Not at all what I meant. I was just explaining that I knew about the book of stories. I wasn't in any way accusing you of being nosy. I don't feel that way at all." My hands were waving in front of my chest until she took them gently, holding them down.

"I'm glad, but I was kind of being nosy." We chuckled together, and Amity tossed the towel on the counter then motioned me to leave the kitchen with her. "I'm worried about him, and I wanted to make sure he was in a good place now. I also think the book has so many great stories and nuggets of wisdom that should be shared. If someone could get him to put them together, I think it could even do well on the market as a life lesson kind of book. His mother was a lot like you. A hard worker and devoted to Beau. At the same time, she suffered a lot in life and struggled through a disease that wasn't kind a lot of the time."

I sighed, and my shoulders slumped forward as we walked into the living room. "Beau told you about my condition." The memory of her holding my hands gently just now was an obvious indicator I had missed.

Amity grabbed her coat off the rack and stuffed her arms into it. "He did. He said it took you a year to tell him, so forgive him for telling us. He just felt we should know, so we didn't shake your hand too hard or wonder why you grimaced a lot."

I took my coat from her outstretched hand and put it on. There would be a fire where we were going, but it was still chilly enough to need a jacket. "It's not that I don't want people to know, Amity. I just didn't want Beau to know about it for obvious reasons."

Amity held the door open for me, so I walked through it, waiting for her on the porch. "Because if Beau knew, then he might decide he couldn't date you since his mom had the same kind of disease."

I held her arm so she couldn't walk down the stairs without me saying my piece. "Beau isn't like that. He loved his mother, and her disease was the smallest part of her. That said, it's different when you have a choice about committing to someone who has a disease like that versus being born into the situation. When he met me, my health was completely different than it is now. I've lost weight, my joints are a mess, and so is my head. I don't have any family left, and Heaven was leaving the ranch too. Risking my friendship with Beau made me very fearful of the future."

Amity rested her hand over mine and patted it. "You're wrong. You have a giant family. All those people out there," she said, pointing at the group sitting around the fire laughing and drinking beer, "they're your family. All my sons back home in Texas, one word from me that someone is messing with Beau's girl, and they're here, too. We have your back."

I smiled, fighting back the tears that were blurring my vision. "Thanks, Amity. That means a lot to me. I do consider everyone here to be my family. They've always got my back, even when it hurts so badly that I can't move. As for Beau, you raised a good man."

She shook her head as we walked down the stairs. "That wasn't me. That was his momma."

"She certainly did right by him, but he tells everyone that you finished the job when you didn't have to. You shouldn't belittle your contribution because he's not your biological child. You didn't have to do what you did and take in another boy just because he was your son's best friend. You changed someone's life at a pinnacle time for them. Remember that."

Amity smiled and patted me on the back. I walked over to Beau and kissed his forehead before taking the empty chair next to him. He was a good man, and I would do anything to keep him.

The fire was dying down, but no one was in a hurry to leave. I'd been listening to Ash tell stories about our older brothers while holding Dawn's hand in one hand and a beer in the other. I was relaxed and happy, something I never thought I could be on a night like tonight. Maybe I had finally found a way through the grief of losing my mom after all these years.

The flow of the conversation slowed, so I cleared my throat. "I got a text after dinner that my client wants to order the retrofit pieces for their daughter's saddle."

Heaven was the first to clap her hand on her thigh and let out a squeal. "Beau! That's amazing! How exciting."

Dawn kissed my cheek. “I’m proud of you. Look at what’s happened because you did something nice for someone else,” she said, motioning at Heaven.

Ash stood and shook my hand, his grin wide, while Amity hugged me around the shoulders. “We’re proud of you, too, son.”

“Thank you,” I said, completely embarrassed by their show of support.

Blaze offered me a fist bump. “I told you when you developed that system for Heaven that you could sell them all day long without even trying. Should I start looking for a new ranch hand director?”

“I’m available,” Tex jumped in, his voice teasing.

“Hush your mouth, boy!” Heaven demanded. “You will not defect. Do you understand me?”

Tex held up his hands in laughter, the excellent food, and beer relaxing everyone.

I cleared my throat again, a little embarrassed by what else I had to say. “The client sort of can’t pay me due to the accident their daughter had. The doctor told them getting her back in the saddle would help her mental health, though. They can’t do that without the retrofit saddle, so they’re stuck between a bull and a fence. He asked if we’d be willing to take a load of hay in exchange for the saddle. I told him no.”

“You told him no?” Blaze asked as though he was clarifying.

I held up my hand so he’d let me finish. “I ta—told him no because he could sell that hay and use it to help dig them out of da—da—debt.” Dawn squeezed my hand gently to remind me to slow down. I changed the direction of my jaw and cleared my throat. “I’ll make the saddle pieces from smaller scraps of leather that I can’t use to make anything else. Their daughter's needs aren’t anywhere near as extensive as what I made Heaven, so it won’t take much leather. Bison leather is ridiculously expensive, so I'll pay you back for what I use. I know you didn't ask for repayment on the one I made for Heaven's saddle for obvious reasons, but this one ain't on you," I said to Blaze.

"You'll do no such thing," Ash said quietly from across the fire. "You'll make the saddle pieces and help the family out. That's what we do as ranchers. We help each other out of tough spots, be it with family or farm. Not everything in life is about payment."

My eyes widened at his statement. This was coming from the man who all my life was about the monetary value of everything.

Amity nodded her agreement. "There's more to life than money, Beau. Those hides don't cost us anything. If you didn't know how to tan and use them, you'd just be selling them off as unfinished hides for pennies on the dollar. Use your talent for good any way you can and anytime that you can, son. That will come back to you tenfold more than any payment will."

Ash spoke up before I could say anything to that. "When someone can afford to pay, take their money, and give it back to someone who can't pay but needs the help. That's how we do it at our ranch. I know I've always come off to you boys as a miserly old man who sits in his house and counts his pennies. The truth is, that was an image I cultivated for your own good. Teaching you to respect the business as a young person was important. Until I did that, I couldn't teach you about philanthropy. I can see I don't need to teach the second half of the lesson anymore. You've got it down already. I'm aware you all thought I was going to screw Heaven out of her ranch. I never had any intention of doing that. I planned to buy her out and bail her out but never take possession of her land and home. That's not me, and I hope you know that now. Life is about giving people a hand up when they need it, but the distance between us can make it hard to show that to you boys."

"Which is why we're thinking about making Wisconsin our summer home," Amity said, a grin on her face.

Blaze and I sat forward at the same time. "What?" we asked in enthusiastic unison.

They both nodded as Ash took Amity's hand and spoke. "We are all but retired from the ranch at home now that the three boys are running it. You know I would never survive the winter here, but I think I'd love the summers."

Amity clapped her hands excitedly. "Don't worry now. We won't be moving in with the newlyweds. We'd buy an RV and live in that if you could find the space on the property."

Blaze laughed, and the sound he made echoed my feelings in a nutshell. Happy. "We have hundreds of acres. I think we could spare some land for an RV, Mom."

"Good, then we'd like to start this summer. We already bought the RV," she said, and that drew laughter from my chest.

"Why am I not surprised? I'm happy to be able to spend time with you guys again. I've missed you a lot," I said, thankful for Dawn's tiny hand in mine when she squeezed it.

"Which is why we decided to take this step," Ash said. "We need to spend time with our family, but we can't expect you to leave the ranch. I don't want to give up another minute of family time. I should never have sent you boys here all those years ago. I see that now."

My mouth dropped open as far as Blaze's did. We glanced at each other, unsure of what to say. "Sir," Blaze started to say, but Ash held up his hand.

"Don't sir me. You know this land has been hard-won, and these beasts hard-fought. I am proud of my sons at home without a doubt, but it is the two here that I have the deepest respect for now. You have had so many terrible things happen to you here, and I have so many regrets, but you soldiered on and made a life for yourselves regardless of those obstacles."

"But so many good things, too," Blaze whispered, holding up Heaven's hand in his while I did the same with Dawn's. "We've struggled, yes, but that is no different than it would be at home. The things we have learned, who we have loved, who we have lost, and who we still have, are all part of that story. By God, if I'm going to be a rancher, then I'd rather be here doing something unique than working a dusty patch of cattle any day."

"I second that," I agreed with a nod. "Perspective is a mighty thing, sir, and we all have our own. I don't expect you to see our perspective as clearly as we do, but I don't want you to carry the weight of guilt where there should be none. You did what a good father does. You sent us out on our own after you taught us what it meant to be a good man. I hope that we have done more than you expected over the years and that you can see we have more to do here. So much more." I winked at Dawn, who smiled shyly.

"I can see that," Ash agreed. "I should have said it the way you said it. When I said I shouldn't have sent you here, it was from the selfish point of view that I'd missed so much time with you. I want to change that now. I want to be part of this. Part of Bison Ridge. Part of the legacy you've built here. Part of Heavenly Lane, if you'll let me, Heaven."

Heaven winked at the man who was suddenly older than I ever remembered him being. "I think you'd fit in perfectly at the dude ranch. I bet you have a lot of tips and tricks to teach Tex and our cowboys who come to stay." She turned to Amity. "I know for sure Cece would love to work with you on some real Texan dishes she can learn to make for the crew."

Amity grinned. "I will bring my cookbook!"

The laughter around the ring broke the tension, which was a relief. Tex stood up, his hands going into his belt loops like they always did when he was fixin' to leave. "Thanks for asking me to dinner, folks. I have to go do my rounds before I turn in for the night." He turned to Ash and Amity. "I'll see you at Heavenly Lane tomorrow at ten for that tour?"

Ash stood and shook his hand. "We'll be there, Tex. Thanks for the invite."

Tex gave Amity a tender hug and nodded once. "No problem. I'm happy to show off our new dude ranch. Besides, I might just rope you into some work while you're there." He waved and jogged off in the direction of the barn to get his horse, leaving just the three of us couples around the fire.

"He's a nice boy," Amity said to Heaven. "Really wants to be Texan, doesn't he?"

We all bit back snorts of laughter in case he was in hearing distance. "So much," Heaven said, nodding exaggeratedly. "But I swear to God he was Texan in a different life. The boy knows more about horses and cows than Blaze and Beau combined. I'm lucky he stays on my ratty old ranch and works for peanuts."

Blaze laughed then, tickling his soon-to-be wife. "Used to work for peanuts. He's got the cushy gig now. Not that he would ever enjoy any of that cushiness. He likes being rustic."

"As did I," I said, laughter on my lips, "until I moved into a cushy house where a beautiful woman resides. Give him time. He might change his mind."

"Where did you find Tex, Heaven? Is that his real name?"

Heaven shook her head. "No, his real name is Caleb North. He said that name isn't fit for a cowboy and insisted we call him Tex. He answered an ad my daddy had in the paper for ranch hands. We knew we lucked out when we got Dawn and Tex from that ad. They both had opposite strengths, which is what we needed. Caleb is from North Dakota. He never talks about his past or why he's in Wisconsin alone. I don't ask too many questions because knowing his past isn't necessary for us to be friends. He needed a place to call home, and we had one, so we hired him on. Best decision we ever made."

Dawn was nodding in the light of the campfire, her lips pursed together. "You could say the same about me, I suppose," she said to no one in particular. "I don't talk about my past or why I rode into Wisconsin at such a young age alone. Sometimes, it's better to leave things in the past when you know dragging them back into the light will destroy your future."

I gripped her shoulder gently but wanted to offer her comfort. "It's okay, Dawn Lee, you don't have to explain."

"He's right," Heaven and Amity said in unison before they chuckled. Amity was the one to continue. "Families are complicated, Dawn. Often, they are the ones who hurt us more than anyone else ever could. Trust yourself to know who has your back."

"And all of us around this firepit do," Blaze said pointedly.

Dawn nodded, her gaze meeting mine for a minute. "I know that because you've shown me over and over what a real family is supposed to be like, even if we don't share blood. I may have been born of one family, but the family of my heart was somewhere completely different. I suspect that's a lot how Tex feels, too. All I'm saying is, we don't take that for granted."

Ash clapped his hands together once. "Then you've got the right idea, Dawn. Families are made in a myriad of different ways. We learned that when we took in a boy who needed us, even though our parenting journey was almost complete. Little did we know what we would have missed if we hadn't made that decision." He patted his hands on his thighs and seemed to think better of whatever else he was going to say. "Anyway, I suppose we ought to let you turn in. You still have to work in the morning. Ma and I can sleep in."

Blaze went to stand, but I jumped in before they could leave. "First, is it okay if I say something?" All their heads swiveled toward me, and I swallowed nervously. "Err, more like, ah—ask something," I stuttered, falling back into that nervous habit of talking too fast.

Dawn put her hand on my shoulder to ground me. "You're fine, Beau. Just say your piece the way you know how."

Amity agreed with her on a head nod. "She's right. You don't have to ask permission to speak. We just established that we're all family here."

I swallowed hard and rubbed my hands on my jeans. "Right, well, I—I, I just wanted to say that we all know what today is. Thanks for being here for me. All of you. And for not taking no ah—ah—ffense at my recent jerkish ba—ba—behavior, drunken door pounding in the dead of night, and acting like a real revolving son of a ba—itch."

Dawn squeezed my shoulder again while Heaven brushed her hand at me. "We all understood, Beau," she promised.

"Dude," Blaze said from where he sat, "you don't have to apologize to any of us. Besides, you weren't that much worse than your normal surly self."

I chuckled and tossed a bottle cap at him, thankful that he broke my stuttering by making me laugh. I always depended on him for that as a kid. Once again, he didn't let me down. "I know you probably think I'm a baby because I'm still mourning a woman who has been dead for twenty years."

Amity stood straight up onto her feet to interrupt me. "Beauregard Theodore Hanson! You are not a baby for mourning your mother on the anniversary of her death! I still mourn my mother's death, and I'm twice your age. Does that make me a baby?"

"No, ma'am," I said without thinking while Ash calmly pulled her back to her chair. "I didn't mean it that way."

"We know what you meant, son," Ash said, patting his wife's hand to calm her. "There is no time limit on grief. It will come when you least expect it, but you will also have longer periods where it doesn't engulf you. Time where you can remember her with happiness in your heart."

I nodded once. "Yes, sir. I agree. For the most part, that's where I am with it now. It is only on the big days, like today, that I struggle. I can say that this time, it didn't have so much to do with momma as it did with my regret for how I treated both of you."

Amity cocked her head. "Whatever do you mean, Beau?"

I reached inside my jacket pocket and pulled out an envelope, nervously tapping it on my pants before I handed it to her. "For you and Ash."

She opened the envelope and held the papers out so Ash could see them, too. "I don't understand what this is."

"It's the paperwork we'd need for adult adoption with the ca—ca—courts," I explained as her hand fell to her lap with the papers in them. "I—I realized that I scre—scre—"

Dawn leaned in and whispered into my ear. "Take a breath. No one here is judging you. Tell them how you feel. Nothing more, nothing less."

I nodded and started again. "I realized that I screwed uh–up," I was finally able to say. "What I thought was most important to remember momma by was—wasn't."

"Her last name?" Ash asked without judgment in his tone.

I pointed at Ash and noticed my hand was shaking, so I dropped it. "When you asked to adopt m—me when I was a teen, that's why I said na—no."

Amity stood and hushed me with a hand on my head. "We understood, Beau. You had been through so much. We just wanted you as part of our family in whatever way you wanted to be."

"You are part of our family," Blaze said emphatically, "same last name or not. That is never going to change."

Amity returned to her seat, and I glanced at the people around me. My tribe. The people I could always and would always count on to have my back. "I know, but now, sitting here all these years later, I've come to recognize that I am more a McAwley than a Hanson, not because momma didn't matter but because she da—did. She wouldn't want me to live in the past. She would have wanted me to grab that new future when I had the cha—cha—chance. I didn't get that right when I was fourteen. I was too young," I explained, clearing my throat again and tapping my fingers on my leg. I had to break the stutter, so there was no mistake in what I was asking tonight. "I've seen a lot here. I've lived through a lot here. I've experienced things I could never think of at nine, fifteen, or hell, even twenty-one. I know what I want now. I want to remember momma for the wonderful woman she was and the strong beginning she gave me. I want to honor you both for the wonderful people you are and the strong love you offered me when I needed it most. If it hadn't been for you, I might never have received the help I needed for my mental health, much less my stuttering and other issues. I don't ever want you to think I don't know tha—that."

"Son, we don't think that," Ash said quietly. "We didn't think that even when you didn't want to take our name. We were adults and understood the intricacies of what you were dealing with even better than you did. All we wanted to do was make sure you were loved and cared for as you grew up. We understood that grief is intricate and different for everyone, especially someone your age who had just had his whole life ripped out from under him. That was why we never pushed it. We all deal with grief in our own way."

Blaze pointed at his father and then me. "For instance, when Callie died, I decided to be a total jackass because I didn't have any other way to deal with it when I had to keep getting up every morning and moving forward."

"We understood you were a jackass because of losing Callie, Blaze," I said immediately. "It was never a question."

Blaze held his hands out and glanced around the circle. "Then, duh. If you had a brain, it would be lonely."

I snorted with laughter and shook my head at him. "Okay, point taken. I guess what I'm saying is, if it's not too late, I'd like to have your last name. I'd like to give my future wife and kids your name. I want to be part of the McAwley legacy, even if it is as a footnote in the family Bible."

"Footnote my foot," Amity said sweetly with tears in her voice. "It will be as part of the family tree, won't it, Ash."

"Absolutely, son," he agreed. "I have called you that since you came to my home for one reason. You were my son then, and you will remain my son until long after my death, but I would be honored to sign these papers and make you my son in name as well."

I put a thankful hand to my chest, fighting back the tears I didn't expect to creep in at his acceptance. "Thank you, sir," I said, clearing my throat while Dawn rubbed my back in a soothing rhythm. "Today, that means more to me than you'll ever know."

I stood and walked to them, hugging them both without words because I had none left. All I had left was a grateful heart for the love and protection I would always find in their arms, even as a grown man.

Twelve

I handed Beau a glass of whiskey that he tossed back in the time it took me to sit next to him on the couch. We had come home and showered, then decided a nightcap was what the doctor ordered.

"I'm proud of you," I finally said, the silence pervasive in the room.

"For not crying?" he asked, setting his glass down on the end table. "I almost did when Ash told me I'd always be his son."

I chuckled and finished my drink, too. "No, and no one would have cared if you had. I was referring to being able to share your feelings without fear of ridicule. For making two people extremely happy when on tonight of all nights, you would have been within your rights to be concerned only about yourself."

Beau took my hand and tapped it on his knee. "It was truly selfish, Dawn. I was concerned only about myself. Maybe, in the end, I made them happy, but that wasn't the angle I was approaching it from."

I tipped my head back and forth a couple of times as if weighing what he said. "You can think that if you want to, but selfish would have been tying one on and not caring about anyone else. Instead, you spent the entire evening engaged with them, encouraged their new dreams, and brought the family closer together. Sure, you benefited, too, but in the end, you were righting a wrong. At least something you saw as a wrong in your life. For that, and for helping the family with their daughter's saddle, I'm proud of you."

He got up and refilled his glass without saying another word. He drank that down and then wandered into the kitchen, coming back with a cream puff. He sat next to me and took a bite of it, holding it out for me to take a bite, too.

"Is that all you feel?" he asked while my mouth was full.

I swallowed and raised a brow, taking a scoop of the cream with my finger and licking it off. Beau groaned and did the same, holding his finger out for me to lick. I pulled his finger into my lips and suckled on it, watching as the front of his Wranglers tightened significantly.

"I feel like we should take this to the bedroom," I said, pulling him up and walking down the hallway, hoping he was following. He wasn't behind me when I made it to my room, so I called out to him. "Are you coming?"

"Hopefully, very soon," he called. When he paused in the doorway of the bedroom, he had the extra bowl of cream I had saved from the puffs.

I lifted a brow when he set it down on the bed. "I was kidding about the extra cream."

Beau's head shook as he eyed me like I was good enough to eat. "I wasn't. I'm a little upset I let you shower. Now I can't rip that blouse off you and cover you in cream."

"It should be a crime," I agreed, standing before him in a flannel shirt and leggings.

"So should this," he said, then ripped the shirt open, the buttons scattering across the floor to reveal my already hardened nipples. "Oops, I think I owe you a shirt." He pushed me down onto the bed and ripped my leggings off until I was completely naked before him.

"I know you owe me a shirt," I moaned as his eyes took an extended tour of my offerings while he stripped off his t-shirt and Wranglers.

He tapped his chin as he took in my now naked form. "Hmmm, where to start." The bowl was in his hand now, and he scooped cream out while my eyes widened. "I know the perfect place."

Beau swiped his full palm across each breast, leaving a trail of the white cream across both nipples, and then took another scoop, trailing it down my belly. He paused as though he was admiring his art before he let his hand roam up each thigh. Beau's eyes twinkled the moment before his fingers trailed the sticky cream around my center to cover it completely. Then his tongue came out to wet his lips before he dove in, licking, sucking, and teasing each breast until they were clean. I was already moaning uncontrollably before his tongue moved down my belly, taking extra time to dip into my navel to taste and tease.

I moaned loudly when his wet tongue traced my thighs upward, and his hands pushed them apart so he could bury his nose inside me. He licked, stroked, teased, and suckled until I couldn't take anymore and came apart in his arms, moaning his name with my hips thrust hard against his tongue.

Beau laughed naughtily, and when I could breathe again, I noticed he was in bad shape. I lifted one brow, scooped out a fingerful of cream, and looked it over. "What's the saying? Less is more?" I asked before I painted his hardness with the white goodness. I suckled the sweetness off my finger, dragging a groan from his lips, his hips thrusting upward, knowing he was next. I took my time with my tongue, returning the torture he'd bestowed upon me, but backed off before he could come too early.

I lay back and beckoned him toward me with my finger. His lips attacked mine while he pushed my legs open with his knee. He was done waiting, and I loved that side of him. When he was done playing, he rode me hard and brought me to life every time. He entered me with a hard thrust, and my pelvis rose to meet his, both of us hungry for the release we so desperately needed. He buried his face in my neck and cussed long and low against my collarbone, the word husky and beautiful even in its vulgarity.

"I need you all the time, Dawn. I don't understand this," he cried, his hips picking up speed as I pushed back, giving him everything he needed and nothing he didn't. "I want to come inside you forever," he cried, his hips stilling when he'd buried himself inside me so deeply that I didn't know where he ended and I began. "Are you ready?"

The only answer I gave him was a squeak as the first wave broke over me. I shuddered, calling his name into the empty night. He fell then, all of him, his breathing ragged against my neck, and his body spasming with such force it ripped a cry from his lips as he neared completion. By the time we collapsed against each other, sated and sticky, we had burned ourselves out with want and need, leaving only raw emotions that I was too afraid to verbalize.

Beau braced his forearms on each side of my head and leaned down for a kiss. "Earlier today, I said, I think I love you. Did you hear me?" he asked. I nodded my head slowly, afraid to speak and make him stop. "Why didn't you say anything?"

I swallowed and shrugged my shoulder against the bed. "Never jump on or hold anyone to anything they say during orgasm. That's the first rule of sex, right?"

"Maybe, but I saw your tears right after that. I was a coward. I should have asked why, but I was afraid of the answer."

"Afraid of the answer? To what question?"

"Were you crying because I thought I loved you or because I only half committed to it?"

"Neither. I wasn't even crying."

Beau smiled, winked, and leaned down for another short kiss. "I may not have done great in school, but I'm not a fool, Dawn. I can even answer the question without your input. You didn't answer because you're letting me decide what's happening between us, right?" I nodded rather than speak and risk my voice cracking. "Then, tonight, I'm going to decide. I don't think I love you. I know I love you, Dawn Briar Lee. I've loved you since day one. I tried to deny it to myself, but I couldn't. You were the last thing I thought of when I laid down at night and the first thing I thought of when I woke up. I love you. I'm not going to pretend I don't anymore. Tonight, I saw what love could do when it is shared honestly with someone else. I want to share my love with you, even if you don't feel the same way. Maybe you don't, I—I don–do—"

I put my finger to his lips. "I love you, Beau Hanson. Since I first laid eyes on you riding a horse that was way too small for you and pretending it wasn't. I have loved you since the first campfire we shared at Heavenly Lane. My tears were out of fear that you loved me but couldn't come to terms with it and fear that you didn't love me at all. Even if neither makes sense."

He kissed my lips again, his finger stroking my cheek. "They do make sense, and I've been feeling the same way. I'm glad we have it out in the open, though. I can't keep biting my tongue every time we make love, so I don't say the words wanting to tumble from my heart. Make no mistake that what we do here in this bed is not sex. It has been making love every time we've come together. I've felt it. I know you have, too."

I laughed, happiness filling every part of my heart. "It feels good," I whispered, running a fingertip down Beau's cheek. "It feels right, finally. I love you."

His chocolate eyes melted into deep puddles before my eyes. "I love you too, Dawn. Sometimes, I think my momma orchestrated everything in my life to make sure I was here, on this night, wrapped in your love."

I trailed my hand down his face to cup his chin. "Maybe she did, baby. If that's the case, I owe her a debt of gratitude. You are the best thing that's ever happened to me. Promise me tonight that you'll always come to me when you need reassurance, Beau. There will never be a time that I'm not here for you."

He leaned down and kissed my lips tenderly before he answered. "Not a hard promise to make, sweetheart. Now, I want you to promise me something." I nodded while he rested his lips on my forehead for a moment. "Never think you can't be honest with me about how you're feeling or if you're in pain, scared, or need help. This is a partnership. I don't ever want you to think you can't ask for help out of some misguided idea that you have to be strong all the time."

I chuckled and rose to kiss his lips. "It's like you know me or something," I said with laughter on my lips and happiness in my heart. "That's an easy promise to make because it feels natural to know you're my resting place."

Beau smiled and then kissed me like a man in love, his eyes glowing in the light from the lamp. "It does feel natural, doesn't it?" he asked, and I nodded again, my hand caressing his face. "It also feels sticky. Can I interest you in a shower, cowgirl?"

"Together?" I asked as he stood up and offered me his hand.

"I wouldn't have it any other way."

The barn was ready if it rained, but the weatherman had called for sunny skies and a warming trend by the time the wedding happened at three this afternoon. I didn't for one minute believe him, though, and decided to move all the horses to the pasture just to be on the safe side.

"Thanks for your help, Tex," I said as we finished cleaning the final stalls.

"No problem, Beau," he said, leaning on his pitchfork. "There aren't any guests at the ranch, so there's no need for me to hang around there. I'm glad Heaven blocked this week off. It would be hard to run the ranch and be here for the festivities."

"I'm just glad the day has finally arrived," I said, sitting down for a moment to rest. "We've been working nonstop already. It won't be long, and the red dogs will start arriving. It feels like this wedding is happening just in the nick of time."

"True, but at least Mr. and Mrs. McAwley are flying home and then heading back in the RV. You'll have a little extra help by the time the red dogs show up."

I waved my hand at my throat. "We don't need Ash's help. We have plenty of hands who know how to deal with these animals. Asking Ash to help is foolhardy and dangerous. Blaze and I have already agreed on that."

"Which is why I plan to keep him busy on the dude ranch," Tex said. "There is plenty for him to do there that's more his speed. I don't want anyone getting hurt either, especially Mr. McAwley."

I laughed and shook my head. "You don't know Ash very well yet, but I wish you the best of luck with keeping him at the dude ranch." I hung the tools back in the tack room and glanced around. "I think we're done here. We have a few hours before we have to get cleaned up and changed. Dawn is keeping Heaven busy at our place."

Tex followed me out of the barn, and we walked toward the house where Blaze was most likely wearing a hole in the carpet while Ash tried to keep him calm. Thankfully, we had reliable hands who would take the chores when the rest of us were busy with lace, tulle, and the I do's.

"I noticed Dawn sure is happy lately. Since dinner last week, come to think of it."

I was grateful I was in front of him and could roll my eyes without him seeing me. "Smooth, Tex," I said, chuckling. "Maybe it's because I finally told her I love her."

Tex grabbed my arm and spun me back toward him. "It's about damn friggin' time," he huffed. "You two are the reason I drink. Please tell me she admitted her undying love back so we can all move on from the last five years of painful unrequited adoration."

I shoved him in the shoulder, and he grabbed it, laughing at me in response. "You're a jerk."

"Who's a jerk?" Ash asked, coming down the steps of the house with Blaze.

"Tex," I said, pointing at the kid who stood grinning like a fool. "He thinks he's funny."

"He is funny," Blaze said, coming to a stop next to us. "Especially when he's hounding you about your puppy dog eyes for Dawn."

Tex gave him a high five, and they busted out laughing.

"You two are less mature than an hour old red dog," I huffed. "Whatever, dude who is about to tie himself to one woman for the rest of his life."

"Yeah," Blaze agreed, hands in his pockets, and his lips turned upward, "but she's beautiful and one hell of a woman."

"And you better not treat her poorly, or you will answer to me," Tex said, the warning real even if the tone was upbeat.

"Heard, accepted, and understood," Blaze agreed.

I clapped my hands together. "Okay, I think we have everything in order. The girls are at Heavenly Lane getting ready, and Amity is helping Cece with the catering. The barn is ready in case it does rain, and the horses are in the pasture."

Blaze turned his head to the endless blue sky for a moment. "Uh, Beau, did love sickness steal your eyesight?"

I turned and punched him in the shoulder, not even budging him from where he stood. "You're a jerk, too."

"Already widely accepted," Ash said, laughter in his voice. "I guess that means we have time for a cigar and a nice shot of brandy before we dude up and ride out."

"Dude up?" I asked, following them up the steps and through the screen door.

Blaze chuckled and shook his head. "Probably something they used 'back in the day,'" he said, putting air quotes around it.

I pulled him to a halt while Dad and Tex kept going into the kitchen. "Listen, I just wanted to say that if you need anything today, I'm here."

Blaze gave me a head nod. "Like you've always been, Beau. You're more my brother than those back in Texas. I know they couldn't come for logistical reasons, but it matters to me that the one who has stood by me all these years is the one who is here with me. Blood or no blood, you're always my brother."

I nodded and accepted his handshake. "Then I'm honored to stand by your side today in that capacity. Maybe you can return the favor someday."

He lifted a brow. "Someday soon?"

I made the so-so hand. "I'm thinking about it. It's probably time, don't you think?"

"You mean because it has taken you five years to get your head out of your Wranglers and figure out that Dawn is perfect for you?"

I slugged him again while laughing. "We haven't even been dating for a month."

Blaze tipped his head back and forth as though he was weighing something. "There's a difference between dating and bedding, Beau. They aren't equivalent."

"Says the guy who got in a fight with a woman at noon and was bedding her by midnight."

He huffed on his fingers and rubbed them on his shirt. "What can I say? I'm an animal. A real smooth talker. Nothing but a Casanova."

"Hang on. I need a barf bucket."

Blaze's laughter was loud and jovial. "All I'm saying is, if you know it's good, don't wait until it's too late. Though, you should probably introduce her as your girlfriend tonight, seeing as you were too much of a bonehead the other night to admit it. That said, I wouldn't even mind if you proposed to her tonight at the reception."

I started waving my hands desperately, my stuttering in full force to the point I couldn't get one word out. He laughed, bending over, and slapping his knee until I thought he was going to pass out from lack of oxygen.

"Dude, that was the best look of bison in the headlights I've ever seen."

I held up my finger to correct him but decided it wasn't worth it. "Have your laughs. You won't be laughing when that girl you're marrying comes walking up the aisle in the dress I've already seen," I said over my shoulder as I walked away. "Then, we can talk about bison in the headlights."

I stepped into the kitchen and heard his laughter turn into a groan.

"Oh, God, I can't do this," Heaven said, standing in front of the mirror. "I can't do this, Dawn. I'm going to throw up."

I stood behind her, my hands on her shoulders to steady her. "You can do this, Heaven. You've wanted to marry Blaze for as long as I've known you. You're not going to throw up, especially not wearing this gorgeous dress."

Heaven glanced down at the gown she wore. It was white, with cap lace sleeves, an empire waist, and an intricate lace overlay that cascaded to the floor where her new rose red boots stuck out from below it. The accent ribbon at the waist matched her boots and her flowers. The seamstress who had altered her gown had used the extra material from the bottom to make her a wedding day shoulder harness to hold her left arm tight to her side. Heaven always wore the brace now, and that told us how bad her arm had become. She didn't need it before the truck accident almost two years ago, but it never recovered enough from that accident to be pain free. I feel better knowing she has some relief from the pain when she wears it, though. Anything is better than it was back then.

"You're stunning. Blaze is going to forget how to breathe the moment he sees you."

"She's right," Amity said as she came into the room. "My son will never see this coming. I'll be surprised if he can utter the two words that he'll need to say to make you his wife."

Heaven finally smiled and let out a breath. "I'm petrified. I haven't been this nervous since I had to drive a white bison to South Dakota."

Amity and I both chuckled at her comparison. "While that was stressful," I said, "this is nothing to be petrified or nervous about, Heaven. In an hour, you're going to be married. After that, the hard stuff is over. Then we can hit back a shot and party like it's 1999."

Heaven turned away from the mirror and grinned. "I'm going to let those words run through my head the whole time I'm doing this."

"Whatever gets you through it, Heaven," Amity said, handing her a box. "Your something old."

I held the box in my hand so Heaven could take the lid off it. She glanced up at her soon-to-be mother-in-law. "What is it?" she asked, lifting the tiny silver ring from the box. "An earring?"

Amity shook her head. "No. It's Blaze's baby ring."

"His baby ring?" Heaven asked in confusion.

Amity smiled and took the ring, tying it to a ribbon in Heaven's flowers before she handed the bouquet to her. "It's something we do in our family. When a new baby is christened, they wear a small silver ring on their ring finger. Then the ring is saved as the first family keepsake for the child to take with them when they leave home. Every bride gets their husband's ring on their wedding day."

Heaven cocked her head and gazed at the woman in confusion. "Blaze has been married before, Amity."

She nodded, her eyes dropping to the floor for a moment. "I know, but we weren't here. Even if I'd had time to send it, I wouldn't have. I'm a mother, and I knew that Blaze and Callie were never meant to be. He tried to break it off with her before they left Texas."

"I know," Heaven agreed, nodding.

"Well, this time, I know. I have no doubt in my mind that you're Blaze's one true love. The ring you carry now, and the one he will put on your finger this afternoon, are the two rings that will join you together as a new family. Trust in that." Amity leaned forward and kissed Heaven on the cheek, patting my shoulder on the way to the door. "I'm heading back to Bison Ridge. See you in twenty?"

"See you in twenty," we both said in unison.

Heaven sighed once we were alone. "Do you think she's right?"

I spun back to the nervous bride in front of me. "I know she's right. Moms know things. Trust in that. Remember, you're only going to do this once, so don't let anxiety or fear steal a single second of your special day. Live every breath you take and love it all, even when things don't go perfectly. At the end of the day, you'll crawl into bed as Mrs. Heaven McAwley. That's the only thing you have to get right."

"And then we'll get busy making sure you are the next one to join the McAwley clan."

Heaven winked, turned, and walked out the door, her laughter filling my head and my heart.

Thirteen

Blaze and I nervously pulled at our ties where we stood at the front of the aisle. Everything had changed in the last two hours. Suddenly, I was not only the best man but also the wedding officiant. The judge they'd lined up to do the ceremony was in surgery for an emergency appendectomy, and while he would survive, he wasn't going to be asking these two if they do. Luckily for Blaze, I had officiated someone's wedding a few years back, so my internet rights gave me legal power to marry them. Tex would have to sign as the witness, but he didn't seem to mind.

So, here we stood, both of us nervous for different reasons. I'd seen Heaven's dress, but I hadn't seen Dawn's, and I wondered if I'd be able to speak once she stood beside me. She was drop-dead gorgeous in flannel and jeans that left me tongue-tied every time I saw her. I could only imagine how impossible it would be once I saw her in that dress. I'd probably stutter my way through the whole damn ceremony with no hope of stopping.

The music started, which meant that any minute, the women we loved would walk toward us, stealing our breath the same way they stole our hearts. I grabbed Blaze's shoulder in support, but in actuality, I was grounding myself. Dawn would be the first to come down that aisle. I inhaled deeply, holding it inside my chest as soon as she appeared. It whooshed from me loud enough that Blaze could hear, and he went from freakin' out to grinnin' in one step of her sweet cowgirl boots. Her dress was lace, red, came to the knee, and left nothing to my imagination. She wore the leather fringe vest I'd made her last year for her birthday over the dress, and it only served to accentuate her sweet breasts. I may have moaned.

"How are you even upright?" Blaze asked from the corner of his mouth.

"Sheer will," I muttered. "Your turn is next."

I smiled and took Dawn's hand to kiss when she was finally within reach. *You're so beautiful*, I mouthed, and that brought a smile to her lips. She stood next to me as the music changed, and Heaven and Ash appeared at the end of the rows of chairs. Heaven was a beautiful bride, but the wanton woman next to me held all my attention. The audience stood as the bride, and her escort began their walk toward us, revealing the whole picture to her groom. Blaze swallowed hard, tipping his hat back and fidgeting with his tie. Heaven wore a shy smile and a white lace shoulder harness that held her bad arm securely, so it blended in with her gown. The florist had made her a bouquet that slipped over her hand and stayed on her left wrist, leaving her right hand free to hold Blaze's.

"I'm going to faint," Blaze whispered as he knelt, the beauty of the woman he loved overpowering him.

I clasped his shoulder until he could stand again, then I leaned over and whispered into Dawn's ear. "Heaven is beautiful, but you take my breath away, darlin'. I love you."

Dawn was blushing when Heaven and Ash made it to us, but I had to turn my attention back to the ceremony at hand.

"Welcome everyone to the marriage of Blaze McAwley and Heaven Lane. None of us ever thought we'd see this day, did we?" I asked. The guests chuckled while nodding in agreement.

"Here we are, though, and so I ask, who gives this beautiful bride to the groom?"

Ash placed Heaven's hand in Blaze's. "Her father, Duane Lane, does. Of that, I am certain." Heaven's chin trembled, and she hugged Ash spontaneously the way a daughter would hug her father. Ash patted her face lovingly and then put her hand back in Blaze's before joining Amity again. Blaze lifted her hand and brushed a kiss across her knuckles while I spoke.

"Today, we gather together to join Blaze and Heaven in holy hell it's about dang time matrimony," I said, dragging laughter from everyone, including the bride and groom. "Welcome to the ranch on Bison Ridge. We promise the party to come is worth sitting here in the beautiful sunshine to watch these two profess their undying love to each other, which I'm quite certain they're about to do. Blaze, do you need to repeat after me, or do you got this?"

Blaze was still laughing when he reached out to punch my shoulder. "I most definitely got this. Heaven, my idiot brother was right. It has been a long journey to get us to this day. But we're here. We're standing in the sunshine, surrounded by our family and friends, and ready to share our vows. We're vowing to love each other through all the good times and the bad. Through sickness and health. To cherish each other every day. While I could easily repeat those simple vows and slip this ring on your finger, there is so much more to say. I vow to appreciate all the little things in life, like nights at the campfire, lazy Saturday mornings in bed, a cold winter morning filled with laughter around the Christmas tree, and warm summer nights watching the fireworks fly high into the sky. Life here can be hard, draining, and repetitive, but our time together will be the greatest reward to cherish. I love you today, tomorrow, and for eternity, Heaven Marie Lane. With this ring," he said, holding it up as Heaven's lip trembled, "I do." He slid the ring onto her right ring finger, signifying their uniqueness as a couple in one motion.

Heaven turned and took the ring from Dawn, who gave her an encouraging smile. "It has been a long road, hasn't it?" she asked, clearing her throat while Blaze offered her another smile. "We've been through more together than most couples go through in a lifetime, yet here we are, still fighting for this thing called love. We have so much living to do, and I can't wait to get started. I can't wait for those nights by the campfire and lying out under the stars while the bison snuffle. We'll ride our horses to visit my daddy and, hopefully, one day, teach our children about the legacy of Bison Ridge and Heavenly Lane. Our legacy of love and laughter, joy and happiness, pain and sorrow through the good and bad times. That is what we've learned together over the painful years that have passed. There is no roadmap for our love, just uncharted fields, and wild paths for us to explore. I loved you yesterday, I love you today, and I will love you for every tomorrow and until I reach the home I am named for, Blaze. With this ring, I do," she whispered, sliding the ring onto his finger.

Heaven had the band specially made. It was titanium and had a never-ending trail of bison around it made from onyx, with one in the middle made from mother of pearl. It was a beautiful reminder of the trip last summer that finally set them on the right path.

I raised my hands to the audience with laughter on my lips. "Looks like they did my job for me. All I have left to say is this, by the power vested in me by the internet and the State of Wisconsin, I now pronounce you man and wife. Blaze, for God's sake, kiss your bride!"

Blaze let out a whoop and grabbed Heaven, bending her over carefully for a kiss none of us would soon forget.

"Good thing we rechecked the fence line," Tobi, Heavenly Lane's new ranch hand, said as we rode back into the clearing.

"Agreed. With that many guests at the bottom of the hill and the herd at the top, it would have been a bad scene if the bison had gotten out. Thanks for following that tingling at the back of your neck. You may have saved lives."

Tobi grabbed Cloudy Day's reins after I dismounted. "No problem, Beau. The animals had bedded down anyway, so I'm sure it would have been fine, but I'm glad we found that hole in the fence and closed it up. Enjoy the rest of your night. I'll put the horse to bed in the barn at Heavenly Lane."

"Thanks, Tobi," I called as she led our horses away.

I jogged toward the giant bonfire where the wedding party had gathered. It had been a long day, followed by a cold night, but most guests had left after the dance. When it cooled considerably after dinner, we did some line dancing in the barn rather than the tent where we held the dinner. I made Blaze eat a little bit of crow since he heckled me so much about having the barn ready for the wedding. We'd had a good time until Tobi rode in, sounding the alarm.

"Did you get it taken care of?" Blaze asked when he noticed me walking toward the fire.

"Nothing to worry about," I said, even though it was. The hole in the fence was extensive and would easily have allowed one of the large animals out to roam. God help us if they had decided to stampede. "It only took a few minutes to repair. We rode the rest of the fence to make sure we were okay. We'll check again in the morning. Don't worry your pretty little head about it," I said when I reached the fire ring.

Blaze punched me playfully on the shoulder and shook said pretty head. "I would have helped."

"Not on your wedding day. Besides, it was an easy fix. I see most of the guests have departed."

Heaven came over and took her husband's arm. "Chores come early tomorrow for all of our rancher friends." She leaned in close to my ear and whispered. "Please, take Dawn home. She's tired. The cold is making her stiff and sore, too. I couldn't get her to go without you."

I glanced over to the fire, where Dawn sat wrapped in a blanket in a lawn chair while talking to Amity. "I was worried about the same. I'll take her home in the truck. It will be warmer that way."

Heaven hugged me tightly with one arm. "Thank you for everything today. Without you, not only would we not be married, but we wouldn't have laughed nearly as much or had as few hiccups in the day as we did. Take the day off tomorrow, Beau. You deserve it."

I patted her back and handed her back to Blaze. "How about I sleep in and show up around ten? I have some work to do on the fences before red dogs start showing up. I don't want to miss my window."

Blaze slapped me on the back. "Sounds great. We're turning in, too. It's been a long day."

We all waved them off as Blaze and Heaven ran for the door, Blaze scooping her up off her feet and whooping as he carried her through the door of the farmhouse, slamming it behind him with the heel of his boot.

I turned to Ash and Amity. "Where are you two bunking tonight? I don't think you want to go in there?"

Ash snorted and pointed at me. "You couldn't pay me enough. Amity moved our stuff over to the dude ranch to stay in the quarters for a few days. We were thrilled when Dawn suggested it. It gives the new couple some time to be alone without the parents in the house. Besides, the bunkhouse at Heavenly Lane reminds us of home."

"Good thinking," I said, massaging Dawn's shoulders. "I need to get her home. Do you want a ride?"

Ash shook his head. "I promised Blaze we'd make sure everything was squared away tonight and put the fire out. Take Dawn home and warm her up. She's not in good shape. We tried to get her into the house, but she refused."

"She is sitting right here," Dawn said from the chair while everyone around us laughed. "They're right, though. I'm not in good shape. A hot shower and some medication will help."

She stood gingerly, grimacing when she took a step, so I grasped her waist and held her close to me. "The truck is by the house. Let me bring it over."

She patted my chest twice. "I'm fine," she promised, then hugged Amity and Ash. "Thanks for a lovely evening. Let's do breakfast tomorrow?"

"Sounds like a great way to start the day," Amity agreed.

"Oh," Ash said, digging in his pocket and pulling out a small envelope. "This came addressed to you about a week before we left. Since we were coming here, I just brought it along. I thought it was odd because you haven't lived at the ranch for years."

I took it and checked the envelope. "No return address, either."

"I figured it was an old high school friend or maybe about your class reunion," Amity said. "The postmark is Dallas. Have a good night, dear," she said, kissing my cheek while I tucked the envelope in my pocket.

"Thanks, Ma— err, Miss Amity," I corrected.

The woman in front of me melted for a moment before she squeezed my arm. "Just Ma will do, Beau. Just Ma will do."

"Okay, just Ma. We'll see you tomorrow." The raw emotion was audible in our voices, so I winked just to keep the tears at bay.

I helped Dawn into the truck and turned the heat on to warm her. The drive to Heavenly Lane was short, but I was afraid it was too late to keep her from hurting all day tomorrow.

Dawn rested her hand on my arm in the darkness. "You probably made her year right there, Beau."

I shrugged, keeping my eyes pinned to the dark road barely illuminated by the headlights of the truck. "I've slipped up and called Amity that before when I was younger. Tonight was just the first time she ever jumped on it."

"She jumped on it because you made her feel secure in your relationship now. That matters. You matter. To them and me. I love you."

I pulled the truck down the lane and parked it in front of the house. "I love you, too. So much so I'm going to carry you inside." I jumped down from the truck and carefully lifted her into my arms. Once we were in her room, I set her on the bed and pulled off her boots. "A shower and then bed, cowgirl."

Dawn opened the nightstand and took out her pillbox, tossing some back and swigging them down with water. "I think I'll need help in the shower tonight," she said as she stripped off the vest in a seductive manner, her voice smokey. "Know anyone who can hold me while I soap up?"

I pulled the bolo tie from around my neck and shed my jacket, starting on the buttons of my shirt. "Darlin', I'm your man," I promised right before I did what I'd wanted to do since I first saw her in that dress. Rip it off her.

The birds had woken me at my usual time, so I grabbed my clothes and cleaned up in the main bathroom to avoid waking Dawn. It was early, but when you've lived the last decade of your life getting up with the sun, that's not going to change just because you want to sleep in one day. I was now in no man's land. I couldn't go back to Bison Ridge and wake Blaze and Heaven, but I didn't want to wake Dawn either. With any luck, Tex was up and had coffee made. I'd grab a cup before I saddled up Cloudy Day and rode back to the ranch to check on the animals and the fences. What's the saying, a cowboy's work is never done? It was true, but I wouldn't have it any other way.

I grabbed last night's pants to find my wallet, and I encountered the letter Ash had given me. Distracted by a beautiful naked woman, I had forgotten all about it. I flipped it over a couple of times in my hand, wondering who it was from before I finally slid my finger under the flap to open it. It was probably some lame invitation to a class reunion I wasn't the least bit interested in attending. If that were the case, Blaze probably would have mentioned it, though. Since they didn't bring one for him and we graduated together, that would be odd.

I snuck out of Dawn's room and into mine, where I pulled out the single sheet of paper. I unfolded it, a picture of myself at about nine or ten falling to my lap. I picked it up and stared at it for a moment before I scanned and rescanned the sheet of paper. I couldn't make the words make sense.

"Beau," I read aloud, hoping that would help. "My name is Travis Pollard, and I was recently released from a Dallas jail. I wanted to get this off my chest with what time I have left on this earth. I am dying of pancreatic cancer, and the doctors have given me a month to live. For that reason, I am sending this letter before I go. I'm your father, Beau. I haven't lived a good life, and I would not have made a good father. Your momma knew that which is why she did everything she could to protect you from me. I wanted nothing to do with being a father, and you were all the better for it. That said, your mother's death was due in part to me. The night she died, I broke in with a friend, both of us high and looking for money. I knew Samantha would give it to us just to get rid of me. What happened after we broke in was not in the cards. My friend refused to let her live, said she'd turn us into the cops. I tried to stop him, Beau. I know you won't believe me, but I did. I've included the picture I took from the house that night, so you know I'm telling you the truth. I never wanted to hurt your momma. Samantha was a good, kind woman who did everything she could to help people. I am not looking for forgiveness or for a way into heaven. I am telling you this so you may find peace about her death that you haven't had in twenty years. If I can offer you that now, I can go to the grave knowing I will suffer the fate I deserve, but you will no longer suffer from not knowing the truth. Travis."

The letter fell to my lap, and I picked up the picture, flipping it over to see my momma's handwriting on the back: Beau ~ fourth grade. My world tipped on its axis to see that writing again after so many years. I crumpled the paper into a ball and smashed it against my forehead. The moment I had feared my entire life had arrived. I knew who had killed my momma. Now, I had to be the man she raised me to be. I had to make it right. I had to avenge her death. An eye for an eye.

No one could save me now.

"Cece, that was amazing," I said, washing down the pancakes and eggs with a sip of coffee. "No wonder every review mentions the food as the reason they gave the dude ranch five stars. You deserve every one of them."

Cece grinned and wiped her mouth before she spoke. "I've always loved cooking, but I hated the restaurant atmosphere. I love the way the cowboys moan and groan as they enjoy a good steak after a long day. The way they wake up with anticipation to see what I'll have on the table for their first meal. It's invigorating and keeps me motivated to come up with new ideas. Amity has sure helped me a lot with new recipes this week."

Amity blushed and brushed her hand at Cece. "I raised a lot of boys while feeding a lot of men. You learn how to take what you have and make new and exciting things with it. I like your idea of keeping it fresh and wholesome for the guests. Hopefully, you can use some of those new recipes I gave you to keep that going."

"I will start incorporating them once you bring me those bags of peppers you promised," Cece said. "You can't get those around here."

Tex nodded and pointed at Cece while he chewed. "I gotta travel to Duluth to get a decent bag of dried peppers. Can't wait to try some real Texas peppers."

Ash shook his head. "Y'all gonna burn the daylights out of your mouth and stomach. You'll have to be careful. Wisconsin and Texas are a long way apart from each other, in distance and peppers."

"Ask Beau. He knows," Amity said, laughing. "Speaking of Beau, where is he? Did he head to the ranch already?"

"He wasn't there when I was," Tex said around the eggs in his mouth. "Jamison was looking for him, too. They have some serious problems with fences up there. I had to help them close more holes. Blaze is spitting mad. He thought he was sleeping in."

My heart started to pound, and I lowered my fork to the plate. "That isn't like Beau," I said, shaking my head. "He never shirks his duties. I know he got up with the birds this morning. That was hours ago now. I thought he'd gone to the ranch." I took my phone out and checked it, surprised when it showed the text hadn't been sent. I held up the phone. "I texted him earlier to meet us here for breakfast. His truck was gone when I got up this morning." I stood quickly and headed for the door. "I'm going to go check the house and see if he came back."

Everyone followed me out the door, and we hurried toward the house, which was too far away for my liking. I wanted to run, the urgency spurring my feet forward, but at the same time, I didn't want to alarm anyone. The fact that the text didn't go through told me his phone was off or wherever he was, there was no service.

I burst through the back door and hurried to his room, glancing around it. Nothing looked amiss until Amity pointed at the bed. "That's the envelope from the letter Ash gave him last night."

I picked it up and flipped it over a couple of times. "It's empty."

It was Ash who noticed a crumpled piece of paper on the floor and picked it up. He uncrumpled it and started to read. The further he got into it, the more desperate his voice became. When he finished reading, we stood in shock for several minutes before everyone started to talk at once.

Tex finally whistled until everyone was silent. "Dawn, when do you think he left?"

"Easily four hours ago," I answered, checking the clock. "Maybe a little bit less."

Ash was tapping the paper on his pant leg and grimacing.

"Say it, Ash," I ordered, stomping my foot. "Whatever you're thinking, say it."

"He once told me if he ever found out who killed his momma, he'd take them out himself. An eye for an eye and all that. He was a hotheaded kid back then, and I told him that violence shouldn't beget violence. I told him he should leave it to the courts."

I motioned at the letter in his hand. "Why would he do that, though? The guy says right out that he's going to die. He could already be dead. That letter is weeks old!"

Amity took my upper arm and held it tightly. "Beau isn't thinking logically right now, Dawn. He just found out who his daddy is and that he killed his momma. Beau has kept Samantha on a pedestal for years. Now that he knows that she died at the hands of the man who created him, Beau will not process that well, especially when he's alone."

My chin fell to my chest in frustration. "I was cold and sore last night, so he didn't open the letter because we fell asleep." That wasn't the entire truth, but I wasn't about to go into my sexcapades with Beau's parents. "He must have read it this morning when I was sleeping. I should have gotten up when I heard him get up!"

"Shhh, child," Amity said, her calmness what I needed right now. "We'll find him. How far can he get in four hours?"

"It's a little bit under four hours to get to the Cities," Tex said, looking up from his phone. "There are nonstop flights from Minneapolis to Dallas later this afternoon."

Ash let out a cuss word I could tell Amity disapproved of, but one that we were all feeling. "We may not be able to catch him in time."

I stood in the bedroom, shaking my head. Anger filled me at the man who wrote the letter and at Beau. "He should have come to me!" I exclaimed. "Dammit!"

Amity lovingly put her arm around me and leaned in. "We'll find him. I know Beau. I know he flies off the handle immediately, but his common sense eventually returns. He's a cowboy. He reacts first and thinks second. We'll find him."

"Okay, but we have to pray Beau thinks before he gets on a plane and throws his life away."

Ash spoke next. "Let's call the airport and see if he's bought a ticket."

"I don't think they can tell you that," I said, but he was already out the door with his phone to his ear. I turned to Amity. "I'm taking my truck and heading toward the Cities. I have to stop him."

"You can't go alone," she said, looking to Tex. "Can you go with her?"

"No, I'm going alone," I said, shaking my head. "If I find him, I don't want him to think we are ganging up on him."

"He hasn't bought a ticket," Ash said, coming back into the room. "At least not for any flights today."

"Do you think he's driving to Dallas?" I asked, my nerves jumping to do something, anything, to find him.

"Doubtful that his truck would make it that far," Tex said. "Doubtful that truck would even make it to the Cities. He took the old ranch one."

I stood there, my hand grasping my neck as I thought about Beau and what I knew about his past. "Amity, where was his mother buried?"

"She wasn't. She left her body to science. While Samantha was murdered and didn't die of natural causes, they still took her body to study the effects of lupus on her organs. She always told Beau that she didn't want to be remembered in one place. Samantha wanted to be remembered everywhere. She wanted him to remember her every time a bird flew over the horizon, when the apple blossoms bloomed on the trees, and when the waves washed over his toes. Samantha always knew she would die young, and she worked to prepare Beau for that. She told him to look for her in nature, not at a gravestone, for she wouldn't be there."

"I wish I had met her. She must have been a fantastic woman," I said, my mind picturing all those things she'd mentioned. I snapped my fingers and stared at her in shock. "I know where he is!"

"Where?" Ash asked in confusion. "How can you know?"

"Trust me!" I yelled over my shoulder as I ran for the back room where my keys hung. "Ash, ride with me. When we get there, I want you to drive his truck back. The spare key is on the hook," I said, motioning toward it before I grabbed my coat.

I hugged Amity and then Tex. "I'll bring him back. Just promise me you'll be patient and don't crowd him. Let me talk him through this, and then I'll bring him home."

"We trust you, Dawn," Amity promised as I ran out the door with Ash on my heels.

If Beau was where I thought he was, it was over an hour before we could get to him. If he wasn't, then it was time wasted. Until Beau reached out, all I could do was follow my gut and my heart. They both told me I would find him watching the birds fly over the horizon with the waves lapping over his toes while he searched for the answers he so desperately needed.

Fourteen

I gazed up at the sky, where the seagulls swooped over the water. What they were looking for, I didn't know. What I was looking for, I didn't know. I tossed a rock into the water and watched an eagle fly over me while it searched for fish.

I probably knew what I was looking for if I wanted to admit it to myself. I was looking for peace. I hadn't had peace in twenty years. That letter and the man behind it didn't offer me peace. All that letter did was create more turmoil and pain. No matter how hard I tried, I was on a slippery slope, and I still hadn't found a foothold to grab.

I turned my face to the sky. *What do I do now, momma?*

I waded into the water to let the cold waves lap over my feet. Momma always told me I should look for her in the birds as they flew in the sky and the water as it rippled over my toes. I walked into the water until it touched my knees. The cold, stark reality of Lake Superior gripped my calves and turned them numb almost immediately. It only took a few more steps before I was up to my hips. My hands balanced on the water, the waves tippling over my fingers as the sun shone down on me. It was beautiful. The water was peaceful. It would be more peaceful under the water, I bet. There, no one would demand anything of me. No one would expect from me the things I couldn't give them. Under the water was where momma lived. She lived in a place that was peaceful and full of promise.

"Beau!"

"Momma?" I asked the air as I lowered myself to my chest.

"Beau! Stop!" the voice called again, closer this time.

It was Dawn.

"Go home, Dawn Lee," I yelled without turning. "You don't want any part of this!"

"You're wrong," she yelled back. "I want every part of this. I read the letter, Beau. Come back to the beach and talk to me."

I shook my head, my hands bobbing in the water. "I'm where I need to be, Dawn. You don't need to be here. You're interrupting my search for peace. I don't want you here."

"You're not going to find peace under that water, Beauregard Theodore Hanson. Turn around and come back to me. We can talk this out. We can find a way through it."

"Leave me the hell alone, Dawn! I didn't ask for your help!" I yelled, anger bubbling up inside me. "Go home to Heavenly Lane and forget that you ever met me. You're far better off that way. Everyone is!"

"You're wrong," she said from behind me. Dawn was closer now, and I scrunched my eyes shut to keep from turning around. "Blaze is holding Heaven, trying to offer her comfort as she cries tears of worry. Cece and Amity are cooking aimlessly to have something to do while they wait for us to find you. Tex is riding the ridges, fixing holes in the fences, and taking care of the animals because he knows you'd do the same for him. Ash is standing on this beach, ready to pull your crazy cowboy butt out of the water if he must. No one, most especially me, is better off without you, Beau McAwley."

"Hanson. It's Beau Hanson! Hell, if you read that letter, it's Beau Pollard, bastard son of a murderer!"

"No. You're Beau Hanson by birth, but you are Beau McAwley. That is the man you are in your heart," she said from behind me.

When I spun to face her, she was up to her waist in the frigid water. One strong wave was going to drag her under and out into the lake. I didn't even care. I warned her to walk away. Instead, she walked in. That wasn't on me. That was on her.

Think about that, son. Instead of walking away, she walked in. What does that tell you?

I glanced up at the sky, looking for the voice but finding nothing but puffy, white clouds. "Dawn, go home. Go home before you get hurt, or this water freezes up your joints. I didn't ask for your help, and I don't want it."

Dawn swung her head back and forth, her hair blowing in the breeze. "You didn't ask for my help, and that's the problem, Beau. When you read that letter, you should have run to me, not away from me. You promised me you would always run to me. We could have talked about it together instead of you risking your life out here."

"Can't a man just be alone?" I exploded, throwing my arms up into the air. "I just want to be alone."

"A man can be alone when he needs to be," she agreed, without wavering. "But that is not what you need right now. Right now, you need your family. You need to be surrounded by people who love you. You need to be surrounded by people who know who you are, even when you don't!"

She's right, son. They all know who you are. You might think you don't know who you are, but you do. Listen to her. Listen to me. Listen to the water and the birds. You are my son. You are the adopted son of Amity and Ash. You are no one else's son.

My eyes closed, and I inhaled deeply through my nostrils at the voice. "I'm no good for you, Dawn," I said, opening my eyes to find her gaze trained on me. "I'm just like him!"

Dawn rolled her eyes. She just stood in the middle of such a powerful force of nature like Lake Superior and rolled her eyes. That gave me pause.

"By him, I assume you mean the man claiming to be your father in that letter?" she asked. "I say assume because you don't know that he is. Even if he is, who cares. It's not going to matter in another few weeks when he leaves this earth. You matter. What you do matters."

"And the first thing I thought to do when I read that letter was fly to Dallas and kill him! I wanted to kill him with my own hands just like he did my mother!" My anger made me shake more than the cold water. I was numb to everything but the truth. "I'm just as evil as the man who made me, Dawn. You don't want me in your life. I will ruin and tarnish the beauty that you are. You can't trust me that way. I could hurt you without even thinking about it."

"No!" she exclaimed, her body shaking. Whether it was with anger or cold, I couldn't say, but her fierceness hushed me instantly. "You would never hurt me, Beau. That is one thing I know for absolute sure." She'd stuck her finger in my chest, but after I blinked, she had disappeared.

"Dawn!" I screamed, searching for her under the water, the numbness in my fingers and legs making it harder than it should have been to grasp her coat when I brushed against it. I hauled her up and into my arms, struggling through the waves to get her onto the beach. "Daddy!" I yelled at the top of my lungs. The massive body of water stole the word, so I screamed again. "Daddy!"

Ash snapped to attention finally and started running toward me.

"You're right. He is your daddy," Dawn said, wrapping her arms around my neck while her teeth chattered. "That man is your father. No one else, Beau Hanson McAwley."

I laid her down in the warm sand, covering her as much as I could with the top layer until Ash reached me. "What happened?" he asked, concern evident on his face.

"She got mad and took a step too far. We need to warm her up quickly."

Ash searched around in Dawn's pocket and came up with a key. "Take her in her truck. It will stay warmer. I'll drive yours back to the ranch."

"I'm fine," she said, her teeth chattering. "I wasn't in the water that long."

I scooped her up and into me again, the sand covering both of us in our wet clothes, but I couldn't think about anything but warming her up. "You will be fine once I get you home and into a warm bed."

I followed Ash toward the wooden walkway with her holding onto my neck tightly. "I'll let Ma know that we're headed back," he said over his shoulder. "What do you need from her?"

"Time," I said, gazing down into Dawn's face. "Time and understanding."

When we reached the trucks, Ash helped me get Dawn inside and wrapped her in an old blanket I found behind the seat. "We understand, Beau," he assured me, his hand on my shoulder. "I know you think we don't, but we do. We always have, son. You don't go through the things you went through and not have it change who you are at your very core. The thing is, you get to decide how it changed you. It can make you the man you were last night. The man who stepped up and made sure his brother's wedding went off without a hitch, and the man who helped keep everyone safe by patching the fence. You can continue to be changed by the past in a positive way. After all, I think that's what Samantha would have wanted the most." He gave me a hug, his clothes getting wet and sandy, but he didn't seem to care. "I'm going to take the truck back to Bison Ridge. You take Dawn to Heavenly Lane and let us know if you need anything. We love you, Beau. Always have, always will. Don't lose sight of that when all you can see and hear are the words of that letter."

I hugged him again in understanding and gratefulness before I climbed into the truck. I turned the engine over and flipped the heat to high. Dawn was shivering next to me, but the color was back in her cheeks, and her lips weren't blue. I noticed a pile of clothing on the floor and couldn't bite back the smile.

"They were making me colder," she said, her hands holding the blanket around herself tightly. "Don't worry. I'm still wearing my underwear."

"I wasn't worried one way or the other," I said, backing out and following Ash out of the parking area. "I'm just glad you're okay. I'm so sorry, Dawn. I shouldn't have put you at risk like that. Do you understand what I meant when I said I could hurt you without even trying?"

"No," she said, letting go of the blanket to grasp my shoulder. "I didn't fall on accident, Beau."

"What?" I asked, completely confused. "It wasn't on purpose. You fell into the lake because you were trying to get to me."

Her head swung back and forth. "No, I went under the water on purpose. I could touch the bottom. I wasn't in danger, but I was proving a point."

I growled, my heart still thudding double time from the adrenaline of her being in danger. "You could have died. As it is, your joints are going to hurt for days."

"It will be worth it because I made my point."

"Did you? Because I still don't know what it was."

"The moment you thought I was in danger, you reacted. You risked your own life to make sure I was safe. You took charge, ordered Ash around, warmed me the only way you could, and protected me. You are not the kind of man who is going to hurt me. You're the kind of man who is going to protect, heal, and love me. Ash and the rest of the family see that in everything you do. Somewhere deep down, you know that's true."

"I don't know what to think," I admitted, my eyes focused on the road in front of me. "Everything inside me is spinning around like the waves of Lake Superior."

Dawn squeezed my shoulder gently while she nodded. "I know, and no one expects you to get that kind of news and then know how to feel about it immediately. Let us help you through it, Beau. Trust the people you've made your family, please. I love you, Beau. I can't lose you now."

Her hand fell to the truck seat, and I rubbed it for a moment. "When I was out there in the water, I heard a voice. I know it was momma from wherever she is now. She said instead of walking away, you walked in. She told me to think about that. Instead of walking away, you wa—walked in." I cleared my throat to keep it from cracking.

"I always will, Beau. You mean that much to me. Whether we stay lovers or go back to being friends, I will always walk in."

"I love you, Dawn. I love you for always walking in."

She brushed a kiss across my knuckles before releasing my hand. "And I love you for running to me when I need you. As long as we keep running to each other instead of away, we're going to be just fine."

I rode along the fence line on Bison Ridge, checking the pastures for the promised red dogs that had begun to arrive over the last two weeks. Sure enough, a few tiny, and by tiny, I mean seventy-pound animals, stood dwarfed by their mothers in the pasture. There weren't many yet, but that would change quickly. Bison have their babies from April through June, and we were only in the early weeks of May. There would be many more to come.

Life had calmed down in some ways since Heaven's wedding. Ash and Amity had stayed a few extra days with Beau before they flew back to Dublin to put their business in order. When they returned with the RV, they parked it behind the barracks at Heavenly Lane. Sure, they could have parked on Bison Ridge property, but Amity and Ash had plans to participate in dude ranch activities, so it made sense for them to be closer to our ranch than Blaze's. Secretly, they wanted to give Blaze and Heaven time to be newlyweds and be closer to Beau, who needed them a whole lot more than Blaze did right now.

Since that day at the lake, Beau had calmed down considerably. He was still shaken by the news, especially once he found the obituary online for the man who sent him the letter. He had passed before Amity and Ash had arrived in Wisconsin. Now, Beau couldn't prove that Travis was his father or that he'd killed his mother. He struggled with it as much as he had struggled with not knowing who had killed her over the last twenty years. I was confident Beau would find his way through it, though. Instead of running away from me, he was running to me, just like he promised. Even if Beau was angry, he didn't try to destroy the life he'd built for himself since he was a boy. Over the last few weeks, he had gone back to his leatherwork, started new projects to improve Bison Ridge fencing, and was living in what was now his new normal.

I guess you could say I was doing the same. As the weather warmed up, my joints didn't hurt quite as much. Then again, that could be from being on consistent medication. It could also be because I had someone who loved me looking after me now. Beau was always mindful of my joints and never pushed me to do more than I could. Usually, he was the one telling me I had to take it easy after a long day. He was never wrong, but I was slowly learning how to do that.

Last weekend, I had my first group of women come to stay at Heavenly Lane. They were there for a work retreat to brainstorm new ideas, do some team-building activities, and enjoy the fun at the ranch, like horseback riding and campfires every night. They had a blast and promised to tell their friends about us. I already had every weekend in June and July booked, and honestly, I could see that if I had a second bunkhouse, I could book bigger groups for a week instead of just a weekend.

I planned to discuss it with Heaven and Tex at our next board meeting. If we started work on it this summer, it would be ready for next summer. The house limited the number of women we could have in the groups and required me to be on call every second of the weekend. At least if they were in a separate bunkhouse, everyone had time to themselves. The women's retreats added extra work to my already full plate, so I could see that we'd quickly be hiring Landry to work full-time. The ranches were growing, and no one would be happier about that than Duane Lane. His legacy was alive and well, even if that legacy looked just a little bit different than he'd planned.

Ahead I noticed flames shooting into the sky, so I urged Black Beauty forward toward the gathering around the fire. I could make out all my favorite people sitting around it, laughing and drinking. Soon, Cece would bring out a platter of bison burgers, and we'd laugh, eat, and smile the way we had for the last few weeks. A week ago, we all went to the courthouse and stood next to Beau while the McAwleys finally adopted the man they'd loved like a son since he was a boy. It was a day to celebrate, and he had changed his name to Beau Hanson-McAwley as a tribute to the woman who started to raise him and the people who finished the job.

I reached the outskirts of the fire and dismounted, hooking the reins to the old-fashioned hitching post by the porch before I joined everyone around the fire.

Beau kissed my cheek and wrapped his arms around me as soon as I reached him. "Did you see the red dogs?"

I gazed up at him and smiled. "I did. They're my favorite part of living here. Not many out there yet. How many are you expecting?"

"Could be fifty more," Blaze said from the other side of the fire. "It's not an exact science when the herd is allowed to roam. I'm hoping for upwards of seventy-five, but I'd be happy with fifty."

Cece came out with the promised burgers just as I sat down, which we promptly made disappear. The darkness had gathered while we ate, and once the burgers were gone, we relaxed back in our chairs to watch the fire and discuss the day.

"Beautiful night out tonight," I said, leaning my head on Beau's shoulder. "I can't wait for summer nights with our guests around the fire and laughter in the air. Bison Ridge has become one big extended family, and it makes my heart happy to be part of it."

Blaze smiled and nodded, his eyes only for his new bride. "Heaven and I agree. To that end, we wanted to tell you all that we're going to be adding to that family."

Heaven gazed at him for a moment before she spoke. "I'm having a baby!"

Everyone started talking at once until Tex stuck his fingers in his mouth and whistled. "One at a time!" he yelled until we all quieted. "Me, first. When, where, how, and why?"

Blaze almost choked with laughter but answered him anyway. "January. The bedroom or maybe the barn? Do I really need to explain how?"

We were all laughing now, but Heaven held up her hand to let her finish. "Why is simple. We want to start the new generation on Bison Ridge. We might be the first, but we won't be the last."

Amity waved her hand in the air. "But you just got married. You can't be due in January already."

Blaze grinned and took Heaven's hand in his. "Let's face it, Ma. We weren't exactly virgins when we got married." He threw his hand against his chest. "I know, I know, I'm sorry to crush your fantasy world, but the truth is what it is."

Heaven shook her head at his dramatics. "We decided to start trying before the wedding once we did the math. I can't be due when the red dogs are and when the work around the ranch intensifies. We had to plan it carefully. If I didn't get pregnant so I was due before spring, we would have stopped trying until that window opened again. I know you understand, Amity."

Amity jumped up and hugged them both fiercely, patting Heaven's face when she stepped back. "Darlin', we all understand. I don't care how this little one came to be. I'm just thrilled they have come to be." She looked up at the sky for a moment. "Let it be a she."

Everyone burst out laughing because if there was one thing missing in the McAwley family, it was a girl to call their own. I got up and hugged Heaven tightly, too.

"I love you, girl. Anything you need, I'm here to do it. I will be the best auntie this little one has ever had. I'm so happy for you both." I hugged Blaze next while everyone shared hugs, handshakes, and congratulations.

Blaze put his hand on Ash's shoulder. "You know what this means, right?" he asked. Ash glanced up at him for a moment, shaking his head. "There are plans for a grandparent's cottage on my desk. Next week we can discuss where you want it on the property and any changes you want to make. It's a prefabricated one, so it won't take long to get it set up. We know you'll want to be here when the baby arrives, but an RV in the middle of a Wisconsin winter is going to be a little too drafty."

Amity burst into tears, hugged her son again, and then jumped up and down. "I can't believe it. I'm so excited to be a grandma again!"

Heaven took Amity's hand and squeezed it. "I'm going to need help with a new baby until I learn how to do it one-handed. We knew we could count on you without even asking."

Amity melted when she hugged Heaven again, gentler this time. The understanding between them was palpable as they held each other. "You can always count on me, but I know you're going to be the best mom, even better than me, one arm or two arms. Your heart is so big that your child will need nothing else."

I sat on Beau's lap and hugged him around his neck, kissing him gently on the lips. "I love you, Uncle Beau."

He chuckled and kissed me back, his tongue taking a tour of my mouth until everyone started gagging with exaggeration while yelling, *get a room*!

We broke apart laughing, and Beau pointed at his brother. "You might be the first to bring a red dog into this world, but you won't be the last."

"Do not refer to my child as a red dog!" Heaven exclaimed with laughter. "There will be none of that!"

Beau held up his hand while I scooted off his lap and sat in my chair. "Never again, but I can't wait to teach the little munchkin about our fantastical beasts and their babies. Before those babies arrive, I have something else to do." He knelt in front of me and took my hand, his eyes glowing with a seriousness I'd never seen before.

"Beau, what are you doing?" I asked in a whisper.

He reached into his shirt pocket and produced a ring that glinted in the light from the fire. "I was fixin' to ask you to marry me. That's why I'm down here on one knee holdin' up a ring. This ring used to be my momma's. She got it from her momma, who got it from her momma. There are generations of love, laughter, happiness, pain, and grief inside that diamond, but it also holds hope. I've had it all these years ha—ha—hoping one day I would put it on the finger of the woman who would carry on the tradition of strong wa—wa—women in my family."

I took his face in my hands and rubbed my thumbs over the corners of his mouth as a reminder he could take as much time as he needed with no judgment.

He cleared his throat and smiled up at me. "I was going to take you up to the ridge and ask you to marry me under the stars but decided everyone here deserved to witness it, at least in my opinion. They matter to us. They matter to me. They are the only reason I can kneel here tonight and ask the woman I love with my whole soul to marry me. Da—da—" He cleared his throat again and changed the direction of his jaw. "Dawn Briar Lee," he said, this time nothing but determination was heard in his words, "you have been my best friend for years. You have taught me to be the kind of man I want to be, taught me to be the kind of man I should be, and taught me that the only family that matters is right here. So tonight, in front of all of them, I ask you the question I've wanted to ask you since the first day we met. I didn't know the long walk we would take to get here or the things we'd learn about each other along the way, but I know this isn't the end. It's only the beginning. There will be times I have to carry you, and there will be times you have to carry me, but as long as we're together, neither will be a burden. I didn't know I had the power to love like this until I met you, Dawn. I came alive that day for the first time. I—I just pray tonight you'll agree to become Dawn Briar Hanson-McAwley. I know it's a mouthful."

Everyone chuckled, and my lips lifted upward at the idea of my name changing in a way that said you belong to someone. You are loved by someone who wants you to have what they have.

"My ma—ma—ma taught me that life is wonderful, but her death ta—ta—taught me life is fleeting. I have put this moment off for years out of fear, but no more, Da—Dawn. You're my whole life now. I love you, sweetheart. Will you? Ma—ma—," he paused and cleared his throat. I winked, and he finally got the words out. "Marry me, that is."

Tears choked away the words I wanted to say to the man kneeling before me, the honesty and earnestness in his eyes leaving me without words. I couldn't speak, so I grabbed his cheeks in my hands and kissed him with a passion that I hoped would answer his question better than any words could.

"Was that a yes?" he asked, everyone around us holding their collective breath.

I nodded with a shaky smile. When I spoke, my voice was barely a whisper. "Yes. Tonight. I'll marry you tonight, Beau. I love you," I said as he slipped the delicate diamond ring onto my finger.

The stone glinted in the light of the fire, and I saw the hope he spoke of inside the diamond. It was the kind of hope that offered love, laughter, trust, and forgiveness in the arms of a tender cowboy.

"We might have to wait until tomorrow, but, darlin', we aren't waiting much longer than that."

He pulled me into a hug and lovingly kissed my temple before resting his lips against my ear. The four words he whispered would be what I remembered years from now when it was long past dawn, and our time together was ending.

"Thanks for walking in."

Also by Katie Mettner

Torched
Finding Susan
After Summer Ends
Someone in the Water
The Secrets Between Us
White Sheets & Rosy Cheeks
A Christmas at Gingerbread Falls

Sugar's Dance
Sugar's Song
Sugar's Night
Sugar's Faith
Trusting Trey

Granted Redemption
Autumn Reflections
Winter's Rain
Forever Phoenix

Snow Daze
December Kiss
Noel's Hart
April Melody
Liberty Belle
Wicked Winifred
Nick S. Klaus

Calling Kupid
Me and Mr. IT

The Forgotten Lei
Hiding Rose

Magnificent Love
Magnificent Destiny

Inherited Love
Inherited Light
Inherited Life

October Winds
Ruby Sky

Meatloaf & Mistletoe
Hotcakes & Holly
Jam & Jingle Bells
Apples & Angel Wings
Eggnog & Evergreens

The German's Guilty Pleasure
The German's Desperate Vow

Cupcake
Tart

Butterflies and Hazel Eyes
Honeybees and Sexy Tees

Blazing Hot Nights
Long Past Dawn

A Letter from Katie Mettner

Let me take a moment to say thank you for reading *Long Past Dawn.* I hope you enjoyed the second installment of the Cowboys of Bison Ridge. I have two more cowboys for you. Well…one is a cowgirl!

A heartfelt thank you to every single one of you who picked up this book and helped make it a success! These cowboys might be rough and tumble, but they are mine to share with you, and I hope you enjoyed every moment of it. If you want to keep up to date with all my latest releases, including more stories from Wellspring, Wisconsin, just sign up at the following link. Your email address will never be shared, and you can unsubscribe at any time on my website.

http://eepurl.com/hl6njH

I love hearing from readers, so please, reach out and tell me what you thought of the book! You can get in touch with me through any of the social media outlets below, including my website. If you enjoyed the book, I'd appreciate it if you'd leave a review on any platform or Goodreads and perhaps recommend *The Cowboys of Bison Ridge* to other readers who enjoy quality romance. Reviews go a long way in helping readers discover my books for the first time. Once again, thank you so much for all your support of *Long Past Dawn.*

Until next time,

Katie Mettner

About the Author

Katie Mettner writes small-town romantic tales filled with epic love stories and happily-ever-afters. She proudly wears the title of, 'the only person to lose her leg after falling down the bunny hill,' and loves decorating her prosthetic with the latest fashion trends. She lives in Northern Wisconsin with her own happily-ever-after and three mini-mes. Katie has a massive addiction to coffee and Twitter, and a lessening aversion to Pinterest—now that she's quit trying to make the things she pins.

A Note to My Readers

People with disabilities are just that—people. We are not 'differently abled' because of our disability. We all have different abilities and interests, and the fact that we may or may not have a physical or intellectual disability doesn't change that. The disabled community may have different needs, but we are productive members of society who also happen to be husbands, wives, moms, dads, sons, daughters, sisters, brothers, friends, and co-workers. People with disabilities are often disrespected and portrayed two different ways; as helpless or as heroically inspirational for doing simple, basic activities.

As a disabled author who writes disabled characters, my focus is to help people without disabilities understand the real-life disability issues we face like discrimination, limited accessibility, housing, employment opportunities, and lack of people first language. I want to change the way others see our community by writing strong characters who go after their dreams, and find their true love, without shying away from what it is like to be a person with a disability. Another way I can educate people without disabilities is to help them understand our terminology. We, as the disabled community, have worked to establish what we call People First Language. This isn't a case of being politically correct. Rather, it is a way to acknowledge and communicate with a person with a disability in a respectful way by eliminating generalizations, assumptions, and stereotypes.

As a person with disabilities, I appreciate when readers take the time to ask me what my preferred language is. Since so many have asked, I thought I would include a small sample of the people-first language we use in the disabled community. This language also applies when leaving reviews and talking about books that feature characters with disabilities. The most important thing to remember when you're talking to people with disabilities is that we are people first! If you ask us what our preferred terminology is regarding our disability, we will not only tell you, but be glad you asked! If you would like more information about people first language, you will find a disability resource guide on my website.

Instead of: He is handicapped.
Use: He is a person with a disability.
Instead of: She is differently abled.
Use: She is a person with a disability.

Instead of: He is mentally retarded.
Use: He has a developmental or intellectual disability.

Instead of: She is wheelchair-bound.
Use: She uses a wheelchair.

Instead of: He is a cripple.
Use: He has a physical disability.

Instead of: She is a midget or dwarf.
Use: She is a person of short stature or a little person.

Instead of: He is deaf and mute.
Use: He is deaf or he has a hearing disability.

Instead of: She is a normal or healthy person.
Use: She is a person without a disability.

Instead of: That is handicapped parking.
Use: That is accessible parking.

Instead of: He has overcome his disability.
Use: He is successful and productive.

Instead of: She is suffering from vision loss.
Use: She is a person who is blind or visually disabled.

Instead of: He is brain damaged.
Use: He is a person with a traumatic brain injury.

Made in the USA
Las Vegas, NV
08 March 2023